STEVE ERICKSON
THE SEA CAME IN AT MIDNIGHT

"A major writer is in our midst. Pynchon, Nabokov, DeLillo—Steve Erickson has approached their heights."
—*Wall Street Journal*

"Steve Erickson is a provocative visionary chronicler of a phantasmagorical America on the brink of the apocalypse. . . . He's not afraid to take chances. . . . Erickson's novel is at once maddening and engrossing, unfolding like an elaborate game in which the rules are ever shifting. He's written the literary equivalent of a tsunami into which the reader must dive headlong or else risk drowning in the author's flood of dreamlike imagery and bizarre imaginings."
—*Toronto Globe and Mail*

"Erickson writes brilliantly sentence by sentence. . . . There's a precision and a humanity to his words. . . . Erickson's concerned with exploring dark contemporary mythologies, those of science fiction, pornography, dreams, sensational news stories, conspiracy theories. . . . His struggles with disorder and myth-making remain as beguiling as ever."
—*New York Times Book Review*

"Steve Erickson has that rare and luminous gift for reporting back from the nocturnal side of reality, along with an engagingly romantic attitude and the fierce imaginative energy of a born storyteller."
—Thomas Pynchon

"Against a background of chaos, Erickson has fashioned an ingenious Mobius strip of a book."
—*The New Yorker*

"Wonderfully scathing wit. . . . A major piece of fiction . . . [that] reveals us to ourselves. And not all is darkness."
—*Locus*

"Steve Erickson is a master . . . a dizzying rewriter of history, myth, and apocalypse. In Erickson's universe, entire cities, entire cultures go insane all at once. From the ruins, the author creates a new tribe, a new kinship map, and a strange new world for his characters to enter into, reunited, close to whole. . . . I started *The Sea Came In at Midnight* sore afraid, running to keep up with a wild pack of characters, and ended calm and clean, ready for the millennium."

—*Los Angeles Times Book Review*

"An astonishing, terrifying novel—the scariest dream you ever had, relayed with unsettling (and technically breathtaking) respect for the leaps and elisions that make dreams what they are. . . . The pace never flags."   —*Time Out* (London)

"Erickson is distinctive and inventive in mining his own field. . . . His new novel is complex, ripe with brilliant sentences, at times surreal, at times bombastic, and as hard to shake as a fever. . . . Erickson pictures a world turning inside out, cannibalizing itself, but he does it with a poet's grace. . . . Not for the faint of heart, but Erickson is after large game in a book that packs a punch."   —*Memphis Commercial Appeal*

"Of all the millennial visions galloping into the marketplace this year faster than you can say 'four horsemen,' *The Sea Came In at Midnight* is likely the most challenging, and the most poetic. . . . If you read one philosophical-doomsday kinky-sex road-trip novel this year, make it this one."   —*Salon*

"Erickson surprises and continually amazes in this novel of mythic circumstance. . . . His writing is ambitious and near flawless—he perfectly contrives this modern myth of the millennium. . . . In doing so, he may well have secured himself a place among the best of contemporary fiction writers."

—*Booklist* (starred review)

"Strip clubs, sexual slavery, Paris dreams, New York horror, and California misery catastrophically define and entrap the troubled margin-dwellers inhabiting this penetrating dream vision of the post-nuclear world. . . . This provocative novel is often funny but always serious and lush with insights that make its often outlandish elements eerily familiar. The razor-sharp narrative balances a nonchalant chaos with an unrelenting stream of violence and tenderness; even the most monstrous psyche in Erickson's ensemble of stoic naifs, murderous sadists, and the sexually plundered is brilliantly rendered as not only sympathetic, but honest, vigorous, and enduring."

—Publishers Weekly (starred review)

"Outrageous . . . *The Sea Came In at Midnight* has everything one could want in a novel. . . . Erickson consistently breaks the most deeply held rules of fiction . . . but does so in a way that keeps the reader focused on the plot and not his style. . . . [It] practically begs its audience for a second read, one that promises to be more enjoyable than the first."

—New Orleans Times-Picayune

"A brilliantly imaginative novelist of the utmost seriousness and grace. All too few contemporary talents are so admirably equipped for the deep lateral exploration of our dire and marvelous era."

—William Gibson

"Erickson has conjured a dreamscape that could be classified as 'future noir' . . . [owing] as much to the likes of J. G. Ballard and Thomas Pynchon as it does to Raymond Chandler. . . . *The Sea Came In at Midnight* provides an inviting introduction to his work."

—Austin American-Statesman

THE SEA CAME IN AT MIDNIGHT

Also by Steve Erickson

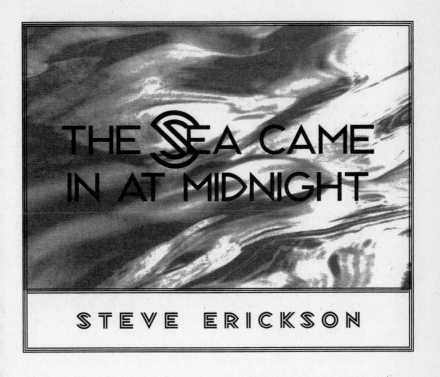

THE SEA CAME IN AT MIDNIGHT

STEVE ERICKSON

Perennial

An Imprint of HarperCollins*Publishers*

Grateful acknowledgment is given for permission to reprint lines from APRIL SKIES by James Reid and William Reid © 1987 Warner Bros. Music Ltd. (PRS). All rights for Western Hemisphere administered by WB Music Corp. All rights reserved. Used by permission. Warner Bros. Publications U.S. Inc., Miami, FL 33014.

A hardcover edition of this book was published in 1999 by Bard, an imprint of Avon Books, Inc.

HarperCollins books may be purchased for educational, business, or sales promotional use. For information please write: Special Markets Department, HarperCollins Publishers Inc., 10 East 53rd Street, New York, NY 10022.

First Perennial edition published 2000.

Designed by Kellan Peck

The Library of Congress has catalogued the hardcover edition as follows:

Erickson, Steve.
    The sea came in at midnight / Steve Erickson.
        p. cm.
        "An Avon Book"
        I. Title.
PS3555.R47S33 1999   98-46851
813'.54—dc21   CIP

ISBN 0-380-80658-4 (pbk.)

00 01 02 03 04 ❖/RRD 10 9 8 7 6 5 4 3 2 1

I HAVE SEEN THE TERRIFYING FACE TO FACE. I DO NOT FLEE
IN HORROR. BUT THOUGH I APPROACH WITH COURAGE,
I KNOW VERY WELL IT IS NOT THE COURAGE OF FAITH.

—KIERKEGAARD

I'M A FOUNTAIN OF BLOOD IN THE SHAPE OF A GIRL.

—BJÖRK

THE SEA CAME
IN AT MIDNIGHT

*want you at the end of your rope, lashed to the mast of my dreams.*

Now she laughs when she reads it. She's trying to remember if she thought it was as ridiculous four months ago, back in L.A. Maybe not; she was a little more desperate then. But now she's almost eighteen, and it just seems very funny to her. That's what a little age and wisdom and perspective will do for you.

IT'S the first line from a personals ad that ran in the newspaper just after the New Year. Crumpled and yellowed as though much older, the ad is now tacked to her hotel room wall.

Also tacked to the wall are articles from travel magazines about mysterious cities such as Budapest, Dublin, Reykjavik and San Sebastian, cities she's always assumed she will never see. But then she never thought she would see Tokyo either. There are also articles from literary journals and art magazines about Flannery O'Connor and Uumm Kulthum and Ida Lupino and Sujata Bhatt and Hannah Höch and Big Mama Thornton and Hedy Lamarr and Kathy Acker and Asia Carrera.

There's also, along with the ad that ran in the personals, a piece from the same day's newspaper that tells how exactly two thousand women and children marched off a cliff in Northern California on New Year's Eve at the stroke of midnight. Or anyway, the piece says it was the stroke of midnight, although the paper isn't quite right about this, and some other things. It wasn't, for instance, quite the orderly mass suicide the newspaper suggests. It also wasn't exactly two thousand. The seventeen-year-old American girl who lives in this hotel room knows this because she was there, number two thousand herself; and now she's here in Tokyo, and, well, anyone can do the math.

A month ago, after arriving in Tokyo but before she moved into this room on the top floor of the Hotel Ryu, Kristin lived for a couple of weeks in a ryokan over near the water.

In her little room in the ryokan, she would tack her news clippings and articles to the wall much like she does here, above the little tea table in the corner. Every day the maid would take them down. The maid never said a word to her, nor did Kristin to the maid, the two of them just locked in a silent battle of wills over the articles tacked to the wall. The maid clearly considered the decor unseemly, but Kristin hadn't come all the way from California so someone could tell her what she could or couldn't put on the walls.

Then Kristin moved into the Ryu, one of the revolving memory hotels of Tokyo's Kabuki-cho section, amid the surrounding bars and brothels and strip joints and massage parlors and porn shops. Since she never dreams, she's particularly aware in her sleep of the hum of the hotel's revolution. It's not exactly the hum of machinery or clockwork, it feels and sounds more like the vibration of a tuning fork, in the walls of her room and in the floor beneath her tatami mat. When the revolving cylindrical hotel slides into alignment with one of the outer exits, it opens up into one of the passages that lead to random neighborhoods of the city. Depending on the time of day, the long pulsing blue corridors sometimes deposit Kristin on the Ginza, and from there she walks to the bay not far from the outdoor market where the boats bring in fresh tuna in the early-morning hours.

HER first couple of weeks in Tokyo, when Kristin was living at the ryokan, she would go down to the market every morning and breakfast on fresh sushi with extra wasabi, the strong green horseradish she prefers to the fish. Now that she lives at the Ryu she still sometimes goes down to the wharves, like this morning when, realizing the vendor was out of wasabi, she gravely rejected the sushi and pushed it back across the stall counter uneaten. Sorry, she shook her head, and the seething vendor exploded in highly indignant Japanese. They got into a heated argument despite the fact that neither actually understood anything the other was saying. "But don't you see that *the whole point* of the sushi is the wasabi?" she kept trying to tell him; he was what Kristin, back in the States, used to call a point-misser.

In the gray day, the gray city disappears. It's possible an empirical investigation would reveal that, during the day, there in fact is no Tokyo, only people wandering an empty plain overgrown with tufts of fog that take the shape of shops, homes, hotels, temples. But at night the city blazes like an aquatic arcade surfacing up through black water, and in the most labyrinthine city in the world, Kristin fixes herself to the cityscape by humming a song, any song, since Tokyo exists in a vibrating lull—a maelstrom of frantic motion in complete silence, no honking cars, no hawkers of goods, no obscenity-screaming pedestrians, just the hum of the Yamanote subway like the sonic spine of Tokyo consciousness, or a hum in the air like the whirring revolution of the Hotel Ryu that Kristin hears in her sleep. The song Kristin sings to herself these days is "April Skies," by an English band from the 1980s. Maybe she sings this particular song because it happens to be April now: *Hand in hand in a violent life, making love on the edge of a knife, and the world comes tumbling down.* At the shores of Tokyo Bay she watches on the other side of the water the bright beacon of light that attracted her attention the first night she was here; she has no idea what makes this light, or where it comes from. At night it's too bright to be a window, too close to be a star. In the daylight neither the light nor its source can be seen at all.

OF course it's very strange to Kristin that, having been hardly anywhere in her seventeen years—having never even left until four months ago the little Northern California town where she grew up—she should have wound up here in Tokyo working as a memory girl in the Hotel Ryu. In her off hours she writes her memoirs in a notebook, saying to herself, Well now Kristin, this is a little presumptuous, don't you think? To be writing your memoirs at age seventeen? But she concludes that, after all, the months since she left home have been interesting, and if she herself isn't worthy of a memoir, maybe they are.

This evening she doesn't feel so well. Lately she's constantly fatigued and her stomach is queasy. But she lays down her notebook and rises from the mat to prepare for her rendezvous with the old Japanese doctor who is her most important client; she puts on the single dress that she brought with her from L.A., a light blue one. In her early weeks in Tokyo she lost enough weight that it finally fit her, but now it's become tight again. She hasn't yet told the hotel madam why.

As Kristin strains to fasten the buttons of the dress, she notes that the number written on her body has now almost completely faded. It's located right above her hip and it says *29.4.85*. To anyone else seeing this number on Kristin's body, it might be a secret code, or a combination; it's even something of a mystery to Kristin. She knows what it is but she doesn't know what it means. The man who wrote it there in indelible black marker ink two months ago didn't know what it meant either, but then, like the vendor selling sushi without wasabi, he always was just a big point-misser. Kristin can still remember the look on his face when he did it, though.

THE old doctor always insists on seeing Kristin and no one else, and his visits have become more frequent, five or six times a week.

The clients of the hotel often establish relationships with certain girls in particular. Unlike the surrounding love hotels of the neighborhood, this is a memory hotel, where girls and clients trade in memory rather than sex, and by nature, memory is more monogamous than desire. A big girl verging on slightly overweight, around five feet eight inches and towering over many of the men who come to see her, Kristin isn't beautiful, though the Tokyo men find attractive the short dirty-blond hair that seemed so undistinguished back in the States. But she's popular because she listens well, and she's smart; much of her young life she's been maybe a little too smart, which she realizes as well as anyone. Sometimes she's thought to herself it's just as well there's a language barrier. She's always had a smart mouth that's gotten her into trouble.

Besides her intelligence and empathy, being American also makes Kristin more valuable to the hotel's clients. As an American, she's considered by Japanese men a natural conduit of modern memory. As a daughter of America, Kristin represents the Western annihilation of ancient Japanese memory and therefore its master and possessor, a red bomb in one hand, a red bottle of soda pop in the other.

AT ten-forty Kristin goes downstairs to the hotel lobby on the main floor, where the girls usually greet the customers.

She finds the old doctor has already retired to the tiny booth where, on the other side of a small table for two, he now sits neatly dressed as always in coat and tie, dozing in the dark. On the table in front of him, before the love seat where he rests leaning against the wall, is a small vase with a single white rose. Watching over the tiny booth from above the doorway is the serene porcelain mask of a woman's face, placed there to transfix the customer and arouse old, impotent recollections.

The old doctor has been telling Kristin his memories of his

life, and she's promised that when he finishes, she'll tell him hers in return. To Kristin it seems an obviously one-sided bargain, her paltry seventeen years for the old doctor's eighty. The old doctor's English is excellent; born in Japan, he in fact spent most of his life in the United States, having returned only in the past ten years. It may account, as well as other things, for the bond he's formed with the American girl.

But tonight when Kristin enters the dark booth, he doesn't say hello. Feeling particularly fatigued this evening, she's momentarily irritated, hoping he doesn't expect too much from her this session. Then she admonishes herself to remember that he's a sad old man, with a sad life and sad memories, and that her kindness is especially important to him. "Hello," she says, not yet having determined whether by custom she's supposed to address him as "Doctor" or "Kai-san." Only after she's sat for a moment next to him on the love seat, looking at his peaceful face with his eyes restfully closed, and only when he remains absolutely silent, does she finally realize he's dead.

KEEPING her composure, Kristin gets up from the love seat and sticks her head through the curtain of the booth out into the lobby and calls Mika, the hotel madam. When Mika comes into the booth and sees the old doctor, her

STEVE ERICKSON

face turns as white as in her Kyoto geisha days. The two women look at each other; turning her back on the body, Mika pulls a tiny cell phone from her robe and makes a phone call. She draws the curtain of the booth closed behind her.

KRISTIN wants to go back up to her room, but can't bring herself to leave the old man alone. Waiting for someone to come for the body, she sits back down next to the old doctor in the dark.

In death he seems less sad than she ever saw him in life. Is he now simply and completely empty of all his memories, or is he afloat somewhere on one in particular that's brought him some peace? As he sat here in the hotel waiting for Kristin, did his thoughts drift and then, stumbling on a memory that would save him, and making a moment's split decision, did he cast his lot, running alongside like a traveler jumping on a passing train, seizing his last and best chance to escape forever?

SEVERAL minutes later Kristin is still waiting. She makes small talk in order to break the awkward silence. Thinking of the ongoing account of his life that he's been relating to her, she says, "Well, Doctor," playfully feigning annoyance, "now I'll never know how it all turned out, will I?" and then she realizes that *this* is how it all turned out. Who would have thought, she wonders to herself, that one's life would run out before his memories? A couple of times she gets up from the seat and sticks her head back out through the curtain into the hotel lobby; Mika is on the other side of the room, still on the phone. A few of the other girls seem to have caught on that something's amiss, and gather around the booth's drawn curtain looking at Kristin. A couple say something to her in Japanese. She shakes her head and pulls it back inside.

After all, she simply can't just leave him here, even if no one has asked her to stay. She remembers how she promised that when he finished telling his story, she would tell him hers; and for all the promises of his life that were broken, none more devastating than the ones he made to himself, she can't bear to break this last one. So as they wait, and as the minutes pass, the west of midnight slowly shifting to the east of it, she begins to speak, and it makes sense to start four months ago, on her last night in the little town called Davenhall, in the Sacramento Delta where she grew up. "Since I've never had a dream," she begins, "one night I woke and went looking for one."

BUT though she'd heard a man has an erection when he dreams, she certainly hadn't wanted the dreams of any of Davenhall's chinamen, old wrinkled dried-up dreams. As she tells her story to the old Japanese doctor now, Kristin sort of glosses over this part, because she doesn't want to shock him, even if he is dead.

"After all," she says to the old doctor, "a dream's only a memory of the future, right? And there I was living in this little town on this little island in the middle of this delta that had no future at all," and so that night she quietly stole from her room in back of the town tavern and into the back alley, after first determining that her uncle wouldn't stir from his drunken stupor behind the bar. Above her, the bare branches of the trees had scraped the moonlight. The dark had hummed with the buzz of mosquitoes.

Soundlessly she had moved down mainstreet past the houses to the town hotel, through the old wooden lobby and up the stairs, from room to room, looking for any random stranger passing through. She knew that the one she found in the shadows was drunk on his back by the way he snored: "I could smell the vodka," she tells the dead doctor in the Hotel Ryu, "I mean, you're not supposed to be able to smell vodka, but remember, I'd been living in back of a bar my whole life," and so she had pulled off her jeans and touched herself for a few minutes until she was wet. Then, straddling the sleeping man, she slipped him inside her.

IMPATIENT for the flash of his dream in her mind, she'd had him faster and faster. As he stirred from his sleep, his erection collapsing in confusion before climax, he murmured a strange woman's name, half desperately and half with hope. "Angie?"

A thousand years ago, in the last moments of the Tenth Century, in an ancient Celtic village twelve kilometers from the coast of Brittany, exactly one thousand men, women and children waited in their wooden boats for an apocalyptic tide to come rolling in at midnight. In the light of the moon one could see across the valley all the boats perched high above the landscape on stilts, which the villagers expected to be washed away by the tide, setting them adrift in the millennial deluge. It was only just before midnight that the leaders of the village realized to their dismay they were missing someone, that in fact they didn't number exactly one thousand, but 999—the name of the year that was about to expire. Since the village didn't wish to expire with it, it seemed an ominous miscalculation. From the vantage points of their landlocked boats, the villagers could see the one-thousandth in the village tower to the northwest, in the direction of the sea, watching from the highest window.

Waving frantically to the villagers, trapped and unable to bear the thought of a colossal ocean wall advancing across the countryside and smashing her and the tower into smithereens, the young girl climbed into the tower window, gazed at the night, spread out her arms, and dove to her death.

In the boats, witnesses shrieked, confusion erupted. The father of the seventeen-year-old girl, who had only belatedly realized his daughter was in the tower, and was restrained from rushing to her by the other villagers who feared he would be swept away by the stupendous midnight sea, wailed at the sight of his daughter's plummeting. "Murderers!" he cried in futility, pointing at the priests watching the drama from the stern of the boat. Later, in the earliest days of the Eleventh Century, after the midnight of reckoning had come and gone with no heavenly wrath manifest, some legend would eventually take shape in the surrounding villages; but in the meantime there were only questions and rumors: Did the young girl in the tower fall asleep, and was then simply forgotten as everyone else scurried madly for the sanctuary of the boats? Did she stay behind on purpose, out of remorse for some transgression that placed her in the tower in the first place? Or, precisely because she was number one thousand, was she intentionally locked away there by the priests, who considered her a suitable sacrifice to whatever pagan god or druid was in control, as the first thousand years capitulated to the second. . . .

In the last moments of the Twentieth Century, with neither protest on their lips nor ecstasy in their eyes, two thousand women and girls—"that's what the newspaper said anyway," Kristin advises her rapt listener in the dark of the Hotel Ryu, "but I can tell you for a fact it was only 1,999"—silently walked off a high cliff of the Northern California coast and plunged to the black waves below. It was impossible to know what they hoped was waiting for them in their last step off the rocks into space. Perhaps they believed some hole would open up in the night, and they would step into infinity. Perhaps they believed the open palm of the cosmos would catch them in midair. Likeliest they had no idea what to believe, since until this very moment they had no idea what rendezvous awaited the end of a migration that had begun eleven weeks before in the desolation of southern Idaho. The cult's male priests brought up the rear, their hands clandestine in their white robes. Only when, at the back of the migration, a few women of less resolute faith finally understood what was taking place and tried to bolt, did there emerge from the white robes into the hands of the priests the long curved knives, swaying as methodically and casually as if they were cutting the tall grass.

 heretic at heart, Kristin had broken for freedom.

"You have to understand," Kristin continues, "I never had anything to do with their cult in the first place. I had just gotten off Davenhall Island as quick as I could, given that . . . well, that part's not worth going into," she assures the dead man, "but let's just say I left in a hurry. So there I am standing by the road somewhere north of Sacramento, with only the clothes on my back and my books"—Brontë and Cendrars and Kierkegaard in a cloth bag—"when the whole migration comes around the bend," and also at the exact moment that the priests were troubling over their latest count of the flock: 1,999, having lost someone somewhere along the way. Which on this particular New Year wouldn't do. Like earlier priests, they believed in nothing if not the precision of their rituals, so they happily scooped up the young girl as the last plump sacrificial morsel.

Such precision "saved" Kristin, if that was the word, on the night of December 30, twenty-four hours before the Great Walk Off, when she had roamed the cult encampment in the dark, up and down the hillside from sleeping bag to sleeping bag, still looking for a dream, just as she had on her last night in Davenhall. Whether the young priest she selected actually slept through her ravishment or just pretended to sleep, no one could know; the impromptu tribunal proceeded on into the early-morning hours amid a flurry of whispered accusations that eventually woke the other campers. Soon, dawn made a decision imperative. The priest was excommunicated. Kristin, number two thousand, was "forgiven," to not much gratitude or concern on her part one way or the other. She would have been even less grateful had she known the evening's plan.

Then at 11:57 on the thirty-first of December, the best-planned mathematics of the priests went haywire. Suddenly aware of what was happening, Kristin ran for as much land as her feet could cross, the ocean furious in her ears, priests lunging this way and that, swinging their knives. "I almost thought of stopping to ask one of them, you know, just how they could be so sure. You know?" For a moment there in the deathly still chamber of the memory hotel with the old dead doctor next to her, she wonders if this entire subject is rather tactless, given the circumstances; but she persists. "How could they be so sure before I came along that the count wasn't really 1,998? You understand? But this one maniac coming at me was swinging a *very* large machete—so I thought maybe I should postpone that particular conversation," and Kristin, younger and faster than the priests in pursuit, and still with a dream to find, alone among the congregation survived the stroke of midnight.

ALMOST a mile and a half down Highway 1, somewhere between Mendocino and Bodega Bay, she finally convinced herself there was no one chasing her anymore, and slowed down. She walked along the side of the road in the dark, panting hard and listening; when she heard a car approaching from the other direction, she stepped out onto the blacktop and into the oncoming headlights, frantically waving her arms. It nearly ran her over, barely swerving as she jumped back out of the way at the last minute. "Two hours later I finally flag a ride— same van, coming back from wherever they were in such a hurry to get to." Two women in their late twenties: the one in the passenger seat didn't look so happy to have stopped. Where you heading? the one driving asked. Inland, answered Kristin.

RELIEVED to be driving away from the ocean cliffs, Kristin didn't care about anything else. Since she never dreamed, she knew the conversation between the two women in the front seat was real, even as she dozed in the back.

They spoke in the same tense whispers of the priests the night before. It was crazy to pick her up, said the one in the passenger seat, what were you thinking? and then the driver, She's a kid, besides she might have told someone she saw us, didn't you see we nearly hit her on the way up? and then the passenger, Well, what now, we can't just drop her off some-where; and then the driver, We'll keep her with us a while, see what happens—and then the driver started giggling as the passenger glanced back at Kristin over her shoulder, checking her out.

Kristin feigned sleep. The driver kept giggling. "Stop it," the passenger spit. The driver stopped, then after a moment said, "Pass it," and the passenger, hesitating, passed a bottle from which the driver took a drink. From her nights in the bar back on Davenhall Island, Kristin recognized the smell of bourbon.

THEY turned left at Bodega Bay and made their way through Marin County, crossing the Golden Gate Bridge and driving up Lombard toward the center of the city just before sunrise. Kristin had never been to San Francisco before, unless one counted being born there, and with the light of day and the suspension of ominous talk between the two women in front, she watched from her window. A couple of times the woman in the passenger seat would turn and look over her shoulder at Kristin, who noticed the driver was also watching her in the rearview mirror. "You hungry?" the driver said.

"Yes," said Kristin.

"We'll stop at a little bakery over in North Beach." She kept watching Kristin in the rearview mirror. "What were you doing out there on the road?"

"Well, now," Kristin said, "you know someone might ask you the very same thing," and then thinking to herself, Kristin, do you *always* have to be smart? "Heh heh," said the driver, not finding it particularly funny, to which the passenger's pointed silence answered, See, what did I tell you? Except for a stray banner blowing down the street, there wasn't a sign of celebration. It would be another hour or two before Kristin could be certain a midnight tide hadn't washed everything away after all, and that this particular New Year had been no different from the ninety-nine that preceded it or the nine hundred that preceded them. The women parked at a bakery on Columbus and went inside. Eating her croissant and drinking her espresso, Kristin changed strategies, employing abject apology: "It's a long story," she said meekly, "but thanks for picking me up. Can I have another of these?"

They bought Kristin another croissant. The two women sat staring at her as she ate, the driver sipping her coffee and the passenger smoking a cigarette. "You can stick around with us for a while," the driver said; the passenger just kept staring at Kristin through the cigarette smoke.

Their names were Isabelle and Cynda. At first Kristin had a hard time keeping track which was which. After breakfast they drove around the city a while, finally parking in front of a hotel on Grant not far from Union Square and sitting for half an hour, looking back and forth between the hotel and each other: This it? Isabelle in the driver's seat kept asking Cynda, who kept checking the address on some piece of identification that obviously wasn't hers. They murmured between themselves and glanced back at Kristin now and then, and finally got out of the van. Nonchalantly the three of them walked into the lobby of the hotel past the front desk and the concierge and the bell captain, and got in the elevator. Using a key, they took the elevator to the top floor.

When they got off the elevator they were in the penthouse. To Kristin, who had never been in a big-city hotel, let alone a penthouse, it seemed lavish and glamorous beyond belief; in fact it was a small though sleek penthouse in a small though chic hotel. The hotel was located half a block from the Dragon Gate into Chinatown, where it wasn't even the new year, let alone a new millennium: I am still surrounded, was all Kristin could think, staring out the window of the hotel, by nothing but old Chinese dreams; and it was the sounds of Chinatown that invaded her sleep at night, Chinese jabber and the clamor of gongs echoing through the cave of unconsciousness.

ISABELLE said the penthouse belonged to her brother. But while there were photos of a good-looking young man with parents and boyfriends and even someone who appeared as though she might be a sister, there was no sign of Isabelle among the effects at all. The two women went through the apartment with the detached curiosity of complete and distinct strangers, picking up things and casting them aside with indifference; they made no effort to tidy up, and gave no indication they expected anyone else to show up any time soon. When the phone rang, they never answered. They stayed for several days, and after a while the messages Kristin heard coming in over the phone machine tended to sound a little mystified and concerned, until Isabelle turned the volume down.

The livelier and more reckless of the two women, Isabelle was prettier—taken feature for feature—than her thin mouth and small eyes would have suggested, with dark hair falling just above her shoulders. Cynda, perpetual passenger, was more pinched, with short blond hair just a little longer than Kristin's. She almost never spoke to Kristin, not over pasta dinners in North Beach or in the afternoons when the women routinely polished off a fifth of Jack Daniel's, or in the morning over coffee when they finally emerged before noon from the bedroom where they slept together. So it was a shock to Kristin, who assumed Cynda hated her, when she tried to kiss Kristin the fourth night, in retaliation against Isabelle, who had kissed Kristin the third night, to Cynda's great rage. "That was when I figured it was time to get out of there," Kristin tells the old doctor in the Hotel Ryu. She now has his undivided attention.

In the dwindling hours of that last night in San Francisco, alone in the dark of her bedroom, Kristin heard Isabelle and Cynda in the next room engaged in a terrible argument. It ranged from matters of fidelity and desire to more mysterious implications that on the one hand didn't explain anything but on the other hand confirmed everything. By now it was obvious that whoever lived in the penthouse wasn't Isabelle's brother, and that in fact his acquaintance with the two women began and ended New Year's Eve, and culminated in a desperate drive to some remote dumping ground a hundred miles or so north of San Francisco. It's insane, Cynda sputtered, that we're here at all, staying here of all places, to which Isabelle had laughed that Cynda worried too much. It's only a matter of time, Cynda had continued, before someone shows up and starts asking questions, and what are we going to do about the kid, it was stupid to pick her up that night, you have to have your toys don't you Isabelle always your toys, and on and on a little more hysterically until Kristin heard Isabelle finally answer, very quietly and evenly, all the amusement suddenly gone from her voice, Calm down, you're losing it. We'll get out of here when it's time, and we'll do something about the kid when it's time.

Then Kristin heard Cynda start to cry, and Isabelle begin to giggle like she had in the van the night they had picked Kristin up. Then Isabelle's giggling tapered off along with Cynda's crying, and about forty-five minutes later—because she had learned that people sleep most soundly after they've first slipped into unconsciousness, especially when they're drunk—Kristin got up and dressed in the dark. She peered through the doorway of the women's bedroom and reached in and pulled a pair of jeans from the nearby chair, and going through the pockets found some money and the keys to the van and the key to the penthouse. "I took the money," Kristin admits now, "and I took the penthouse key—I needed the key to operate the elevator." She was sure the noise of the elevator was going to wake them, since the shaft was right behind the wall of their bedroom; as she waited in the dark, it seemed to take forever.

HER bag of books had gone the way of the old millennium, smashed on the ocean rocks in her place, so she had nothing but the clothes on her back and, adding the money she took from Isabelle and Cynda to what she had brought of her own from Davenhall, $319.

Part of that got her a ticket on a bus out of San Francisco down Highway 1 past Santa Cruz to Monterey. Then the bus cut inland to avoid the winding and perilous road through Big Sur, then back to the coast picking up Highway 1 again at San Luis Obispo, proceeding to Santa Barbara and many small stops in between. Mexican laborers, for whom the coastal trek was as routine as a crosstown line, got on and off. Kristin arrived in L.A. at the Hollywood station on Vine Street, five days into the new year at one in the morning in a rainstorm, when it was impossible to know if the hush of the place was from sleep or the sort of anticlimax that comes so naturally to a city unimpressed by time.

What remained of the $319 lasted three days. In the first early-morning hours of her arrival, she walked about two miles west on Sunset Boulevard in the rain, cop cars pulling up alongside and slowing, studying her and then moving on. She would have been just as happy to spend a night or two in jail. She would have been just as happy to confess to whatever felony might have gotten her there. The next day, exhausted but still going on the adrenaline of her near brush with salvation five nights before and whatever fate her deadly dalliance with Isabelle and Cynda had held in store for her, she checked into a hotel called the Hamblin just south of the Strip.

The hotel was just dilapidated enough that Kristin's remaining funds covered three nights, paid for up front. Stiffing the hotel for the fourth night, she slipped out at three in the morning and pressed her New Year survivor's luck by hitching a ride on Santa Monica Boulevard with a man whose predilection for molestation was fortunately disposed to seventeen-year-old boys rather than seventeen-year-old girls. Her size and cropped hair, seen through his windshield at three-thirty in the morning, fooled him just long enough to get her inside the car; disgruntled, he reluctantly drove her to Century City. She slept in an alcove of one of the towers until a little past eight, when a security guard woke her.

By now all the New Year adrenaline was wearing off. Her focus was sharpened only by the fact that there was nothing behind her to which she could return. She wandered Century City raiding trash cans like an animal, then walked down to Pico Boulevard, where she hitched another ride with a boy about her own age whom she could handle if she needed to. Once they reached the beach he seemed, if anything, all too happy to drop her off. Stumbling through the streets of Baghdadville, as lacking in prospects as she was in dreams, she begged for food outside restaurants until she was chased away, scorn and hostility the only interruptions in the hush of anticlimax that still gripped the city. She spent that night in an alley and then the next in the kitchen of a seaside grill where the late-night cook took pity on her. Twice she nearly prostituted herself, first with a huge black man in a red Chevy who kept circling the block, and then with a bisexual art dealer who craved diversion, soul-numbingly bored in his empty gallery, surrounded by a dreary series of eight black canvases. Even Kristin couldn't entirely be sure whether her rejection of him was an act of morality or aesthetics.

LATER, after she moved into the spare room of the Occupant's house in the Hollywood Hills, she would understand a little better what mysterious force had directed her attention to the advertisement in the week-old newspaper.

I want you at the end of your rope, it read, back among the personals, *lashed to the mast of my dreams*. She was sitting in the seaside grill sipping a bowl of charity soup, having just read, on page five, the sketchy details of the mass murder/suicide of two thousand women and children off the coast of Northern California. *I do not want a wife, I do not want a girlfriend. I do not want a mistress or a maid or a cook or a cleaning woman. My heart has no needs, except to be left alone with the memories that have already wounded it. Beauty is as unnecessary as intelligence. Best if you are desperate. Best if you are either absolutely self-knowing, so preternaturally secure about who you are that no* *physical defilement can violate it, or absolutely empty of self-concern, so primally attuned to basic appetites that pathology is beside the point. The naturally indignant need not apply. You will be given a place to live, a room of your own, access to the kitchen and most parts of the house, a weekly stipend of $100, and whatever free time in which you are not otherwise needed. Of course you are free to end the arrangement and leave at any moment. Auditions voluntary.*

"Well," she sighs now to the old dead doctor, "that part about not being beautiful was certainly a relief, even if there *was* a post office box to send a photo." In fact, Kristin secretly held out hope she wasn't as plain as all that: "I know my eyes are a little too far apart," she acknowledged, "and my mouth's a little too thin," but it did have an appealing way of curling up on one side into a sly smile. Her hair was its dirty and undistinguished blond chopped to prisoner-of-war length. A big girl, she nonetheless had an exaggerated sense of her own size; she certainly regretted about ten pounds, none of which had the decency to accumulate in her breasts, of course, but steadfastly located themselves instead on her hips. Rereading the ad, she wondered if it automatically assumed she was stupid too. He probably thinks I'm another idiotic seventeen-year-old who doesn't know what preternatural means, she said to herself.

Still, she felt as though the ad had been written expressly to her. In the hope that the call would ultimately lead to her departure, the bartender let her use the phone; he rather liked her, actually, but could already anticipate a moment in the very foreseeable future when she would overstay her welcome. Along with the post office box there was, at the bottom of the ad, a phone and reference number that connected Kristin to a voice-mail service. "Yes, well," she said into the phone, clearing her throat, "we girls at the end of our rope don't happen to have our portfolio of eight-by-ten glossies with us today. I'm at Jay's Grill on Ocean Avenue in Baghdadville, near—" She turned to the bartender.

"Pico Boulevard," he said.

"Pico Boulevard. It's . . . Wednesday—"

"Friday," the bartender corrected.

"Friday the . . . eleventh—"

"Thirteenth."

"The thirteenth of January. And I'll be here at noon tomorrow . . . on Saturday, and the day after that." The bartender winced. She hung up. She slurped down the rest of her soup and wandered out toward the beach, and slept that night on the pier, smoking cigarettes to suppress the hunger. It rained Saturday, and in the rain on the beach in the broad gray daylight she took off her clothes and laid them on a rock and washed herself. Several people passing by on Ocean Avenue saw her, and two members of what she concluded to be a distinctly cretinous strain of teenage boydom watched devoutly. For a few seconds she caressed her breasts at them suggestively, just for laughs, and then decided she better stop when they looked like they were going to start bouncing off the palm trees.

But no one showed up that day at the grill, and she spent yet another night on the pier sleeping behind the old carousel. By now she was almost nostalgic for the good old days of Isabelle and Cynda. Up and down the pier in the rain she rummaged through the garbage with little success, reduced to licking the browning mustard off hot-dog wrappers and the pink residue of sugar off disposed cotton-candy cones. By Sunday she was staggering deliriously between exhaustion and starvation, and pedestrians on the street gave her a wide berth, assuming she was drunk or on drugs. By Sunday the bartender and the cook at the grill weren't nearly as friendly. "You can't come back here anymore," the bartender said when she showed up out of the rain a little before noon on Sunday.

She was weaving in the doorway as though she would faint. "It's Sunday," she murmured shamelessly, perfectly ready to try whatever worked. "You're not going to feel so good later, making me leave on a Sunday."

"Probably," he admitted. He didn't look like he felt so good about it now.

"I'm really hungry," was all she could think to add.

"I'm sorry," he just kept saying, "you can't come back any-more." The rain fell harder. They both turned to look at it through the window; one lone car was parked across the street, metallic blue like the rain and the water rushing by in the gutter. "When the rain lets up, you have to go." When the rain let up she lingered for a moment, and as she lingered the door of the car across the street opened and a man got out. He wasn't wear-ing a coat, and he didn't run in the rain but walked across the street with his hands shoved in the pockets of his pants, staring at the ground in front of him. He looked to neither left nor right; a truck could have flattened him as easily as not, and he gave no indication it would have mattered to him in the least.

He came into the grill and gazed around. Other than Kristin and the bartender and the cook, no one was there. Kristin sud-denly felt a lot more lucid; she stepped toward the stranger and said, "It's me." He was around six feet tall, a bulky man in his early forties with black hair and a black beard splattered white with premature age, disheveled in an absentminded way, a shirt button in the wrong hole and the collar askew. He looked as exhausted as she felt; later she would learn he had aimlessly driven the city in clockwise circles the entire night—racked by one of his excruciating headaches—having come by the grill the previous day without stopping. His startling blue eyes were filled with hurt.

In the booth where they sat down, the man kept shifting fitfully, eyes darting. Well, Kristin said to herself, I've now met a lifetime of psychos in a week and a half. She examined him so as to take the full measure of his derangement and weigh the risks, evaluating the situation as fast as her exhausted brain and famished body would allow. "Would you like," he said in a voice of great intensity she nonetheless could barely hear, "something to eat?"

"Yes."

"Do you serve lunch?" he asked the bartender, still barely audible.

"Sandwiches," the bartender answered, "soup."

"A hamburger," Kristin announced.

"Two," the man said with a shrug to the bartender. The cook brought two hamburgers. It took ten minutes to prepare them, during which time the man in the booth didn't say a single word or look at her, but stared out the window in dismay as though Kristin couldn't possibly be the one he had come to meet, and the right woman would surely appear soon. It's because I'm not beautiful, she thought, though for the time being—enthralled by the extravagant promise of a hamburger—she didn't give a flying fuck. She pounced on the burger while thinking things through. "You're not eating your hamburger," she said, almost finished with hers.

"Oh," he said, shifting in his seat. To her great disappointment he began to eat it.

"Maybe, before you leave, you could order me something else I could take with me."

He seemed perplexed by this request. "Well," he finally said in his hoarse whisper, "you understood the ad?"

"Oh yes," she assured him, "I would like to think I'm in the 'self-knowing, preternaturally secure' camp myself. Defile away."

"How old are you?"

"Nineteen."

"Really?"

She almost said, All right, eighteen; but since that was untrue too, it seemed better to stick to the first lie: "Almost twenty, actually," embellishing it instead. She stopped feeding her face for a moment to give him her best sly smile, and hope that in the previous forty-eight hours she might have lost a few of those ten extra pounds. Later she would have to analyze it for herself in order to truly understand the insight, but there and then, in the booth at Jay's Grill in Baghdadville near the beach, Kristin had her first realization of how pathetic male sexuality really was. It has nothing to do with their dicks at all, she thought to herself with some amazement; rather it's all there in that ludicrous little lump of lapses and impulses they like to think of as a psyche. We've had them right in the palms of our hands all along. There in the grill it was all she could do not to burst out laughing.

But because she was even more desperate for what he offered her than he was for what she offered him, she submitted herself recklessly. Blindfolded in the backseat of his car on the way to his house, of course she considered the possibility he would chop her up with an ax or sell her to sex-crazed Moroccans or maybe, if she were lucky, only lock her away in an attic for two or three years until he was bored with her; but now all she really cared about was the prospect of spending a night indoors, perhaps even in a bed, regardless of whose it was or what happened to her in it. That seemed worth risking everything: take me home with you, she had said to him in the booth of the grill, and if you like me, you can keep me. If you don't, you haven't lost anything. On the other hand, lying blindfolded on the backseat and aware of his many quick and erratic turns as he drove, as though he was trying to lose the psychotic boyfriend he suspected was following and for whom she would unlock the front door of his house in the middle of the night, she tried to reassure herself that he was vulnerable too, a hope emboldened by the way she later noticed he had stripped his house of all identity—photos removed and no name on the mailbox, no bills in sight or any personal correspondence, the address labels torn off all the magazines and every possible self-reference hidden from her except the junk mail addressed to "occupant." The only personality the house had was someone else's: a woman's jewelry box in the main bedroom, in the bathroom a woman's lipstick and eyelash curlers that appeared to have been there for some time, and, saddest and most mysterious of all, the empty bassinet in what would come to be her room, with soft cotton blankets arranged on the chest of drawers alongside, awaiting a baby.

When they got to the house an hour after meeting at the grill by the sea, she was led, still blindfolded, into what she figured was the middle of the living room, the sound of the front door closing behind her. After a moment of waiting for him to say something, she broke the silence by taking off her clothes. In the dark of the blindfold she stood nude until she finally said, "I need a bath." All right, he answered. She took off the blindfold and he was still standing at the front door, as though to stop either her or himself from escaping; and her clothes that she had dropped to the floor at her feet were nowhere to be seen, as though they had evaporated, falling into the silvery afternoon light that came through the living room window.

SHE supposed she was already violating the spirit of the arrangement, but she locked the bathroom door behind her. While the bathtub filled with hot water, she analyzed the remnants of a lost female presence, the small blue art-deco atomizer and the bottles of French bubble bath, the old hair spray canisters and the little plastic bottles of nail polish remover, all beginning to crust over and take on the film of age. For an hour she sat in the tub drifting dreamlessly in the steam, wondering if he would break down the door for her.

Please don't fake it, she heard him whisper harshly in her ear that first night. She wasn't aware she had been. After her bath and a meal, which she ate alone, she had gone to her room as instructed and lay on the bed, where she waited three hours in the dark until he finally came for her. Don't pretend, he said, because you think it will please me. I would rather you said nothing at all. I would rather you showed no feeling whatsoever. So she refined her impassivity. She was naked on her bed most of the days that followed, industrial rave and Liszt's "Transcendental Etudes" playing in the background, viscera twinkling along the flesh horizon of her body like the lights of the Hollywood Hills. Through the open window of her room she could smell the eucalyptus and the smoke of the city. Some nights he took her to his own bed, always dismissing her when he finished except once when he drank too much and, unable to perform, passed out and she fell asleep next to him. In those first few weeks he often came to her in the dark early-morning hours when she was still asleep. She would stir awake to find he had slipped into her soundlessly, pinning her to the bed by her wrists as if afraid she would run away, even though she was barely conscious.

Up and down the house stacked against the hillside in three narrow stories, she wandered aimlessly, standing naked for hours in the large windows overlooking the city, while he vanished into a room on the bottom floor that he always kept closed and locked. Be ready in an hour, he would tell her before disappearing for three or four, commissioning her to her room to wait on her bed, in the dark, in her daydreams.

THEY didn't converse at all. Everything about his manner discouraged conversation. After a couple of days she couldn't remember whether she had even told him her name, and once when she almost blurted, I'm Kristin, he looked at her as though he knew exactly what she was about to say and adamantly didn't want to hear it.

They didn't eat together or pass time together otherwise, and the house became more hers than his, since he confined himself to the locked room on the bottom floor. He had no hours or daily clock, from what she could tell, his days and nights running together. He never slept, as such; rather he just passed out now and then from exhaustion or drink or terrible headaches that plagued him on a regular basis. Sometimes the headaches incapacitated him, sometimes he seemed to draw energy from them as though the pain radiating from behind his hot blue eyes propelled him through the day and his work. Sometimes he would lie on the sofa or his bed holding his head in his hands, his unblinking eyes focused straight ahead of him as though he was staring into a piece of blue sky lodged in the ceiling above, waiting to catch sight of something. "Are you all right?" she asked one afternoon, finding him like that in the living room.

She didn't know which startled him more, the question itself or just the sound of her voice. "Yes," he finally answered quietly through his clenched teeth. He lay there with his eyes closed a few more minutes before opening them to see her still there: "It comes and goes," he added, more as a dismissal of her than an explanation.

Oh, excuse me, she almost answered, did I cross a line? Did I overstep my bounds, trying to relate to you as a human being? But she bit her tongue and came over and knelt down on the floor beside him and began to rub his head.

"What are you doing?" he asked.

"Rubbing your head."

"Why?"

She nodded. "Good question." She stood and turned and walked away, stopping at the stairs only when she thought he might say something. But he'd already forgotten her.

Downstairs, when he was inside the locked room below her, she could hear the vodka bottles rolling around on the floor. But he never sounded or smelled or staggered like a drunk man, the way her uncle did back on Davenhall Island, and he never became violent with her like a drunk man, though the sounds that came from the locked room were often violent, hoarse cries of desperation, either from the headaches, she imagined, or some mysterious thwarted effort. The Occupant's behavior was more possessed than anything: Kristin noted, for instance, that he always moved in a clockwise direction. His furious pacing was always clockwise; if there was a light switch to his right just beyond his reach, he would get up and circle the room to the left to turn it off, like his life going down a drain.

The terrible sounds that sometimes came from the secret room, the crashing and thrashing like a trapped animal, were always left behind, locked away, when he emerged. When he emerged, all he brought with him was the look in his eyes, anguish invaded by fury; she could anticipate when he would come for her, always after he had been in the secret room a particularly long and sullen time, or when he had been passed out and would wake wanting her. After a while she stopped being afraid of what he might do. Once she woke in the middle of the night to hear him pacing in the dark, no doubt in clockwise circles, at the foot of her bed; for fifteen minutes she lay there holding her breath, but he just went on circling and finally she fell back to sleep. When she woke he was gone, nothing having happened between them. Once, in his bed after he had finished with her, he pulled her to his chest and held her, absently caressing her hair, until he suddenly realized he was verging on a moment of actual feeling and fled from the room in terror. Later, when she finally got up the nerve to go looking for him, she found him back upstairs in the living room, sleeping on the sofa.

When he had no interest in her, or when he left the house, she would halfheartedly search for a clue to who he was, reading her way through his library on the lookout for an old forgotten letter or maybe a memo tucked among the pages of a book. From the windows of the house all she could tell was that she was somewhere in the hills of a city that was strange to her; as part of the first generation of human beings to have been born with an actual photographic knowledge of what the Earth looks like from outer space, for a while she found something psychically reassuring, even profoundly secure, about living her life entirely within the walls of a space she had never seen from the outside. She relished the times the house was empty. She liked walking up and down the stairs from room to room and staring out the large drapeless windows at the panorama of little houses and little trees, and little cars driving up and down the winding streetlit roads that seemed to drop off in midair, and white satellite dishes erupting from the hillsides like monstrous mushrooms in the rain.

Sometimes she noticed the satellite dishes had been painted black in the night. Sometimes at night she could even see them vanish one by one, and the dark form of a clandestine figure fleeing the scene of the crime. The morning always brought a truck of huge new dishes; it was driven by a young Japanese boy who regularly replaced the vandalized black dishes with pristine white ones. Once, having just finished unloading a dish for the next-door neighbor and installing it on the hillside, he turned to see Kristin naked in the window, watching him.

There was a time, not so long before, she might have stepped back from view. Now she just ate a plum and watched him back.

IT was an old house for L.A., dating back to the Thirties, with the main floor at the top, at street level. There, perched with the library and kitchen, was the living room, shaped like a large half-moon, walled in white brick with a wooden floor and fireplace and a small empty piano in the corner, circled by the large bare windows with window seats.

On the level below were his bedroom, with a window facing east, and hers, with a window facing west. The locked room was down on the third floor below that. After a week or so, she began taking liberties with her room, putting away in the closet the bassinet that so unsettled her, anticipating a furious response from him. But he said nothing, maybe because he didn't notice or maybe because he too had wanted to move it but for some reason couldn't bring himself to.

The house offered few signs of either a life or a life's secrets. There was nothing on the walls except one overwhelming black-and-white print of a particularly desolate stretch of Route 66 in

Arizona, circa 1953, a Texaco gas station and a motel in the background, and back beyond them a car disappearing under a sky of delirious clouds. The old dirty-white piano in the living room sat undisturbed, never played; there was something barren and forsaken about it, as though recently abandoned by someone who sat behind it often, as though recently vacated by some significant memento that sat on top of it. In the library, that stray letter or photo, filed away among the pages of a book, wasn't to be found. This wasn't the kind of man who left, in the wake of his life, purposeless miscellany.

Soon she began smuggling books out of the library down to her own room. These included volumes of the Brontë and Cendrars and Kierkegaard she had originally brought from Davenhall, novels of Traven and Toomer and Bowles and Dostoyevsky and Oë and Woolrich and Silvina Ocampo, *The Ogre* and *Arabian Nights* and *The Book of Lilith* and *Confessions of an English Opium Eater*, the nightmare woodcut epics of Lynd Ward and the autobiography of Vincent van Gogh, a volume of suppressed Egon Schiele comic strips and the collected letters of Edgar G. Ulmer, and the lost unexpurgated diary of Kim Novak. She put them on the shelf below her window. On the wall above her bed she pinned photos and articles she tore out of his magazines, stories of writers and musicians and faraway dream-places like Morocco and Venice and Ireland, as well as a clipping she had managed to keep through all her travails: the news story about the New Year's Eve in Northern California.

"They must have believed," he said, in that strangled whisper of his, "that whatever was coming at midnight was so terrible any risk was worth taking." She had been sleeping in the sun in one of the windows upstairs and, upon waking, had ambled lazily down to her room; she was startled to find him sitting on her bed, where she supposed he had come looking for her in one of his stormy carnal fits. He had taken the clipping down from her wall and was studying it, not looking up as she came into the doorway. "They must have believed any consequence of whatever risk they took would be preferable to an apocalypse they couldn't imagine."

"They didn't know what they believed," she answered.

"No?" Now he looked up. "How do you know?"

"I was there."

"And what did you believe, that led you there?"

"I was running away from home."

He nodded absently, looking back at the article. "Walking off a cliff is an act of faith. So they must have believed something."

"What are you," she got up the nerve, "a philosopher, a sociologist?"

Until later, when she was able to sound it out and write it down and look at it, it sounded like an unspeakable medical practice: "I'm an apocalyptologist," he answered, still studying the clipping intently.

"Walking off a cliff," she said, "may be an act of faith, but that doesn't mean they knew what they believed in." Talking to him like this, she felt self-conscious about her nakedness for the first time in three weeks. "Isn't faith just believing in believing? Not wanting to *not* believe, knowing you simply *can't stand* to *not* believe? So you blindly take whatever faith offers you." She sighed in exasperation. "You're a point-misser."

He appeared annoyed. "I thought you said you were only nineteen."

"Actually I'm seventeen."

"You said you were nineteen!" he cried, aghast.

"I lied. I was desperate, remember? 'Best if you are desperate,' I think was the way you put it. I'll bet you just thought you were being pithy. That will teach you to write pithy sex ads. You want desperate, you'll get a liar every time."

"Yes, you're right." He tacked the clipping back on the wall where it had been. "You get a liar every time." He stood up from the bed and looked at her carefully, and she smiled ingratiatingly, because she was afraid now she had made a mistake. Silently he brushed past her in the doorway and then reappeared, moments later, with her clothes neatly folded in his arms. "Don't make me go," she said, looking at them. "I'll be nineteen if you want. Maybe I really am nineteen and I just told you I was seventeen because I thought you would like that." Her throat was tight with the prospect of being cast back out into the street. "I'll be stupid if you want. I'll tell any lie that pleases you. But I can't leave yet. I wouldn't last half a week, OK? Don't make me go. Please."

"I wasn't going to make you go," he said. He put her clothes on the bed. "I just thought maybe you would want to take a drive with me. You can stay here if you want, but I just thought we would go out for a while and take a drive."

The clothes on her body had a stunning weight and texture. Having fully adjusted to the initial vulnerability of always being nude, she now felt almost claustrophobic in her clothes. But it was exhilarating to be outside, riding in the car with the window down and feeling the breeze, once she assured herself he wasn't going to abandon her somewhere. He didn't blindfold her or put her in the backseat. They descended the hills and cruised through Hollywood and spent a couple of quiet hours in a cafe where he read old newspapers. He was surprised to see that her taste ran to literary journals rather than fashion magazines. "Oh, I'm not nearly intelligent enough for fashion magazines," she said witheringly. "All those conceptual juxtapositions of shirts and skirts—and of course the phylogenetic manifestations of makeup application are beyond me. Don't you have to have an advanced degree in art philosophy or something to understand that stuff?"

"It doesn't change anything," he said, "us sitting here talking, me taking you out for a drive. If you want to live in my house it has to be on the same terms, because it's what I need and it doesn't matter to me if it's right or wrong, it doesn't matter to me in the least if you think I'm exploiting you or if anyone thinks I'm exploiting you. It's what I need."

"Actually," she answered, "I thought I was the one exploiting you."

He went back to his newspaper for a moment and then looked up. "Where did you get those books in your room?"

"I've been stealing them from your library."

After another moment looking at the newspaper, he said, "I don't believe in them anymore."

"Not any of them?"

"Not any of them. I don't believe anything a single fucking one of those books says. I was desperate for what they said once, but like you said, desperation will get you lies every time."

"I don't think I meant it like that."

"You may not think you meant it like that," he whispered furiously, "but someday you'll find out. Someday when you're not just seventeen. You'll find out you meant it *exactly* like that." In that moment he seemed to hate her last shred of innocence as much as he coveted it. They left the cafe and drove west on Sunset Boulevard almost to the old abandoned freeway, and then he parked the car at Black Clock Park, where they strolled the time-capsule cemetery looking at the headstones where the capsules were buried. It started to rain; it seemed to rain all the time, a growing freakishness of the weather, strange guerrilla assaults of jigsaw lightning and increasingly torrential downpours. Up and down the rows of capsules they walked as the rain came down harder. As their clothes soaked through, he barely noticed. We're getting soaked, she finally said at one point, and he told her to go wait at the edge of the park beneath the trees. She went over to wait where he told her and then he walked back alone to one grave in particular several hundred feet away and stood staring at it for almost an hour, as the rain kept coming down and Kristin became colder and wetter.

When they got back home he stripped her and had her in the window where she had slept in the sunlight earlier that afternoon. She could see out the corner of one eye the storm clouds racing past the moon and the trees in the hills below them swaying in the shimmering patches of rain. In her mind she had an image of the window shattering and the two of them tumbling out over stalagmites of broken glass, plunging bloody to the little road that wound far below.

SHE figured out soon enough that an apocalyptologist wasn't a doctor. In the three weeks she had been living with the Occupant he had no contact with the outside world at all, as far as she could tell, except when he went out driving alone, communing with his buried time-capsule at the cemetery.

The phone never rang. There were no visitors. He had cut himself off from everything, having placed between himself and everyone else first the hills, then the house, then the door to the room on the bottom floor. She was the sole occupant of this designated no-man's-land between him and the world, wandering the house for hours and watching from the windows as the Japanese boy unloaded the new white satellite dishes off his truck and loaded the defaced black ones in their place.

She came down with a terrible fever from the hour she had waited for him in the cold rain at Black Clock Park, although in the fit of the fever she wondered if it was something more, her New Year survivor's luck exacting its toll. He brought to her soup and bread and juice, protecting his investment, she told herself cynically, in the rare moments amid the fever's throes when she was lucid enough to be cynical. Finally, by the third day when the fever had finally gone, he couldn't resist having her again, and seemed to find her new enervation particularly thrilling.

She had expected to be filled with dreams by now. She had expected by now she would be awash in them, dreams lapping at the coves of her body in white tides. But she was still a dream-virgin, her sleep a long black moonless expanse: it's my luck, she ruefully realized, to have sold myself to the one man in Los Angeles who has no dreams. If a dream is a memory of the future, she had found the one man with no future to remember.

She was there in the house alone on the one afternoon that the telephone finally rang. She stood staring at it, wondering what to do. Perhaps it was his usual complete obliviousness to her that made her blurt out later that night, just as he was disappearing into the downstairs room, "The phone rang." His door didn't quite close. It lingered uncertainly between closing and opening until he stepped back out into the hallway. "What?"

"The phone rang."

"When?"

"This afternoon."

"Did you answer it?"

"No."

He pondered her. He turned and went back into the room, but she noticed he still didn't entirely close the door. She had been lying on her bed reading a book for almost an hour when she came out into the dark hallway and found him standing there on the stairs, staring up at the telephone in its small cubbyhole in the landing on the first floor. There he stood in the dark, staring at the phone. She saw his silhouette turn in the dark and heard it say, "Did it ring a long time?"

"I don't know."

"You don't know?"

"What do you consider a long time?"

"A long time," she heard his silhouette say heatedly, "you know what a phone sounds like when it rings a long time. Each ring gets . . . worse. . . ." He didn't know what he was trying to say. He turned in exasperation and then once again vanished back down the stairs into the room at the bottom. Kristin went upstairs to get a glass of water and when she came back down she once again found the Occupant at the foot of the second landing, watching the phone. "Why didn't you answer it?" he said.

"Why should I have answered it?"

"If it rang a long time, anyone would have answered it."

"I didn't say it rang a long time," she said, "you said it rang a long time. 'I don't need a maid, I don't need a cook,' that was what your ad said, right? You never said you needed someone to answer the phone."

"Look," he whispered, taking a threatening step toward her up the stairs out of the shadow. His hovering dark form bled into the shadow so that all she saw were his throbbing ice-blue eyes and the floating spots of white in his black hair and beard. "You're a very smart seventeen-year-old, I know that. But keep your bright little seventeen-year-old mouth and your bright little seventeen-year-old mind to yourself, please. I don't care that you didn't answer the phone, do you understand? Look." He charged past her to the cubbyhole with the phone and grabbed the instrument and tore it from the wall. The wire whipped past her head in the dark. "See? I don't care. I don't care if the phone rings now, because now when it rings, it won't ring. Now if she calls, it won't matter. What do I need her for, I have you. That's why I have you, so I can do whatever I want with you and I don't have to need her anymore. See? Now we don't have to talk about this again. Now if the phone rings again you won't have to not *not* answer it. It will be like it never rang at all." He yanked more phone cord from the wall. "Here, let's do this. Let's do this, all right?" He grabbed Kristin and dragged her down the stairs with one hand, holding the phone cord with the other. He pulled her into her room and threw her on the bed and got on top of her and tried to tie the cord around her wrists, but the cord kept getting tangled and somehow he couldn't manage a knot. "Let's do this," he kept saying, "let's not answer the phone anymore." Finally he formed a haphazard knot and tied her wrists to the bed. He took her legs and opened her thighs and lowered himself to her and put her in his mouth.

She was shocked by it. Though she could have easily slipped from the phone cord around her wrists, she suppressed every instinct to, instead gripping the bedposts in rage trying to concentrate on the moon through her window, full and depthless like the moon that had shone her last night in Davenhall when she had awakened and gone looking for a dream. She kept concentrating on the moon and then closed her eyes and held the white sphere of it in her mind and imagined herself floating in space; feeling the breeze that came through the window, she imagined herself alone and falling into the moon with the breeze brushing her face and blowing between her legs. Just as she realized in horror she was about to have an orgasm, he fell away from her, half growling and half crying as he crumbled against the wall. "Angie," she heard him mutter before collapsing in grief.

He lay naked on the floor and wept. Kristin sat up in the moonlight of the bed, torn between rage and terror and a sense of violation she didn't understand. It took her a minute or two to place the name he had spoken and the voice in which he had spoken it, and then she felt betrayed or tricked, as if he had known it was her all along, though the rational part of her understood this wasn't a reasonable conclusion. She was enraged at how he had taken her in a way that somehow seemed beyond the unspoken bounds of their agreement—a rape of her erotic will rather than simply her body, by nearly bringing her to the point of orgasm. And she was enraged at the way he now lay on the floor and wept into his hands, as though there could possibly be something purifying about it, as though, she thought to herself bitterly, it was supposed to tear her heart out or something, as though she was supposed to extend to him some kind of compassion just because the way he used her had been premised on a secret grief. She didn't see that his grief was her responsibility. She had never presumed, after all, that her alienation should be his. And now it was all coming out, his grief, and she hated the hypocrisy of it, as though it was supposed to absolve him of everything; and she didn't owe him absolution, it was too much for him to ask, he didn't have the right to ask for it in words let alone sobs.

As for the terror she felt with the rage, that lay in knowing that everything their arrangement had been was about to change; and perhaps particularly because she was still feeling weak from her fever, she didn't believe she had the strength for whatever was next. The other thing, the deep, personal violation she had no name for, came from something else: that not by his cock but rather by his loveless kiss on her, she had just had her first dream, of the morning almost a year before when the Occupant woke to find his wife, nine months pregnant, vanished from their bed.

FOR a while after that he didn't come for her. "Look," she tries to explain now in the dark of the Hotel Ryu in Tokyo, "I certainly didn't care about the sex one way or the other. But I was a little concerned maybe his need for me had already exhausted itself, and I didn't want to have to leave yet. Life . . ." she says, not at all sure she's communicating clearly, "life's really just a process of trading on your most valuable commodity, isn't it? Intelligence, strength, talent, charisma, beauty. Well, in order to survive I traded on my nakedness, in the way I trade on my memories now, here, and on yours too," she says to the dead doctor. "I traded on my nakedness till a more valuable personal commodity presented itself. It never crossed my mind that anything but my body was subservient to him. There wasn't a moment my mind or spirit submitted to him, I knew that and I think he did too. . . . Then one night I went into his bedroom, where he had collapsed unconscious and drunk." She had knelt by the bed and looked at his face; it seemed to her his beard had gotten much whiter in just the few weeks since she had come to live there. "Are you awake?" she had said to him.

He didn't stir, snoring deeply, like she had heard him in Davenhall.

Kneeling there by his bed, she whispered in his ear, "How ridiculous," her face inches from his, "how absurd. Didn't slave girls and tying up women sort of go out with the Twentieth Century, even for pathetic middle-aged drunks? Whose life do you think you're saving anyway? Not your own, and not your wife's or your baby's"—and she could almost swear she saw him wince, and for a moment she wasn't sure he was unconscious at all. For a moment she was sure he was entirely awake, listening to her words only inches from his face; but she went on anyway—"so whose life, then, tell me. Is it possibly mine? You don't think for a second you're really saving *my* life, do you? That can't really be what this is all about, can it? Or is it just to lose your own life altogether? Is it that you've simply become that broken now, you've simply become that pitiful, that you've decided everything is just beyond saving?"

She stopped and waited five, ten, fifteen minutes just to see if he stirred, the courage of her words succumbing to her instinct for survival; she really had to watch her smart mouth. She really couldn't afford to so alienate him as to wind up back out on the street. Not only had she come to see this life, in this house that she loved with all the books that she read, as not such a bad one for the time being, less dreary than many lives, but she also understood—maybe he did as well—that though he had brought her home as his prisoner, he had become hers, or at least his own, locked up in his little room while she had the run of the rest of the house, as though he had relinquished his life to her.

And so her nights continued to pass dreamless as ever, as well as the days in which she sometimes daydreamed of being back in Davenhall. She daydreamed of lying on the deck of the boat that ferried tourists back and forth to the island, on the rare occasions when there were tourists, and wishing on the usual occasions when there weren't that the boy who navigated the boat would stop just gazing at her longingly *and do something*. Such daydreams, however, ultimately led back to thoughts of her uncle and the mother who had disappeared when she was a baby—such an abstraction for Kristin it barely seemed worth thinking about at all—and then she stopped thinking about home altogether.

Now this house in the Hollywood Hills was as good a home as any, and if it meant being jailer to some old drunken crackpot under the illusion he was having his way with her, fine. One evening she went downstairs and stood for a while outside the locked room, staring at it; suddenly the door opened and, framed by the doorway, his silhouette stared back at her in the dark of the hallway. "What do you think you're doing?" he whispered. Tonight he sounded especially nuts.

"Nothing," she said.

"You were going to lock me in, weren't you?"

"What?"

"You were going to lock me in."

She snorted, incredulous. It had never dawned on her. For the rest of the night her thoughts were swept by the idea: locking him in the room—could she do that? And if she did, then what would she do with him? The next afternoon it made even less sense, when the Occupant was gone and she went downstairs to the room and examined the door, and saw that it locked not from the outside but the inside; so it wasn't possible to lock him in even if she wanted to. For a moment she became frightened. He was really losing his grip now, she thought to herself. But it wasn't nearly as terrifying as what she found beyond the door.

Not entirely to her surprise, the door was now unlocked.

Perhaps this was because he had accidentally forgotten to lock it, or perhaps he had left it unlocked on purpose, or perhaps at this point his accidents and intentions had become one and the same. In any case, stepping into the afternoon shadows of the room and wading through the empty vodka bottles, she saw the Apocalyptic Calendar for the first time.

A couple of hours later she was still sitting on the small footstool in the middle of the room, looking at the calendar, when she heard him behind her in the open doorway.

Not daring to turn, she braced herself for the repercussions, and for some time could feel him standing there, silently raging, she supposed. Finally, when she couldn't stand it, she looked up at him only to find him studying the calendar as she had been, unperturbed. It appeared as though he, like her, was seeing it for the first time. Or as though, with her there, he thought there was a chance he might finally understand it.

The calendar entirely circled the room. It covered all the walls except the door, a sky-blue mural blotting out the windows and overflowing the walls onto the floor and ceiling. The dates on the calendar were not sequential like on an ordinary calendar but free-floating according to some inexplicable order, in some cases far-removed dates overlapping, in other cases consecutive dates separated by the length of the room. In varying shades of red and black, apparently senseless timelines ran from the top of the calendar to the bottom, from one end to the other.

"Look here," the Occupant finally said, and began tracing the lines for her. She nodded as though everything he said made perfect sense. He was explaining that, after twenty years in which he had become the Western world's foremost apocalyptologist, he had made the startling discovery that the new millennium, which he called the Age of Apocalypse, had not begun at midnight New Year's Eve 1999 after all. This was because, he went on, over the course of the last half century the very definition of apocalypse had changed, as empirically and quantifiably as a virus changes, or a galaxy: "You see, sometime in the last half century," he said, "modern apocalypse outgrew God." Modern apocalypse was no longer about cataclysmic upheaval as related to divine revelation; modern apocalypse, the Occupant told Kristin, speaking with more passion than she had ever heard him express before, was "an explosion of time in a void of meaning," when apocalypse lost nothing less than its very faith—and in fact the true Age of Apocalypse had begun well before 31 December 1999, at exactly 3:02 in the morning on the seventh of May, in the year 1968.

"How do you know?" she said.

And exactly as she had answered his question about that New Year's Eve on the cliffs of Northern California, he replied, "I was there."

For instance, the Occupant went on, by the modern definition of faithless apocalypse, the assassination of America's greatest civil rights leader in April 1968 was not a modern apocalyptic event, because it had a rationale, however villainous the rationale was. The assassination of the civil rights leader's *mother,* on the other hand, on the thirtieth of June 1974—Year Seven of the Secret Millennium, he pointed out to Kristin on the Calendar, down along the baseboard—*that* was a modern apocalyptic event, because it had no rationale at all: the woman had simply been playing the organ in church, when a maniac started randomly firing a gun.

Such incidents littered the Calendar in sensurround, connected by red and black lines. These included irrational assassinations and killings: nuns in El Salvador (Year Thirteen or, by the old, now obsolete calendar, 27 December 1980), Hollywood Eurotrash in L.A. canyons (Year Two: 9 August 1969), benign Swedish prime ministers walking home from the movies (Year Eighteen: 28 February 1986). Such crimes fundamentally defied whatever conclusions commentators and sociologists and ideologues frantically tried to offer. Incidents of the New Apocalypse included mass exterminations so detached from cogent explanation that tragedy could never quite overcome absurdity: airplane explosions off the coast of Long Island (Year Twenty-Nine: 17 July 1996), schoolchildren beheading other schoolchildren in Kobe (Year Twenty-Nine: 27 March 1997), billowing toxic clouds from East Indian insecticide plants killing two thousand (Year Seventeen: 3 December 1984), nuclear-reactor meltdowns in the Ukraine radiating 400,000 (Year Eighteen: 26 April 1986), 1,400 panicked Moslems on the way to Mecca crushed in a 110-degree tunnel when the air-conditioning failed (Year Twenty-Three: 2 July 1990), thirty-nine members of a religious cybercult, in the hope of riding a passing comet to the next world, committing suicide in Southern California (Year Twenty-Nine: 26 March 1997), and a recently added item, Kristin noted, dated Year Thirty-Two: two thousand women and children walking off a cliff in Northern California. "I can tell you for a fact," Kristin murmured, just trying to be helpful, "it was no more than 1,999."

The Calendar's apocalyptic flotsam included the emergence of figures of such dazzling dementia as to momentarily mesmerize even thinking people: military buffoons in Uganda (Year Three: 25 January 1971), "holy" men in Iran (Year Eleven: 1 February 1979), megalomaniacal novelists in Japan (Year Three: 25 November 1970), genocidal schoolteachers in Cambodia (Year Seven: 13 April 1975), Nazi war criminals winning presi-

dential elections in Austria (Year Nineteen: 8 June 1986), psychotic Texas billionaires polling one vote in five in presidential
elections in America (Year Twenty-Five: 4 November 1992), and
ludicrous duets in which it was difficult to know who was loo-
nier—the memoir forgerer, or another psychotic billionaire so
reclusively and obsessively shrouded in secrecy for so long it
might be argued that the man who appropriated his memories
became more the real rememberer than the real rememberer
himself (Year Four: 13 March 1972).

More than these, the crucial reference points of the Apocalyptic Calendar were moments of nihilistic derangement no scheme
could accommodate. If the various connecting timelines that the
Occupant had drawn in red and black between murder and may-
hem and madmen were secret tunnels running through a mansion of memory, in which history was only the floor plan, certain
insane events large and trivial eluded the Calendar's geometry
altogether. They included the erection of London Bridge in Arizona (Year Four: 10 October 1971), the gassing of a subway in
Tokyo (Year Twenty-Seven: 20 March 1995), the discovery of a
burial ground of slaughtered eagles in Wyoming (Year Four: 3
August 1971), the disintegration of an American spaceship and
all its crew due to the erosion of a tiny rubber ring (Year Eighteen: 28 January 1986), the discovery and announcement that
video games triggered epilepsy (Year Twenty-Five: 14 January
1993), the decapitation of a notorious snuff-film director in a
Manhattan traffic tunnel (Year Fourteen: 3 October 1981), the
hounding unto death of an English princess by tabloid photogra-
phers in a fatal car crash in Paris (Year Thirty: 31 August 1997),
and the mass marriage of four thousand people performed by a
cracked Korean minister who chose their spouses for them, on
16 July 1982 (Year Fifteen), which by sheer coincidence happened to be the same day Kristin was born.

But finally, the Occupant told Kristin, he had determined that
the true center of the Apocalyptic Age, and the true center of
the true millennium that began on the seventh of May 1968,
and the true center of the Apocalyptic Calendar among all its

crisscrossing lines and floating anarchic events, the true vortex where all meaning collapsed into blackness, lay between two abysmal events so beyond the pale of unreason that a civilized person could barely bring himself to contemplate them. One, on 5 May 1985, was the pilgrimage of an American president to a German cemetery for the express purpose of laying a wreath in honor of the most singularly vicious, sadistic and incontestably evil human beings of the Twentieth Century. The other, only twelve days before on 23 April, was the utterly arbitrary decision by America's greatest soft-drink company to immediately discontinue the single most successful product in the history of modern commerce, in order to produce in its place a bad imitation of its obviously inferior competitor.

BY the time the Occupant had finished talking, afternoon had given way to dusk and dusk had given way to night. No light came through the pale blue calendar that papered over the windows except small throbbing white orbs of streetlamps on the road below the back of the house, that curved to the east before curling down the hill.

Bonkers with a capital B, Kristin said to herself. Around and around in the dark, in clockwise circles, the Occupant paced furiously. It was not unlike the night Kristin had awakened to hear him prowling the foot of her bed; mindlessly he kicked vodka bottles out of his way. She could see his blue eyes glittering in the dark. "What?" she said nervously to his silence.

He stepped toward her. He pulled her up from the small footstool where she'd sat almost motionless for hours and ran his hands over her body, as though searching for a particular spot on her thigh, along her forearm, under a breast.

"What are you doing?" she said.

"Not so long ago," he said, "I made this . . . confounding determination."

"OK. Confound me."

He knelt at her feet and ran his hands up one leg, as though looking for the button that would open a hidden door. "I determined," he said, "that if modern apocalypse is indeed an explosion of time in a void of meaning, then time is moving, and the timelines of the Apocalyptic Calendar are moving as well. All the routes and capitals of chaos on the Calendar are constantly, imperceptibly rearranging themselves in relation to each other . . . do you understand—?"

"Let's pretend I do."

"Which means the Calendar is always . . . out of whack. You know? Too static on the walls to accommodate, you know, shifts in perspective. Like an ancient starwatcher who always watched the sky from the same place and assumed the stars were moving, only because he hadn't learned to take into account that it was the earth he was standing on that was moving." Still on his knees, he touched the hinge of her thighs, and in the dark she could see him looking up at her. "It's not there."

"What's not there?" she said.

"The *place*. Do you understand what I'm saying?"

"It sounds like physics and physics was never my strong suit."

"It's not physics," he said, "it has nothing to do with physics. It's far beyond the meaning of physics. The Twentieth Century spent far too much time paying attention to physicists. It has to do with . . . For the calendar of modern apocalypse to be accurate, its nihilistic center—floating in Year Seventeen between the twenty-third of April and the fifth of May 1985—needs to move in relation to the timelines of chaos."

"Yes?"

He found a spot above her spleen, and his eyes shone in the dark: "*There*," he whispered, in that same whisper in which he had spoken since the first day she met him. Even in the dark, she thought she saw him smile; it was the first time since that first day and she shuddered. "Right there." Right above her spleen in black ink he marked the spot, the twenty-ninth of April 1985—*29.4.85*—in the Year Seventeen of the Secret Millennium, and then he stood on his feet and stepped back and kept staring at her, his eyes still shining with such a crazed look that he frightened her more now than he ever had before. He grabbed her by her wrists. "No," she said.

He pushed her to the wall, and then to the floor.

"No."

"There are no noes between us," he hissed, "you know that. No noes, no maybes. Only yeses. You know that." He lowered her to the floor and fucked her not far from the assassination of an Indian prime minister by her bodyguard (Year Seventeen: 31 October 1984) and the murder of a Sixties soul singer by his father (Year Sixteen: 1 April 1984), his black-and-white beard in her face, rapture displacing grief. Now he had her so as to shoot himself into the vortex of chaos rather than simply empty himself of memory; and she had a hundred dreams in a single climax, until she thought she couldn't stand one more revelation.

Her body became part of the Calendar, the traveling center of apocalypse. Over the course of the following days and weeks, he positioned her everywhere, studying how the dates shifted in accordance, how the timelines rearranged themselves in relation to her. He had her walk the room in circles for hours, from one corner to the other, in the light cast through the papered window or the shadow beyond the light. He perched her high on ladders and lay her facedown on the floor; he pinned her against the wall and placed her outside the room in the hallway or on the stairs. He took her outside the house to the base of the hillside below, posing her naked where he could see her in relation to this year or that, through a peephole he cut in the Calendar in some frivolous, expendable date; astonished drivers nearly drove off the road. He set her on the next hill over, far out of sight and beyond the range of what even he could see, and finally took her to Black Clock Park, standing her at the grave of his time-capsule in an old long blue coat he gave her, with a stop-watch and instructions that at an exact designated moment, after enough time for him to return to his house and his room and his calendar, she would drop her coat and stand naked among the tombstones while he plotted the shifting courses and charted the swirling clockwork.

By this time she had gotten so used to being naked that she wore her nakedness like a persona. The sex between them changed to something no longer indifferent but, for his part, possessed, like the rest of his life. At his insistence she began sleeping with him in his bed, even when they didn't have sex, and she would wake in the morning with his arms clutching her close. *Of course you are free,* she remembered his newspaper ad had read, *to end the arrangement and leave at any moment,* but the very nature of the arrangement had changed now, she knew that, whether or not he acknowledged it.

So she never doubted what he had in mind the night they drove out to the desert. By now night and day meant nothing to him, he slept only moments here and there; and the night they drove out to the desert, three hours northeast of Los Angeles, the sky was on fire with stars. She was uneasy the whole way, exhausted, but her anxiety and the cold kept her awake, and he kept looking over at her as though trying to de-cide exactly what to do with her, as though he was as uncertain as she exactly what desire or revelation or madness was dictat-ing the moment. They drove out toward San Bernardino and then up through the Cajon Pass, flying out across the desert highway in the dark, Liszt and industrial music on the tape player. Somewhere in the desolation between Barstow and Las Vegas, he finally pulled over. He turned off the engine but not the ignition, turning up the music because it had gotten particularly depraved and he wanted to be able to hear it outside the car. He got out of the car and went around to the other side and opened her door. "Get out," he said.

"What are we doing," she said.

"Just get out."

"No."

"No noes," he snarled, "just yeses."

"No," she said. She sat in the passenger's seat looking up at him. She knew what he was going to do, she knew exactly what he had in mind: "I know exactly what you have in mind," she said. "You're going to drag me out into the desert and stick me next to a cactus and then you're going to drive back to L.A. and study your fucking calendar. And then you somehow think— because you've gone completely off the deep end—you somehow think you're going to drive back out here in seven or eight hours and just pick me up again. And what you don't understand, *because you are completely out of your mind,* what you don't understand is that in seven or eight hours I'll be dead. I'll be dead because I'll have frozen to death or some motorcycle gang will have come by and raped me and killed me, or some wild animal will have eaten me or . . . or maybe I won't be dead, maybe I'll just have had *a really unpleasant experience.* No. I quit. We can waive the pension plan. 'You're free to end the arrangement and leave at any moment,' that's what your ad said. This is the moment."

"No noes"—his whisper rose to a pathetic howl—"just yeses." He stumbled out into the desert, thrashing clockwise among the overgrowth; she could tell one of his headaches had returned. He kept pressing his temples harder and harder, blue eyes about to pop from their sockets; and then trampling the desert shrubbery, he clutched his head as though barely containing it in his hands, trying to hold it together. "Timelines of chaos!" he cried hoarsely to the desert night, "the anarchy of the age!"

"Jesus," she muttered, reaching over and pulling her door shut and locking it, though she wasn't really sure who was the bigger point-misser here, the Occupant or her. She slid over to the driver's seat, closed the door on the driver's side and locked it too, and stepped on the gas. Because she had never driven a car before, she had to figure out how to shift it into gear, and while she was figuring that out, he finally understood what was happening and began pounding on the passenger door. As best she could, she appraised the mechanics of reverse, neutral, drive; found a gear and hit the gas and the car lurched; and kept on lurching for a couple of miles before she realized that if she continued, she would lurch into Las Vegas completely naked. She had no way of knowing this was the one American city other than New Orleans to which such an entrance might have endeared her, so she turned around and went back. When she came to him standing in the middle of the highway, pacing in circles in the dark talking to himself as though her abandonment of him was only the most temporary distraction from his obsession, she slowed and then stopped. They looked at each other through the windshield and finally he walked over. It took her a minute to figure out how to lower the window on the passenger's side. "Do you want a ride?" she said.

"Move over," he said, "you don't know how to drive."

"I'm driving, you're riding," she answered.

"You don't know how to drive," he quietly insisted, "move over. I'm not going to leave you out here in the desert. I'll drive us back to Los Angeles." She saw that he could see how she was looking at him. "Whatever else I've done," he pointed out, "I don't think I've lied to you yet."

"Not yet," she said. She slid back to the other seat and he got in the car and they drove home.

NOW when he had his headaches, he would lie in the dark of his bedroom and let her rub his head for hours.

One night when he came for her, she grabbed his hair in two handfuls and even in the dark of the bedroom he could see her looking him squarely in his blue eyes. "What are you doing?" he whispered in alarm.

"I'm making you look at me," she said. "I'm making you look in my eyes while you fuck me, I'm making you see me while you do it."

He cried out, pulling away from her. On his knees he tried to scramble back to the far end of the bed, and all the while she held onto his hair. When he tried to stand, he pulled her up with him, she was clutching so tightly; the whole time she kept staring determinedly into his eyes. "What are you doing," he kept saying.

"Don't you think it's time?" she said. "Don't you think it's time you looked in my eyes?"

"What are you talking about?" he choked. Together they tumbled to the floor and into the dark corner of the room.

"It's time you looked in my eyes," she answered, but she meant: time I looked in yours. Time for a personal act of revolt.

Time to throw your oh-so-highly intellectualized sense of chaos into a true chaos of the heart and senses. She didn't much care anymore if he tossed her out of his life for it; she had about decided it was time for that too. They had never understood each other. If she had understood him, she would have known that for almost a year now, since his wife had vanished with their child in her belly, in his mansion of memory he had become increasingly lost and trapped. If he had understood her, he would have known she was a dream-virgin when he met her, and so wouldn't have been surprised to wake one morning soon afterward and find that she had vanished too.

LET'S say I'm a monster. Let's say I was never capable of love. Let's say down in the pit of my soul, beyond whatever I tried to convince myself I believed, everything was always about surrender and control, so the bond I formed with the girl I brought home was true to who I really am, because it was base and hungry.

Let's say I never really believed in anything but myself. Let's say my soul was so impoverished I never really believed in anything but my appetites, because of all the things I've felt, appetite was beyond my control. This assumes I ever really believed there was a soul to be impoverished. Let's say from the first moment of my life, everything's always been about me and nothing else, including apocalypse and chaos; let's say even apocalypse and chaos have been conceits of my psyche and bad faith—this assumes I ever kept any kind of faith at all, bad or otherwise. . . . Let's say I'm faithlessness made flesh, the modern age's leap of faith stopped dead in its tracks, fucking around with apocalypse and chaos only because in some broken part of me, among any wreckage of honor or altruism or commitment or compassion, or the bits and pieces of moral vanity, I really believed the abyss was always just the playground of my imagination, and I was its bully.

How do you know, the girl said the afternoon she found the Calendar in the downstairs room, when I told her about the true millennium of the modern soul, and I said, I was there. I was eleven. My father was a semi-celebrated, proverbially lion-maned American poet and romantic egomaniac, larger than life and moving us to Paris when his political activities made staying in the States uncomfortable. Dragging Mama and me from one forum to the next, from one podium to the next, from one adoring standing ovation to the next, from Boston to San Francisco till institutional harassment and ominous threats and anonymous phone calls seemed to make exile the only viable option. He reveled in exile more than he ever really agonized over it. . . . Mama, half French half Russian Jew, determined self-sacrificer and silently suffering martyr, first went to America as a student after the second world war had cast across her family twin shadows of looming extermination on the one hand, rumors of collaboration on the other. What was exile for my father, she was determined to call home. Back in Paris maybe she was also determined to stop either the suffering or the silence, if she couldn't stop both.

I was asleep in our flat at the corner of the rue Dante and rue Saint-Jacques, on the left bank of the city, not far from Notre Dame, when I woke to a sound unlike any I'd ever heard before. People always say it's like a car backfiring but hearing it anyone can tell it's different. Years later I still don't know whether the gun was Mama's or my father's, or belonged to the dead girl in their bed. One of the smaller mysteries. Like lots of things, it never got explained. But when it woke me, even at age eleven I knew something was wrong, and I ran out my room in my underwear straight to my parents' bedroom and Mama catching me in her arms, and I didn't ask what happened . . . in my eleven-year-old life I already hated anything that might constitute emotional upheaval. I just wanted her to tell me everything was all right, that I could go back to sleep, that it was only a sound from out in the street.

Then there was a sound from out in the street.

It was the night of 6 May 1968, or to be exact 3:02 in the morning of 7 May. The shot that woke me woke the modern age. Echoed down the rue Saint-Jacques to the boulevard Saint-Germain and the university a few blocks beyond, where a few thousand students had taken over, thrown out the professors, draped red and black flags over the statues of Hugo and Pasteur, hoisted banners that read FORBID THE FORBIDDEN and BELOW THE BOULEVARD, THE BEACH, and waited as what seemed like tens of thousands of cops surrounded the school waiting in turn. Who knows what any of them took the sound of the gunshot to be. Years later, for everything that's been written about it, there's no record of any student having a gun, and the police weapon of choice was the truncheon, when it wasn't a tank . . . did the cops really think some student had fired a gun? Did the students really think some lone cop had fired a gun? Maybe they thought it was the snap of a truncheon across some anonymous body. Maybe it doesn't matter in the least. Maybe in the early-morning hours what mattered was the sound's sheer explosiveness not its source, and it cracked the waiting in two—and cracked in two there could be no waiting anymore. The cops charged.

Upstairs in our flat Mama, half hysterical, held me in the dark of the hall and I could smell gunfire through the door of their bedroom, open just enough so I could see in the light of the bed lamp my father standing there holding his head in his hands. A lifeless feminine arm jutted into view. Bedlam exploded in the streets. Tearing myself from Mama I ran downstairs as she chased after me, and in the dark of the rue Dante up and down the rue Saint-Jacques people were yelling and running, ripping cobblestones up from the road, hurling them aimlessly, pushing cars over on their sides and setting them on fire. Cops were swinging at everything. They surged against the sidewalks, uprooted the chestnut trees. Glass glistened everywhere. Tear gas canisters rolled in the gutters. The air was thick with fumes and smoke and there was a chant in the distance I didn't recognize as *Métro boulot dodo* till I read it in the papers later.

It meant, more or less, *subway, work, sleep*—a bitter reduction of everything the modern age had become. It was the moment when the meaning of the modern age unraveled. In the years leading up to this moment there was an incontrovertible moral logic to upheaval, upheaval was the instrument of morally distinct aspirations, whatever you thought of those aspirations. In the minutes before 3:02 on the morning of the seventh of May, the students who seized the Sorbonne did so on behalf of complaints that ceased to matter at all by 3:03 . . . by 3:04 upheaval lost all rationale, it was the expression of a spiritual chaos no politics could address; by 3:07 I was running in my underwear in the street, sprung loose of moral meaning along with everyone else, time exploding in a void of meaning; at 3:08 I turned to see Mama behind me in the door of our apartment building, not running after me but just looking as if to commit me as fast to memory as the moment allowed. And then she just walked from the doorway into the crowd as calmly as everyone else around me ran insanely. . . .

I stopped and said, Mama? and stepped toward her, when someone knocked me over. When I picked myself up, she was gone.

THERE I am crying in the street. Around me there's a sound that's more than just the collective voice of upheaval, it's the collective voice of the age growing into a din like I wouldn't hear again for years . . . the louder it grew the louder I tried to call her, till I was screaming so loud finally my voice was gone. It would be seven years before I got it back.

Timelines of chaos! Anarchy of the age! It wasn't possible everything could have happened in that one night, it just seemed like one night. Had to have been nights and nights, weeks of nights. . . . The last lucid memory I had was standing there looking for Mama in the riot, then turning back to the doorway of our building on the rue Dante waiting for her to come back and somehow knowing she wasn't going to come back. And I wasn't going back upstairs, back to the gun on the floor and the smoke in the hall and my father in the bedroom, so I took off down the boulevard Saint-Germain in the direction of the very café where I would meet Angie years later, and up the boulevard in waves I could see them in the streetlights, tanks rolling, cops marching. In their black helmets in the night they looked headless, thousands of headless cops snapping truncheons in their hands and a sound from the helmets like black hail bouncing off, handfuls of bolts and nuts thrown by students. I traveled below the sight lines of chaos. I moved unscathed, except to be drenched by erupting water mains and buckets of water that Parisians in the upstairs windows kept dumping on the students below, whether to douse or revive their fury I never knew—I don't think they even knew. Medical students in white frocks streaked with blood ran back and forth shouting at everyone to calm down, but no one wanted to calm down, the spectacular disintegration of everything was too exhilarating, and now everyone existed just to be exhilarated.

The smell of exhilaration's smoke settled over everything. From one end of the city to the other . . . but I never found it as overpowering as the smoke in the hall of our flat that last time. *That* was the smell of years to come. What would have been one of the more sensational murder trials in modern France just happened to coincide with the country's most anarchic days since 1871, if not the last years of the Eighteenth Century, so, busy picking through the rubble of the following weeks, France barely noticed. The dead girl in my parents' bed was a literature student at the Sorbonne, part of the protest only hours before she was shot, maybe destined to be cut down by a charging cop, dying for anarchy instead of desire. I'd seen her once before, actually, one afternoon when I was with my parents at the Deux Magots. She was a couple of tables over, red hair and freckles and a smile I still remember. The position of the gun on the bedroom floor near her hand indicated the possibility of suicide, maybe like it was meant to, a conclusion the police rejected when they charged my father with second-degree murder. He went first to trial then prison stonily and uncharacteristically silent. The romantic in him, compelled by a personal code that was narcissistic at heart but still had its occasional heroic results, I guess, may have been protecting Mama after she caught the girl in bed with him and killed her. It wasn't till years later it occurred to me it might have been Mama, sick of her silent suffering and feeling unleashed in a Paris flirting with havoc, who was in bed with the girl, something my egomaniac father would have been too proud to explain to anyone let alone police and newspapers, and which wouldn't have absolved him in any case.

In any case Mama disappeared. Into the Apocalyptic Age! Into the Secret Millennium! The next couple months, as the country descended into disorder, the closest exit out of France was Belgium and you had to get there first, presumably on foot since no cars drove because they had no gas, no trains ran because they were on strike, no planes flew because they were grounded. . . . I never saw her again, or my father. I was shuffled around a while among friends in Paris, then shipped back to New York and New England to be shuffled among friends there. Didn't communicate with my father in prison before leaving Europe, hadn't communicated with him when word came of his death—by then I was sixteen, deposited at a commune in upstate New York and finding the loss of my voice altogether convenient . . . when I got the letter, I read it once, and went into town to catch a movie. I was unmoved by the lost opportunity of reconciliation—let's say I never would have believed it. Let's say I saw nothing to reconcile. Let's say I'm a monster.

Years later, after I married Angie, the day we moved to the house in the Hollywood Hills, I stumbled on a box of letters. Flipping through, I found an empty envelope addressed in a woman's hand I knew immediately, though I hadn't seen it since I was eleven. I kept blinking at it as if something would click in my head that explained it. I had no recollection of receiving it. Though the envelope was torn open at the top, I had no recollection of having read it. In a panic I went through the box knowing the letter had to have fallen out, but it wasn't there. I went through the other boxes and for a long last time stood in the middle of the empty apartment knowing that letter was there somewhere, slipped through some crack, and that if I left now I'd never find it.

Finally, of course, I had to leave. Kept the empty envelope

with its postmark faded and obscured, the date lost forever and the origin a tiny French town I never heard of called Sur-les-Bateaux, about twelve kilometers—according to the atlas—from the coast of Brittany.

OH I'm sorry. Have I spoken too loudly? Have I raised my voice? Have I taken a tone? Have I transgressed my station in life as chaos assigned it to me, to always exist just above a whisper? Would I have just gone on never living beyond the sound of my own voice, if I hadn't rescued Jenna's copy of Gorky from the gutter on Central Park West that spring day in, what, 1975? . . . I was nineteen. Eighteen. Don't even remember what I was doing in the city but there I was, and when I picked up the book that slipped from her arms, she gave me as radiant a smile as I was ever going to get from her. Jenna was a card-carrying Stalinist, an exotic and preposterous bird even in the zoo of the Seventies . . . now, of course, when I think about her at all, which isn't much, I realize that—dialectical materialism being what it was—the odds of Jenna giving herself to me were always exactly zero. But I didn't know that. I was historically naive, as she would have been the first to tell you or me or anyone else.

She'd just gotten back from studying abroad in Madrid,

where by some machination far too mysterious to divulge to an inescapably bourgeois American boy—the son of a poet, no less: a *bohemian*—she'd gone to Moscow for two weeks as part of some sort of "friendship" program that opened her eyes forever. . . . All right, I went a little around the bend for Jenna that spring in New York. Followed her to secret meetings and clandestine rendezvous with this or that comrade, at the headquarters of this or that cadre where she would spend the night while I stood on the curb outside counting the windows up the side of the brownstone to the one I decided was hers. . . .

A stalker is just a particularly dedicated romantic, right? Next morning I'd still be there, slumped against a tree. In a way she gave me back my voice, seven years after it was drowned out by revolution, the anarchic kind that disciplined Stalinists had no use for—gave me back my voice albeit in whispers and mutters, and I sat up nights rewriting her speeches for her, the language of her convictions having either failed those convictions or eluded her altogether. I didn't believe a word. I didn't believe a word I wrote or a word I said. I didn't believe a word I whispered or muttered. I believed in the way I wanted her, and when I realized I wanted her so much I'd mutter or whisper almost any conceivable horseshit for her, I knew I had to get away, and hope my voice went with me.

Got away, back to Europe, where else. To Amsterdam, where I lived in the red-light district above a bakery now converted to a nightclub, with the usual haze of hashish and the house chanteuse who sang nude every night with the broken line of a highway painted up the front of her between her breasts. A month later I got Jenna's card casually announcing she'd be in Madrid in two weeks, and my instinctive reaction, so fast I barely noticed, was not to go at all. My next was to immediately check out of the hotel and head straight for the central station, where I bought a one-way ticket on the next train out, somehow assuming life would get warmer the farther south I got. . . . I was a little surprised to find the train getting colder the closer it got to Spain, and by the time I reached the frontier in the middle of the night I was feverish in a way that had nothing to do with her. I had a seat in a second-class compartment with an older Spanish businessman who looked and dressed like he should have been up in the better part of the train, and the whole trip we didn't say two words until crossing the border, where Spanish soldiers went through my bag and found my bundle of old articles and news photos. One magazine cover in particular, from May '68, was of a car exploding spectacularly in the Paris streets. Are you a revolutionary? the border guard said very calmly. Once back on the train, I asked the businessman what was going on, was it always like this, the guards and soldiers, and he didn't say anything, just stared back at me and then back at his newspaper, the same paper he'd been reading for twelve hours, and then without lifting his eyes from the paper, as though speaking to no one at all, he answered, "The General is dying."

On and on he'd been dying, an endless dying, days and nights, weeks and months, and by the time I got to Madrid police and guns and martial law were everywhere, with everyone else behind closed windows and locked doors. No one was in the streets, no one was in the bars or *tascas* or cafés, even the famed fountains of the city seemed frozen. So it was very deliberately into this Madrid that Jenna came, on orders from some Spanish-lisping apparatchik no doubt, to prepare for and bear witness to the reclamation of a Spain that had slipped from her comrades' fingers thirty-six years earlier. That it was her Stalinists who had stabbed the Republic in the back while Hitler's Stukas flew overhead was precisely one of those unseemly loose ends for which history is so conscientiously and completely re-written from time to time. In Madrid, Jenna was in her element. "Anarchists," she advised me, "are only bourgeois turned inside out," but as far as I could tell she thrived in the anarchic Spanish air. If anything it brought out the flushed carnal glow of her, her red lips all the more luscious with paranoia.

I had grown a beard in Amsterdam. . . . Jenna wasn't so impressed. She didn't find it radical or dangerous, in the fashion of glamorous Cubans, but self-indulgent and undisciplined, in the fashion of odious hippies, the dregs of capitalism—first thing she said when she got off the plane was, "Why did you grow that awful beard?" In her very smart little cocked red beret with the little red Soviet star pinned to the front, she had big brown eyes, a moist mouth that glinted with the gold earrings that hung from her strawberry hair, a body capable of evoking such wild and meaningless upheaval as to completely disprove the "science" of her ideological certainties. The Party back home in the States didn't get so many gorgeous recruits. Actually the Party back home hardly got anyone at all anymore under seventy years old, so already they were grooming her accordingly, to fill the ranks with new recruits, young men in particular, although to anyone giving the matter careful consideration there was an obvious contradiction inherent in the advertising: Comrades! Check it out! Under socialism this is the sort of foxy chick you would get to fuck *if* socialism were as corrupt, decadent and self-indulgent as capitalism! If it was as corrupt, decadent and self-indulgent as capitalism, then the Party could afford to be generous with Jenna's body since she had already given it her heart, a softer slushier more malleable organ of less functional value than shoulders, back, hands, feet, but certainly more useful than a brain, which could be troublesome when it had an inclination to operate on its own. Jenna's never presented that problem. Compliant as the Party could ever wish for, Jenna made all the necessary dialectical transitions with utmost agility, even aplomb—the gulags were a myth, the purges a hoax, invasions of various countries a matter between comrades and none of the West's business, the Nazi-Soviet Pact of 1939 a complete invention of the bourgeois press.

When Jenna wasn't talking Party politics, her other overriding object of interest was her father, who she hated, and who I'd been hearing about from almost the moment I met her. From the cafés of New York to the cafés of Madrid, she'd sit staring and sputtering at the photo of her father she always carried with her. "We don't look anything alike," she'd say. . . . of course they looked exactly alike. She also had, crumpled in the back of her wallet, a photo of her mother, with whom she was on good terms and to whom she bore no resemblance at all. She also had a brother, or half brother, though which half was which was so unclear to me I wasn't sure Jenna herself knew who mothered who, who fathered who, a confusion that terrified her. Jenna's involvement with the Party was a secret her family agreed to keep from each other in mutual pretense, with the exception of the father, from whom it really was a secret. The idea of her father learning the truth was so mortifying to her she couldn't stand it.

What did she expect of fathers in this day and age? At the time I couldn't figure out if Karl Marx was Jenna's surrogate father or surrogate lover, when now the answer is so obvious. Night after night the three of us slept in the same bed, though every once in a while I'd wake to find myself on the floor, Karl having rolled over in his sleep. Up and down the Gran Via, from one end of the Sun Plaza to the other, from Hapsburg Madrid to Bourbon Madrid, from the Prado to the Toledo to the Convent of the Barefoot Nuns, from the Moorish shadows to the white doves dissolving into foam on the fountain waters, day after day I tagged along after Jenna and Karl on their rounds, waiting plaintively in black archways as they visited friends, attended meetings, plotted history. "You treat me so well," she sneered.

"Yes," I agreed.

"You're so understanding, aren't you," she said, "you're so caring. But what you don't understand is that history doesn't care at all about how caring you are, about how understanding you are. History doesn't care at all what you want or need from me."

"I don't give a fuck about history."

"Exactly," she said, "that's how limited you are. That's how narrow. You don't see the big picture. In the Soviet Union everyone sees the big picture."

"This isn't the Soviet Union."

"Not for the moment," she allowed. "You came all the way

down to Madrid just to see me, didn't you? All that way. You came all that way just to see me—and it isn't fair. I have work to do. I'm part of something bigger than me, bigger than you, bigger than us, that's what you can't understand." In the meantime the old Spanish General went on dying. By now he'd gotten it down to such an art there was no big rush to finish. He's dead! word would filter out into the street, and then, Uh, no, actually, he's not dead. A day or two later, Yes! this time he's *really* dead! and then a few minutes later, Well, actually, he's *almost* dead. As Spain became a ghost country, riots and demonstrations broke out across the rest of Europe, I'd seen one myself from the train leaving Bordeaux, marchers pouring up the boulevards by the thousands under red banner after red banner, chanting *Fran! co! As! sas! sin!* over and over. . . . On the face of it there was a rationale for this. Five Basque separatists had just been put to death by garrote for the alleged murder of some Spanish cops. But of course that wasn't what the riots were about at all.

The riots were a release, after thirty-five years of suppression and silence. The riots were a cheer, urging the old General on to his end. The riots were a protest, that death and time had let him off so easily. The riots were a complaint, that he wouldn't be around to hate anymore, that he wouldn't be around to fear anymore, that the last monster of a clearer, more morally delineated age was now exiting the premises and leaving everyone else behind to sort out the moral confusion.

Jenna, I whispered in her ear one night as she slept. By now I'd lain chastely beside her five consecutive nights.

"Is he dead yet?" she murmured back.

No he's not dead yet—and in her sleep she swooned. Then she blinked her eyes open in the dark, and turned to me, and saw I wasn't who she was looking for. Where's Karl, she said, glancing around. Karl's not here, I said. Karl went down to the corner for a beer, or maybe he's in the toilet jerking off because he's become bored with you, Jenna, as I have finally become bored. I moved to her and she tried to pull away and I held her.

I was naked. Not bad, eh, Jenna? tell me Karl is this big. Tell me you'd rather be lying with his corpse out there in the street. I lowered my mouth to her and put my tongue inside her. "What are you doing," she said in horror, trying to twist herself away from me. Her climax wasn't a moan or shudder or even a cry, it was the scream of a woman in labor, it wasn't a climax but deliverance, and I especially enjoyed the wracked humiliated sobs afterwards, the way all her comradely discipline was in shambles, the way the fragile sense of herself she had created so carefully and artificially out of her inane ideology was smashed. When she finally began to calm down I did it to her again, till I was confident I'd taken her far beyond the point of ever again entertaining even the fleeting conceit of knowing herself, of ever being so smugly certain of anything in her life. I got up, dressed, walked out the hotel, flagged a cab in the street, and went to the train station.

BY the time I got on the train, news that the old General was dead had spread up and down the platform. Descending the Meseta, winding alongside the Manzanares, the train headed north, into the face of an Andalusian rain from the south that had swept through Madrid the night before; and as dawn came over the plains I could see peasants dressed in black darting furtively through the tall golden fields. . . .

Back to New York. Spent the last days of summer '76 moving up and down Third Avenue from a small sublet on East Fifth to a flat on Bond Street, where I crashed from time to time with the editor of a literary magazine who viewed every night as a race to the finish with Jack Daniel's. Dawn always lost. I was almost twenty. In the quiet of my muteness over the years, besides the clothes on my back, all I had was a box of tapes I had collected—bits and pieces of Indonesian chants, surreal bebop, gamelan rain songs, war-documentary soundtracks, Saint-Saëns, water chimes, Jamaican dub, police radio signals, recordings of howler monkeys, all smashed together on a single soundloop and broadcast from a pitiful little tape player run by ever-dying batteries. . . . Then, soho and noho, I heard something else.

Downtown was littered with punk enclaves now. From Broadway to St. Marks, the musical center of the Village had shifted from west to east, its hub a vertical bomb crater of a club at Bowery and Bleecker: I cared nothing about the Scene. I cared nothing about the hair or ripped clothes. I cared nothing about the pierced flesh. I cared nothing about the piss on the floor or the posturing in the dark, about the quaaludes or the coke or the needles in the backstage toilets. I cared nothing about the graffiti on the walls or the charred hallways. I cared nothing about the bikers or the junkies or the vampires or the groupies or the backstreet dadaists, or even the people who made the music itself. I didn't care in the least about whatever inane blurtings were passed off as polemics. I found the professed rage of the Scene amusing to the extent I found it to be anything, I found the bodies slamming at the musicians' feet tedious to the extent I paid any attention to them at all. I found every other thing about the Scene an affectation except the sheer shimmering beauty of the racket it made.

They considered me a slummer, they were right . . . but I was slumming not inside their noise but outside my silence— that was the difference! I confounded them with tenacity, night after night, week after week, month after month, till one night after finishing her set Maxxi Maraschino took me home. Max was the one who looked like Bardot and served as the Scene's resident blond sex goddess when she wasn't working her day job at an uptown strip joint . . . secretly pushing thirty-five, some years earlier she had made a film with the notorious New York pornographers Mitch Christian and Lulu Blu, and many years before that, when she was seventeen, rumor had it she was the long-lost member of the Shangri-Las, expelled from the group before their first hit record for the one night she went down on an entire college fraternity. . . .

Now Maxxi had a three-bedroom flat at Second and Second known as Depravity Central. It was across the street from the most popular drug house on the Lower East Side and provided an emergency landing-strip for every crashing drooling smack-shooting would-be rock-and-roll colossus in the neighborhood. Three in the morning was the designated Suicide Hour, when people routinely passed through threatening suicide or, in a smacked-up and otherworldly stupor, claiming to have in fact already committed suicide. Bandage-bound wrists were chic. I lived for a while in Max's apartment, where she gave me a tiny bedroom to myself, with its own bathroom and a window that looked out on a vacant lot and the building next door where the kids lined up on the sidewalk for their daily score. There I fooled with my shitty little tape player as the traffic of musicians and hookers and strippers streamed in and out of the rest of the flat.

"What are you doing," Max said like Jenna had, the first night I woke her in a cloud of vodka to slip my tongue up inside her. "What are you doing," whispering it even though on this particular night there was no one else at Depravity Central to hear us, "and why are you doing it?" and I said, Because I want to.

Oh, well, in that case. As long as it was because I wanted to. As long as it was for me, not her. As long as I didn't care in the least whether she wanted me to or not. As long as I expected no sort of response from her whatsoever, as long as I wasn't trying to resurrect something from the dead. As long as it was because I couldn't stand to leave untasted every last drop of her. In that case she would collapse back into the pillow, feel every part of her implode to her core, grab my hair in her hands and hold on with everything she had. *I fell into the arms,* went my favorite song of the time, *of Venus de Milo*—like I was in a universe of sound surrounded by a curtain of pink water, the slim white disembodied arms of the world's most beautiful woman reaching through to me.

I fell into the soundtrack of the subterranean imagination. The nine years since Mama disappeared into the riots of Paris came bubbling up around my ankles like the sound that rose around me and drowned out my eleven-year-old cries for her. In the moment of the gunshot there was a whole world unto itself, and I came back for the dark and the noise again and again, standing in the back of the clubs at the edge of the gorgeous black din while everyone around me got more and more deranged. My drug of choice—not that I chose it but it chose me—was bargain-basement fiorinal for the blinding headaches I was starting to have around then, chased down with Black Russians and suspending me in an incandescent blast of vodka and caffeine and painkiller. . . . Word spread. Guys hated me. Twenty-five years later they probably still hate me, if my name should happen to come up or if they should happen to have survived the years' cocaine not so dream-exhausted and sensually constipated they can't remember it. I kissed all the girls. Poised between my teeth every one of them gasped, caught her breath, held it. Before placing it on the lips of their sex I tasted it on the tip of my tongue: the Kiss of Chaos! an apocalyptic delirium exhaled into all of them . . . and in response there came from out of them the music of the subterranean imagination like the tapes I played—squalling guitars, pirate chanteys, pygmy tribal prayers, Four Freshmen outtakes, shrieks of sea buffalo stranded by high tides. . . . And though I didn't know it at the time, with every kiss another day was marked on the Blue Calendar of years later, every woman marked by the Kiss of Chaos became a day in the Apocalyptic Age, so years later when I went back to New York I kept my eyes peeled for punk goddesses I knew in the Year Eleven, on the twenty-fifth of July 1978 (first baby born from a test tube) or the second of September (first girl murdered in a snuff film) or the twentieth of November (mass religious South American Kool-Aid suicides). . . .

By the time I was done with them, in the waning days of '78, with the Scene only a winter away from rigor mortis, the girls of chaos were crawling the Lower East Side with a thousand anarchic anniversaries and a thousand nihilistic holidays in their throbbing little wombs. In the clubs in the dark, from under the glorious sublime howl of the music, at first barely discernible, the sound of the subterranean imagination poured out of them between their thighs, rising to their waists then their breasts, then to their necks, till everyone's ears was full of it and the music couldn't be heard at all, only the cacophony of oil wells exploding in the North Sea, jumbo jets colliding in the Canary Islands, rioting Persian Moslems protesting the Twentieth Century, Manhattan serial killers murdering on the orders of barking dogs, firing squads carrying out executions in Utah, missionaries executed for no reason in Rhodesia, thousands executed for no reason in Uganda, millions executed for no reason in Cambodia, restaurants blown up for no reason in Belfast, gas tankers running aground off the coast of Brittany, not far from the tiny village of Sur-les-Bateaux. Only thing anyone could hear anymore was these girls transformed by the Kiss of Chaos into human jukeboxes of the apocalypse, till their last song, most deafening of all, was the final death throe of the Scene itself— the suicide of the Scene's most notorious and pathetic figure, following the murder of his hooker lover, a crime for which he was the prime suspect. With that, everyone knew it was all over, including Maxxi Maraschino when she heard the news at dawn from a junkie on the street . . . and then she came back up to the flat, stepped among the various unconscious bodies crashed out on her floor, looked in my room to determine I was still asleep, and locked me in.

Actually I wasn't asleep, I was just lying there with my eyes closed. And in the rare quiet of dawn I might have heard the click of the dead bolt, but in fact my life wasn't quiet anymore, the roar of chaos was always in my ears now, the roar of Paris when I was eleven, the roar unleashed with a kiss in all the human jukeboxes of the Scene's women . . . I couldn't even hear my tapes anymore. And it wasn't till I got up and used the bathroom and tried to open the outer door to the rest of the flat that I realized I was locked in. Like anyone suddenly and unexpectedly trapped, my first instinct was to free myself. I rattled the knob, started banging with my fist. On the other side of the door, various denizens who had spent the night either slept through the ruckus or were just cognizant enough to laugh at what they considered an amusing situation. On the other side of the door, I could hear Max writing something.

Over the course of the following days then weeks, I alternated between desperation to try and free myself, and an acceptance of the boundaries of my new universe, along with the consolation that if I couldn't get out, no one else could get in. I stared out my window for days on end at the vacant lot below and the drug house next to it, where the line of kids on the sidewalk grew longer or shorter depending on the weather or the whims of the pharmaceutical market or the popularity of the drug du jour or the news on the street—good or bad—and the circling squad cars. I could never shout to anyone outside my window or outside my door because my cries never rose above the whispers and mutters that chaos had left to me when it took my voice in Paris years before. . . .

Max always had an uncanny sense when to unlock the door and slip me a sandwich and water or juice or a soda while I slept. Meanwhile, with the roar that I always heard in my head, my headaches got worse, to which she responded with some generic painkiller she scored on the street . . . coming to me in the dark as I lay on my mattress in a blinding incapacitated delirium, Max would withhold the painkiller till I serviced her to satisfaction and then leave as I slept off the pain and the stupor of the drug, turning the dead bolt locked behind her. "Baby?" I heard her through the door one afternoon.

Through the roar in my head I could barely make out her voice. "What?" I said.

"Are you all right?"

"Am I all right?" Through the pain and noise I think I still managed to sound a little testy. "I'm locked in a room."

"Yes," she admitted, "is it so bad?"

"I can't get out. I'm a prisoner."

"Try to learn to accept it," she explained gently, and so for seven months I lived in the locked room. In my hallucinations from the headaches, I began to see for the first time the time-lines of chaos on the walls around me, on the ceiling above me, and the whole Calendar started to take shape. If I'd had anything to write with I might have drawn it all out right then and there, and then and there it would still be, in some hovel down at Second and Second on the Lower East Side of New York City. On the other side of the door, I heard the Scene come and go, sound of chaos slowly transforming from exhilaration to despair . . . sometimes I thought I could make out the whimper of death. Max would return from a gig in the early-morning hours and call through the door. "Baby?"

"What?"

"You all right?"

"I'm still here, if that's what you're asking."

"You missed my show tonight."

"Yes, I was detained." I could hear her discouragement. "How was it?"

"I don't know," she'd say. I could hear the Scene's collective faith ebbing from her voice. "I wish you'd been there, you could tell me."

"Yes," I said, "it seems like something we should share to-gether. As part of our ever-deepening relationship. Sometimes," I said, "I can almost hear it from here."

"You can almost hear it?"

"Almost. I lie on the floor and put my head next to the vent and I can almost hear it, your voice, your song, coming through the vents of the Lower East Side, traveling up the Bowery from Houston, taking a right at Second, coming through the vent into the room."

"How's it sound?"

"Hard to say. By the time it gets here, sound traveling at the speed of chaos as it does, you're into the next verse."

"I wish," she said forlornly, "you could hear it better. So you could tell me."

"Me too."

"It's hard to know whether it's good or not, without someone I can trust there listening."

"I know what you mean," I assured her.

"I miss you."

I said, "Max, I have an idea."

"Yes?"

"Tomorrow," I said, "I'll come to the show, and I'll listen, and I'll be able to tell you then, because I'll be right there."

For a while I didn't hear anything. I wondered if she was saying something and I was just missing it through the door and the roar in my head. "But then," she finally answered, "I'd have to let you out of the room."

"Yes."

"No," she said through the door, "I don't think that will work out."

"I'll be right there, so I'll be able to hear everything."

"I don't think so, no," she said.

"It's a very good idea, actually."

"No, actually, it's not so good. Really, it's not that great an idea."

"Absolutely."

"No, actually," she said, "thinking about it, having given it some thought, really, I think the show tonight went well."

"You can't be sure."

"I think it went quite well, giving it some thought. I'm quite happy with the way it went."

"From here," I tried to point out, "it seemed like . . . it seemed like it went well, but maybe it could be . . . better. It seemed . . . maybe it might have just missed being perfect. If I was there listening, I could tell for sure."

"No," she said through the door, "I don't believe it missed at all. I think it was divine. I think it was groovy. I'm tired now, you know, baby? It's been a long night. How's your headache?"

"Open the fucking door, Max."

"I'm going to sleep now, baby. I'll come see you again soon."

"Max!"

"Good night." I didn't get out of the room till one afternoon when, with neither the sound in my ears nor the pain in my head as bad as usual, I heard the voice of yet another woman outside my door. Hello? I heard her, and on my knees I scrambled from the mattress to the door and pressed my ear against it. Hello? she said again, and I felt a very strange confusion as to whether to answer, as if, faced with the prospect of release, I wasn't as sure anymore I wanted it. When I tried to call back, for a moment I found my voice failing again, till I finally managed to croak out a strangled response: Yes, I said, getting on my feet, Yes! and then rapping on the door. Are you all right? the girl on the other side said, and when I tried to answer, once again my voice failed, and so I just kept rapping on the door. I stepped back from the door to see if it would open. But nothing happened, and after a moment to my great fury I could hear amid the sound in my head footsteps of the girl leaving. I slammed my hand against the door and returned to my mattress on the floor and dozed. . . .

A few minutes later I woke and got up and went to the door and turned the knob and found it unlocked. I went out into the apartment, like a man emerging from the underground into the sunlight of the earth's surface, gazing around at the empty flat. Looking back at the door of the room where I had spent seven months, I saw Max had written, in black marker ink, OCCUPIED. I left everything behind—including my tapes—took fifty-five bucks from the cigar box where she kept her spare cash, and got out.

LET'S not analyze too much why I went back to Paris in '82. The timing was probably random anyway . . . sooner or later I was going back, and it just happened to be then. Got fired—for "insubordination" and being a "disruptive influence in the office," but that's not worth going into either—from a job with a research firm where I had a thousand facts of chaos at my fingers . . . and fleeing that and an affair with a recently separated woman still feeling bad about her ex-husband, I went to Paris. So there I was. I lived for a while with some anarchists on the rue de Vaugirard, not far from the Eiffel Tower, then moved into a hotel on the rue Jacob, just off the boulevard Saint-Germain, where the concierge supplied me with toothpaste and toilet paper and aspirin for my headaches while deferring payment on the hotel tab.

"Can we make a deal," Angie said at the Brasserie Lipp the first time I saw her, "we won't ask too much about the past?" How much of a past can she have? I thought. She was a daunting nineteen. I was an unconvincing twenty-five. It was July and she was the only person on the boulevard that afternoon sitting in the sun, with no use for the shade, the slimmest of breezes moving the long black hair that fell on her shoulders. I would have thought she was so sophisticated in the black boots she wore outside her jeans like the French girls, if not for the ridiculous little stuffed bear she sat in the chair next to her. Later the only thing besides the bear that betrayed her was the way, forgetting herself, she would bite her nails, because Angie biting her nails was as fully incongruous with the rest of her as she meant it to be, the rest of her such a practiced determined cool.

She never broke a sweat. Amerasian, she wasn't quite beautiful, but near enough to confuse and unsettle the passing guys. Twenty years before, her mother met her father in Tokyo while on leave from duty as an army nurse in Korea, and after that they settled near Las Vegas, where she was born. Her father was a physicist, Rising Sun expatriate among a half-dozen Third Reich expatriates now working for the victorious Americans in the Nevada desert, and in the afternoons her pregnant mother went out on the patio and lay on the chaise lounge sunbathing in the nuclear light of the tests her husband worked on just beyond the backyard fence. . . . This was as much of Angie's past as I was going to find out right away, drinking my vodka tonic and wondering if I said something wrong trying to make conversation: "Four thousand people," I read out loud from the *Herald Tribune,* though my voice was still such a hoarse whisper I wasn't sure anyone could hear me, "married in New York by a crazy Korean who picked their husbands and wives for them," and then thinking, Shit (as I said it), maybe she's Korean.

"Maybe," she said instead, "he would have picked us."

That answer alone probably got us through the next three years. For that answer alone I avoided certain magazines at the newsstands, certain movies in dark moviehouses full of men, from which your doomed eyes and sorry smile and all the naked rest of you would have stared back at me, if I had gone looking for trouble. . . . I don't know whether not looking for trouble was a sign of maturity or cowardice—whatever, Angie had left something behind in New York, and whatever New York had done to her, it was lousy enough that Paris seemed liberating in comparison, for all the ways the city was so ragged around the edges that '82 summer, hot and overrun with beggars and trash piling up on the streets and people getting pushed in front of oncoming Métro trains. After buying her dinner at the Lipp, I got her to come back with me to my hotel and we climbed the five flights to my room and in one hand she held her stuffed bear and in one hand I still had a white rose some old woman had given me in the Luxembourg Gardens that afternoon. . . . At the Lipp I kept trying to give you the rose and you kept pushing it back. So it lay on the table, next to the profiteroles. . . .

Back at my hotel, five flights up, the room was stifling. I opened the window that looked out on the street, worked on the cork of a Côtes du Rhône, and turned to find a naked girl on my bed, in nothing but knee-high boots as black as her hair. She lay on her stomach reading the *Herald Tribune,* spread out on the bed before her, her elbows getting black from newsprint, legs swaying back and forth in the air behind her, stuffed bear on the pillow at the head of the bed and the white rose I thought I'd finally gotten her to take tossed on the table next to the bathroom door.

All right, I was stunned. I admit it. I stood there with the bottle in my hand staring at her, till she looked up. "So if he'd married us," she said, "how long do you suppose it would be before you left me?"

"How do you know I would leave you? Maybe you would leave me." I sat next to her on the bed. She was very casual about the way she read the newspaper naked, lazily swaying her legs back and forth behind her, and I'd almost say there was no sexual suggestion about it at all except for the boots—such a hackneyed and effective male fantasy, for her to be wearing nothing but those boots, like she just neglected to remove them, though of course she couldn't have taken her jeans off without also taking off the boots. In the few seconds that I'd turned my back to open the window and uncork the bottle of wine, she'd taken off her boots and then all her clothes—and then put the boots back on. . . .

"No," she assured me with utmost seriousness, "you would leave me, I don't think there's any doubt about that. I wouldn't assume," she added, now obliquely addressing the subject of her nakedness, though it took me a moment to catch up with the shift in conversation, "I wouldn't assume, if I were you, that things are as easy as they appear. For all you know," she said, "it's my way of seizing control of the situation. For all you know, I may just be trying to intimidate you. Are you intimidated?"

"Not in the least."

"For all you know," she went on, "it might be much easier for me to take off my clothes in front of a strange guy than to sleep with him. You shouldn't assume, just because many men might have seen me naked, that many men have had sex with me."

I took a drink from the bottle and offered it to her. "I didn't necessarily assume many men had seen you naked."

"Don't you have any glasses?" she said, looking at the bottle disdainfully, and I got up from the bed and got her a glass from the bathroom and poured her some wine. "Don't assume," she said, sipping the wine, "I've had sex with more men than I can count."

"I don't assume that."

"I can count them. I don't need all my fingers either." She wiggled the fingers of her free hand at me. "I may not be able to name them, but I can count them."

"Is this the part of the past we aren't supposed to talk about?"

"Yes," she admitted. She tapped the *Herald Tribune* in front of her. "So how do you think this guy paired them up?"

"What?"

"This Korean guy, Reverend Whatsis. Who married these four thousand people in New York. He chose all their partners for them, it says. How did he do that? Did he choose them by age, did he choose them by height? Did he choose alphabetically? Did he have a file on them, did he match up their interests, hobbies, college degrees? That doesn't seem possible, does it, that he would have a file on all these people?" Unconsciously she began to bite her fingernail on one of the fingers that she didn't need to count all the men she'd had sex with, then she caught herself and closed her hand in a fist, burying it beneath her breasts. Outside, the noise of the street was starting to die and the summer light that doesn't die in Paris till after ten o'clock was finally dying too. "So on the one hand you figure he doesn't care if any of these marriages are successful, or happy, or if any of these people belong together—all he cares is that he can snap his fingers and everyone just does what he wants, right? Everyone just surrenders to him the single most important decision of their lives. That's the point."

"Yes."

"That's all he cares about."

"A demonstration to the world of his control over chaos."

"You think?" she said, frowning. "Except," and now she rolled over onto her back staring at the ceiling, raising the finger she had been biting and blithely showing me the rest of her, "if all these marriages fall apart later, then the point he's making sort of falls apart too. You know?" She twisted her head around now, looking at me half sideways, half upside down. "Bad public relations really, to perform whatever it is, two thousand marriages as the world watches, and then, you know, nineteen hundred of them don't last. Not a very convincing demonstration of control."

I was still distracted.

"You're distracted," she said.

"I'm listening."

"But you're distracted."

"Not at all."

"Not at all," she scoffed.

"I don't think there was any grand scheme," I said, "that was the real point. That's the real power. That he can be so completely arbitrary. It makes him that much more powerful to be able to marry anyone to anyone without any rational reason. People's lives completely changed through a whim. You see?"

"I'll bet he just threw a bunch of names in a hat and picked.

They're probably lucky he even matched guys to girls." She thought about it. "In its own way, it's completely evil."

"Is it?"

"Yes," she assured me, "it is. I know. I've seen evil," she said quietly, "not evil in the abstract, but in the concretely tangible. I know what evil is, and I can now tell you for a fact it's not me lying on this bed in nothing but my boots drinking red wine with you. That isn't even close."

"And the four thousand people who blindly deliver themselves over to his decision, are they evil?"

"That's not evil. That's faith."

"Where does there stop being a difference?"

She rolled onto her side and closed her eyes. "Confusion," she said, concluding the argument, but at the time I had no idea what she meant. We fell asleep without making love. Sometime in the early-morning hours I woke to a kick from one of her boots, and thinking I might close the window, I got up, but it was still so warm I left the window open, and then I pulled off her boots in the dark and pulled the sheet up over her. I was about to take from her arms the small stuffed bear she was clutching when she muttered from out of her sleep, "I would seriously advise you not to try and come between me and my bear." I sat on the bed a while and noticed, in the dark, that the white rose I got in the Luxembourg Gardens that afternoon, which had been lying on the small table by the bathroom door, was now stuck in the bottle of wine I'd opened. I had no idea why or when she put the rose in the wine, but since there was still wine in the bottle, the next morning when we woke, the white of the rose had turned a deep and saturated pink.

BY the next night she had moved in. I never fooled myself into believing it was for love, even with that crack about the Korean minister choosing us for soul mates. It's possible if I'd thought for a moment it was for love, I would have had nothing to do with it. On my part it was to have her: she let me. On her part it was to survive: I saved her life. My specialty. I was the evangelist of romance. Every time I needed to justify my existence I could pull her life out of my pocket and say, See this life of yours? I saved it. Every time she nearly slipped from my fingers I could snap her back into my arms and hold her life up in front of her eyes, so she got a good look, and say, See this life of yours I saved? Please don't thank me. Think nothing of it. And by the way, where do you suppose *you're* going?

"Truthfully," Angie answered, "I have no idea," because she was too young to know who she was, let alone where she was going, and too wise to pretend otherwise. Her identity surfaced in bits and pieces—a head for higher mathematics, and how she was called Saki as a girl, and the afternoon in, where, London? months after we'd been together, when she sat down to a piano in someone's flat and out of the blue started playing Debussy and Liszt and Duke Ellington. She clung to the little girl in her,

sometimes clutching that fucking little stuffed bear as if the innocence of it could cleanse her life of those moments when sometime, somewhere before, in the same hand she cracked a whip
in black leather. Was she trying to live down the sleek sophisticated side of her that was still hard from at least one teenage
suicide attempt—if I read between the lines right—as well as
whatever was the source of the bad dreams at night? She labeled
her emotional responses. Instead of laughing she would say,
"Haha," with just a hint of humor in her eyes. Instead of groan-
ing she would say, "Groan," with something in her eyes between
exasperation and disdain. She translated her own feelings first
to herself then to everyone around her, and the truth is, it was
probably what kept us together so long, because then I could
deal with her as though her feelings were only signposts on the
highway of our relationship. Lanes merging, detour here, danger
ahead. Slow down. Stop.

Fleeting revelations about her parents . . . their early
expectations. . . . Hints about the angry and bitter estrangement
from them at least three or four Nevada winters past, from what
I could gather, when they must have wondered if she was dead
or alive. I guess this accounted for why at first Angie didn't much
give a damn whether I saved her life or not. The streets of
Paris might threaten her life, but something in New York had
threatened her soul. That was the real difference between us;
she valued her soul more than her existence and I had it the
other way around. It didn't seem such a great incompatibility.
Seemed a minor difference compared to the way she never confronted me and the way our sex never demanded to call itself
love, a minor difference compared to whatever erotic radar existed between us that led my lips straight to hers in the dark
and reduced all our other language to non sequiturs. "How arrogant of you," she'd say, "to assume my mouth is always right
where you want it. What if I slept pointed the other direction?"

"I would kiss your toe. I would believe your head had gotten
very little."

"Haha," she said, sounding all the more solemn in the dark because I couldn't see her eyes.

Because I valued my existence more than my soul, I had no need of my memories. Because I valued my existence more than my soul, I didn't go looking for Mama after she disappeared. Because I valued my existence more than my soul, I didn't see my father before he died. Because I valued my existence more than my soul, there was a certain corner in Paris I avoided altogether, just a half mile down the boulevard from the Lipp. Once we almost happened upon it, strolling along, when I suddenly realized it was only a café or two away, and I turned us abruptly the other direction, yanked her along with me down the boulevard Saint-Michel toward the river. "What is it?" she said.

"I thought we agreed we weren't talking about the past," I said. August now, a month since we'd come together, Paris all ours. . . .

"No," Angie explained, "we agreed we're not talking about *my* past. We never said anything about your past."

"Well, now we agree we're not talking about my past too."

"I don't agree at all." She stopped on the sidewalk to look in a shop window as she continued to talk. There really wasn't anything in the window that interested her, it was just a place to stare while she bitterly pointed out the ways I shut her out of my thoughts and feelings. "When we first met," she said, "we agreed we wouldn't talk about my past. You should have said right then if there was something you weren't going to talk about, if you were going to shut me out. It might have made a difference." She stood so close to the window that, from the side, I couldn't see her face through the black hair that fell down her profile. . . . "It's a betrayal to tell me now there's part of your life that's off limits. You should have told me from the beginning, the way I told you."

"I don't see how it matters when I told you," I said, "I'm telling you now."

"Fume," she said. "Dismay."

If it had been anyone but Angie, I would have kept on walking down to the river. I would have kept on walking down to the quays, heading west toward the Eiffel Tower, looking for a houseboat navigated by some other desperate female sailor begging to be bailed out. But instead I told Angie about what had happened in Paris when I was eleven, if not every detail then most of it, and then I had to tell her about the Calendar, at that point just a grand scheme more than anything else, points of seismic apocalyptic activity still uncharted and undetermined . . . and when I told Angie all that, she was inside the walls of my life for good. She had all my most important secrets and I had none of hers, and I had no choice but to keep a close eye on her from then on, and try not to let her out of my sight.

Once winter came, we watched Paris from that beginning stage of a fever when consciousness is dimmed and everything seems dark, slow songs from the next room always like an echo, and distant memories jangling with present dreams, riddled with the sound of someone saying something you can't quite hear. Riding through the Bois de Boulogne where prostitutes had fucked men in the summer trees, with the calamitous crash of sunset and the ferocious rattle of the foliage through the taxi window, autumn colors of death and rouge buried by winter, woods gleaming with semen and snow, Angie sat with me in the back of the cab biting her nails without realizing and then, looking at her fingers, suddenly lurched into my arms and held me. In the rubble she obsessed me. In the ruins I was both her pimp and john, selling her to myself. In the decay it seemed all the more suitable a place to have her however I wanted. Through the lace of the curtains in the hotel window I could watch young girls in the vacant room across the courtyard while I was behind her. Rock and roll was in the halls, guys hacked tubercular on the stairs, sink pipes rumbled like the streets. Drains gurgled near the sidewalks. Whispers from 1968 rose to a wail from the river, windows banged open and shut in the gust, the heads of the girls across the courtyard dropping from their necks, hair hanging to the gutters . . . and from the streets I can hear it now, the waves of truncheons and swaying clubs, cops wearing empty tear-gas canisters around their genitals, flagellating dead revolutionaries. Chaos banal and splendid—black workers killed in Johannesburg on 3 July, IRA bombs in Hyde and Regent parks on 20 July, grenades lobbed into a kosher Paris restaurant on 9 August—marks my violations of her. "*Insist*," Angie hisses in the dark, digging her nails in my thighs; first I take it for one of her signposts, but it's a command. "Insist on what you want from me. Make me do what I can barely bear to do," she says, turning beneath me, thrusting herself onto me. "Make me do something nearly as bad and depraved as I am," and I do, down all the days and weeks and months to the very hour Christian militiamen in Beirut randomly slaughter Palestinian peasants: "Moan," she sighs in the Paris twilight.

Went to London and fell in with a debauched couple who had nothing but money and looks and antics. An older South American woman and her young Englishman. I knew immediately everything they proposed didn't shock Angie in the least but bored her. Soon she had no more interest in antics and I was outgrowing my own capacity for them too, feeling too absurd to succumb. Besides, it was now 1983, the newspapers full of deadly new statistics, desire's new mortality rate. "I have to go back to New York," I said a year later on Boxing Day, in Piccadilly.

"Regret," she answered quietly, "sob."

By the time she followed, five or six months later, it was unaccompanied by promises. "Maybe it's for a month, or a week, or a day . . ." she said on the phone from London, sounding confused, and at first I took it as a good sign she hadn't simply announced, "Confusion." Having gotten what I wanted and left to question only whether I really wanted it, I wondered if it meant she was slipping, that maybe she was now an altogether less postmodern Angie, maybe her survival instinct kicked in after all and she had decided it was time to call the expert on Angie-saving. It put me in control, the way I liked it . . . but now I also realized saving Angie made me *responsible*, a thought I pushed from my mind the moment it entered. And then in New York I saw how she peered around every corner before turning it, how she scoured the shadows of every doorway before entering it. . . .

It was now seven years after the Scene. The Girls of Chaos were gone! By tracking them down I had hoped to plot chronologies, lay out the temporal schematic, because I didn't have the sound in my head anymore, and had to rely on memory, even as I already knew memory was the first casualty of the new calendar, that the Calendar would have its own memory. . . . Spring of '86, the Calendar's blue panorama was already creeping its way round the walls of my Upper West Side apartment. By then Angie had been with me in the city a year, and that was when I found out what it was in New York she so dreaded all that time, what it was she so feared. It was me.

The day that the letter came with the news about her mother, I was sitting in a chair by the window overlooking Broadway and Seventy-first, Angie at a piano I had bought for her. I could tell she didn't think it was such a great piano. The keys were cracked, and I couldn't explain why I considered this a virtue, she would have had to hear the music of years before. She hit a discordant note and looked at me, and then at the letter, and for a while it just sat there on the piano—did she somehow know what it was, and just couldn't bring herself to open it right away? She kept hitting the bad note on the keyboard till I'd gone into the back of the flat awhile and then from the back room heard her note just stop, hover in the hallway, in a way that made me go find her again. . . . As far as I could gather, her father hadn't even written it himself. Still so alienated and furious, even in a moment of mourning and grief, he wouldn't even break the news to his own daughter. He'd had someone else write it for him.

Well, what did you expect, Angie? What did you expect of fathers in this day and age? What did you expect of mothers, for that matter? What did you expect of me—wasn't this our bargain, to leave the past out of it? To leave mothers out of it, and fathers? What was the point of our pact if, in the end, we have to deal with these things, what was the point if, in the end, I have to feel it tear my heart out just to look at you so desolate there in the corner of the flat with the Blue Calendar looming over you like a wave, with your bedraggled little bear close to you as though it could explain everything, as though it could give you a comfort I could not or would not. So don't look so betrayed. Don't look so abandoned. This paralysis of mine was part of the deal, from our first moment at the Lipp on the boulevard Saint-Germain.

It was later that night I dreamed the walls were raining. I dreamed the Blue Calendar was swallowing up the apartment like the sea flooding in around my head as we slept, splashing on my face. Only when I woke did I realize the walls were not raining, the Calendar was not the sea, and Angie was crying on my pillow. It was the first time I'd seen her cry. I'd felt her hold me tightly before, in the backseat of cab rides through the Bois de Boulogne, I'd felt in rare moments, hard as she tried to conceal it, a need from her I never answered. It wasn't till years later, thinking back on our time together, and thinking back on this particular night, that I understood both the power and powerlessness of our bond, and that what I thought made her so powerful before—the confidence into which I had taken her when I told her what happened to me as a boy in Paris—was in fact only a testament to how powerless she really felt. She needed to know my secrets without divulging her own, just to feel she had a fighting chance with me. And what I thought made her so powerless, her tears on my pillow, was in fact a testament to how she was coming to finally deliver herself from the past by no longer denying it.

Years later I also understood, when it was too late, that had I been a better and wiser man, I would have pulled her close to me that night and made her tears into a new bond between us, and maybe even cried with her. But I didn't do that. I just lay in the dark listening to her, dreading both the sound of her and the brief glimpse I had of some larger insight that hid in the shadows of me, and having the terrible suspicion that my failure to really understand the moment, or to even want to, was the irrevocable cowardice I would never redeem.

TWO years later in the fall of 1988—Year Twenty-One of the Apocalyptic Calendar—somewhere on the highway between his old life and his new, as the Occupant drove across the country from east coast to west in clockwise loops, somewhere in the wake of the phone call from Angie ten months after another split-up and after she had left New York and gone to Las Vegas in order to let her Rising Sun father know she was still alive and to try and make some sort of tattered peace with him if possible, her mother having died from a cancer born of too many afternoons in her father's nuclear sun, sometime after Angie had then moved to L.A. where she was cobbling together several part-time jobs into one full-time life, teaching English to the children of Asian immigrants and piano to the children of movie producers, somewhere on the highway after he received her call and immediately packed everything up in New York and loaded his car with what he could without thinking about it two seconds, because he missed her and it was nothing more complicated than that, somewhere past the Texas-New Mexico border and then the New Mexico-Arizona border in a shambling little motel on Route 66 just east of Kingman, with its windows tightly closed to discourage the sandy grit of the relentless desert wind and the small determined dust devils that smuggled their way into his room anyway, somewhere past half a bottle of cheap vodka that he picked up at a liquor store in Williams because they had nothing better, sometime after sitting in the motel room listening to the wind and trying to call her and then pouring the rest of the vodka down the sink, and after going to bed and slipping off into the wail of the desert wind that reminded him of a long-ago music whose euphoria he believed he had forgotten, while he wondered how in their six years he and Angie managed to circumvent love altogether, and where things went wrong, and realizing there's never any one point where it goes wrong, that the flaw is there in the original mold and then the question becomes whether the crack is deep and fundamental, bound to lengthen with time and finally break altogether, or can be lived with if not entirely mended, somewhere before reaching L.A., he realized something and dismissed it so quickly that it would be years later—on the morning he woke to find she had disappeared from their bed with their first and only child inside her—before he admitted it to himself again: and that was that she had saved his life more than he had ever saved hers.

MY bright little star, Angie's father had called her when she was small.

Now he was sixty-nine years old. He still lived in the same little tract house in the Vegas suburbs where he had raised his family since first coming to the United States from Japan. When Angie returned home after almost ten years, she found him sitting in the same room where she had slept as a little girl; on the outside of the bedroom door hung a very old sign that had been there since the day Angie, then named Saki, left at the age of sixteen. It was made of cardboard and written in black marker ink, in English letters that nonetheless had the quality of Japanese characters, frail and slightly open-ended and not quite connecting: LOST, the sign said. After standing in the front yard a long time wondering if someone would see her, after knocking a long time at the front door wondering if someone would answer, Angie had finally let herself in to prowl the dark house that now seemed much smaller than she remembered; and upon finding her father in what was once her old bedroom, she noted the sign ruefully.

He sat before the large window through which, as a little girl, she used to watch the desert sky go dark, when her father always made her go to bed at seven o'clock. In the distance he could see the neon halo of Las Vegas in the same way that, one August morning around eleven o'clock in 1945, he could see from his hometown of Kumamoto the nuclear halo of Nagasaki across the bay. A great glowing star, he had said to himself that morning; he had been twenty-six then. For Angie's father this wasn't the birth of the new age, as Westerners so arrogantly assumed—he could see it in the smirks of the American scientists out at the test site: *we gave you a new millennium*—but rather the death of the old, the past of his country blasted into the future at the speed of annihilation. For Angie's father the new millennium, the age of nihilism, was born on the first of January 1946, with the mortifying confession by the Emperor to his people that he was, in fact, not God. That was the day the Emperor told his countrymen and Angie's father that his descent from the sun goddess Amaterasu was—how did he put it?—"a false conception." Now there was no god, only a new sun in God's place. In annihilation there had been honor, in God's disownment there was the void. Forty-three years later, Angie's father sat in what had been his little girl's bedroom, watching a similar light rise from the casinos and hotels and clubs where he had once heard that his daughter danced in nothing but her shoes; and he was sitting there watching the light when she came through the bedroom door behind him.

WITH a start he thought at first it was his wife, before he remembered a moment later that wasn't possible. "It's Saki, Papa," she said. He didn't answer, either that night or the next day, and Angie had decided the possibility for reconciliation was lost forever until, as she finally came to tell him goodbye, he suddenly took her hand in his own, still staring out the window, still conceding nothing, still disowning her with his silence, but holding her hand in a grip that wouldn't let go.

My bright little star, he had whispered in her ear at exactly 7:02 on the evening of 6 May 1968, as he slipped her stuffed bear from her arms. For a moment little Saki, lying in her bed, was confused: my bear, she called, reaching for it in her father's hands. Looming over her, her father shook his head. You're not a baby anymore, he answered, closing her bedroom door behind him as he left, so stunning her with both this news and the loss of her companion that it was several minutes before the enormity of it all sank in and she began to cry. Outside, other kids still played as the Nevada desert sky faded to dark. Four months shy of her sixth birthday, she was already precocious in all matters except stuffed bears, including her sleeping habits; she was quite certain she didn't know a single other kid who had to go to bed at the ridiculous hour of seven o'clock. But her father was as unyielding about it as he was about the bear, as he was when he had insisted on naming her Saki, as he was when he whispered in her ear My bright little star, not as an endearment, not as an encouragement, not as a hope or even a demand, but a warning.

When she started kindergarten, he began to hang the sign on her door every morning, in the form of a single word. At first it was a game for her, to wake each morning with great excitement and see what waited on the door. Early on, the daily sign reflected his expectations and aspirations in the first words of English he had so resolutely taught himself upon his expatriation from Japan to the United States: EXCELLENT. AMBITIOUS. DETERMINED. SUCCESSFUL. Only as the years went by did the sign on the door monitor both her fall into trivial girlish adolescence and the commensurate, steady deterioration of his approval, branding her life with the ways she let him down: DISAPPOINTING. LAZY. SILLY. FAILURE.

Saki Kai was the only child of parents who assumed that when it came to the matter of producing superior children, one opportunity should be sufficient. What need was there to have more than one child when the first should turn out so well? Already displaying the potential of a clear prodigy, she showed early talent at the piano and tested high on all her early intelligence exams, with scores in mathematics near genius level. Nonetheless, except for the piano lessons which she loved, she was bored by education, and in school her grades were mediocre, baffling her mother and enraging her father. By the time Saki was fourteen, the battle lines between the three of them were drawn, and at sixteen she rescued the stuffed bear from an old box under the stairs and moved out of the house, working underage as a waitress in a seedy downtown bar and as a dancer in another club up the street where all the girls took stage names, not in the interest of self-invention but confidentiality. Hers was Angie, inspired by a popular rock and roll ballad she had loved at the age of ten, and which happened to be the song playing when she auditioned for the job. She wasn't certain which she hoped for more, that her father would never find out, or that he might happen to stroll into the club one afternoon just in time to see her standing on a table in nothing but her black high heels. That would have been a revelation for both of them, and might have rendered the old battle lines suddenly obsolete.

AT this point in her life she had had sex exactly twice, with neighborhood boys. Of course neither was for love, both were for rebellion. In the club she was a bad dancer, either too shy to dance sober or too drunk to dance at all. For some of the older men, however—in a way she was still too innocent to understand—her awkwardness stirred a kind of debauched wistfulness.

An investment analyst from New York in his early sixties, flying into Vegas every three weeks for the weekend, became particularly attached to her. She would sit and listen to him talk about things she didn't care about in the least, and he would ask her questions about this and that, and over the course of several conversations it came out she wanted to become a concert pianist, which he found so wonderfully absurd it practically made his mouth water. After they talked a couple of more times, he called long distance just as she was coming on to the afternoon shift, and explained that if she had the wherewithal to get herself to New York, he would set up an appointment with the musical director at Carnegie Hall, and reserve her a room at the Hilton down the street.

It was now the autumn of 1978, when it was apparently still possible for a precocious teenage girl from the Nevada suburbs to be a little stupid about some things, even one who had danced in a strip joint four or five months. Angie packed one suitcase with as much as a small stuffed bear left room for, took every penny she had, which just covered the plane ticket and the cab ride from JFK to the Hilton on Sixth Avenue, registered at the front desk as Angie Kai, and checked into her room, where she ordered room service and delighted in signing the bill she so blithely assumed was being taken care of by Carnegie Hall. When the telephone rang that night at eleven o'clock, it was not Carnegie Hall but the investment analyst down in the hotel lobby, explaining that the audition was "all set up" for the next afternoon and perhaps it would be a good idea if he came up to the room and explained some things to her, just so as to assure everything went well. A little stupid or not, Angie was finally beginning to have a not-so-great feeling about the situation when she hung up the phone. She was trying to dispel this feeling when the old man showed up at the door with a bottle of champagne.

Twenty minutes later she screamed persuasively enough to send the barely dressed patron of the arts scrambling out into the hallway with her naked disillusionment trailing along after him. "God, Saki," she said, sitting in front of the hotel mirror looking at herself and wondering what the sign on her bedroom door back home would read now if her father knew; and there and then she began to write the shorthand of her broken heart: "Disgrace. Disgust. Humiliation. *Lost*." Ten years later, when she once again saw the sign on the door, she would find she had known her father pretty well at that.

She had no money. Any hope she had of squeezing another night or two out of the hotel was dashed with a call the next morning from the manager. "We have just been notified," he explained, "that the gentleman who placed the deposit on your first night will not be paying for the second." A pause. "How do you wish to handle the charges?" Up and down Sixth Avenue she dragged her suitcase in a daze, even to Carnegie Hall, where she lingered outside on the sidewalk in the long-shot hope maybe an audition really had been scheduled after all. That night she spent constantly on the move, darting from one dark and dangerous street to the next, eventually discarding everything but the bear; by the morning of the second day she was hungry and exhausted, by the morning of the third desperate and terrified. By the evening of the third she had forty dollars for doing something she would never speak of or think about again. By the evening of the fourth there was just enough of the forty dollars left to buy dinner—a can of cream soda and an over-the-counter bottle of sleeping pills. When she woke, her head pounding and her stomach very sore from having been pumped, she wasn't sure whether it was still the fourth day or the fifth; she was in the indigent ward of a county hospital that almost anyone else would have reasonably considered a horrorshow. But in a bed under a roof, with a meal in front of her that by subnormal standards was nearly edible, she was as happy to be there as she would have been anywhere, assuming being alive was the only option offered to her.

She was perfectly content to stay on a while, in fact, until a nurse told her that the hospital had been trying to notify her parents. Please not my father, Angie begged; there was no way of fully explaining the overwhelming oppression of his disapproval, the unbearable burden of his disappointment. He hangs a sign on my door that says FAILURE, she tried to explain. The doctors and nurses and hospital administrators seemed more confounded than sympathetic. You don't understand, she finally cried when all her pleas had fallen on deaf ears, *he named me after a nuclear holocaust*. Next thing they knew, they turned around and her bed was empty and, except for the bear, she had left behind all the last remnants of Saki. By the end of her first week in New York, she was Angie through and through, hitting the strip clubs of Times Square where the owners took one look at her and saw she was a bad dancer and that it didn't matter, and didn't ask too many suspicious questions about how old she really was.

She went to work in a place at Forty-sixth and Broadway, where the owner was willing to advance her a hundred bucks, and one of the other women, who called herself Maxxi Maraschino, put her up for a while. Maxxi, brushing up against one side or the other of thirty, was a Bardot-look-alike blonde who also sang in a punk club downtown. At night in Maxxi's flat at Second and Second, known to the punk scene as Depravity Central, where someone or another was always slumped in the corner, Angie slept on the couch while Maxxi explained the situation: here's how it works. The club doesn't pay you, you pay the club—a percentage of your tips for the high honor of getting to take your clothes off there. Not every guy is the kind who will go into a strip club, Maxxi went on, but the same hunger that makes some guys go into strip clubs exists in every guy. Some guys have suppressed it, some are threatened by it, some feel bad about it, some like to think they've outgrown or civilized it, but they've all got it. There's the weirdo so incapable of relating to a woman that his interest in that little bit of tissue between your legs is virtually gynecological. He's too pathetic to think about, like worrying about a gnat watching you undress. There's the loudmouth who's there to convince himself he exists, there's the quiet one who's there to convince himself he doesn't exist. There's the tourist whose whole life is a tour. There's your bread and butter, the obsessed romantic—he starts coming just to see you. He's your best opportunity and your biggest problem, because somehow he's got it in his head he's going to fuck you, or rescue you, or maybe even marry you, except if you ever did marry him, neither of you would ever be able to forget for a minute what it was you used to do for a living.

The whole thing about a strip club, Maxxi went on, is that it's set up as though the guy's in control, when anyone can see that the guy is the only one in the situation who's *not* in control. Anyone with a tenth of a brain is going to figure out he's never going to lay a finger on you, let alone put any part of him inside you. He's never going to know your name, he's never going to have anything to do with you whatsoever except to keep giving you his money, again and again and again. You're in the lights and he thinks you're exposed, he's in the dark and he thinks he's hidden. But he's not hidden, he's dead, and you're not exposed, you're alive.

After a month Maxxi told Angie about a photo session for a magazine layout, which led to another magazine session, which led to a movie in which Angie had sex for the third time in her life, a fact she protected as carefully as her date of birth. The seduction of making these movies was unmistakable and nearly irresistible; whatever was happening in front of the camera could almost seem vindicated by the very glamour of the process, even if it was a distinctly seedy version of glamour. More than this it offered Angie an identity that was tangible and attainable, in terms that, for better or worse, were completely her own and no one else's. Being fucked by several men on film, she didn't say to herself or to her father or to anyone else "Shame," in the way her father had taught her to proclaim "Failure," reducing everything she felt to a defeated emotional monogram. Rather, for the moment her shamelessness so demolished any last possibility of shame she was almost euphoric. Shame wasn't just a foreign concept, it was beyond the given psychological physics of the universe she lived in.

It became clear to Angie from the beginning that there was a choice to be made. Many of the girls in these films were aspiring actresses hoping to go legit sooner or later, but as one told Angie on her second shoot, "There's no doing both. You can't do this"—waving her hand at the bed a few feet away—"*and* do legit too, it's one or the other," and for a while Angie fell in with this tribe of actresses and directors and cameramen, moving out of Maxxi's place and staying with one or another of the other girls. Though she had no particular interest in being an actress, it seemed to her one also couldn't live in both the world of shame and the world of shamelessness, it was one or the other, and she might well have chosen the world of shamelessness if, five films into her new career, someone didn't finally get more inquisitive about her age. When it got out she was barely seventeen, the films she made had to be pulled from circulation by a distributor so enraged—and with enough underworld connections—that Maxxi Maraschino strongly suggested Angie lie low for a while.

Angie got a job with an escort service and moved out of Depravity Central and into her own place near Seventy-fourth and Third. The afternoon she went back to Maxxi's to finally get the few things she had left behind, Maxxi was gone and the place was empty, no rock stars or groupies or junkies laid out on the floor, no signs of any life at all except in the back bedroom, where she herself had slept a couple of times: now, written on the door in the kind of black marker ink her father had used, was the word OCCUPIED. From behind the door, she thought she could hear a strange sound like the echo of a distant, cavernous roar. She went over to the door and stood for a while, her ear pressed against it, until she finally called out. She thought she heard someone moving around inside the room, and maybe someone answer, though she couldn't be sure, and so she called out again, "Hello?" and now someone distinctly answered from behind the door, Yes. It was such an emphatic yes it frightened her, and she stood back from the door, again reading the word written on it in black ink. She was afraid to open the door and let out whatever was behind it. Then whatever was behind it began beating on the door furiously, and that frightened her even more, and she backed away, and turned and looked around the flat again to see if anyone else was there. She had to use the toilet. When she came back out of the toilet the flat was still empty, and the sounds from the back room, including the beating on the door, had stopped. She crept back to the door and listened for a while, and though not at all confident of her intu- ition, she unlocked the dead bolt as quietly as possible and left as quickly as possible.

Though no one yet knew it, she was living in the dawn of the moment when chaos would kiss love with a new malevo- lence. Waiting for this fatal unforeseen future, the women of the age writhed in their beds, veins flooded with the recognition of their desires, the air of the dying Seventies full of a sex both voluptuous and revolted, with the membrane between the two soon in tatters. During these months Angie's only romance was a brief one with an aspiring playwright in his mid-twenties named Carl, whose day job was as map master for the city of Manhattan. Carl had a hundred maps at his disposal, maps of streets and maps of bridges, maps of sewers and maps of sub- ways, maps of power grids and maps of water ducts, maps of sound currents and maps of wind tunnels; on the walls of his tiny St. Marks apartment he had maps of his entire life, coordi- nates for where he first got drunk, where he first had sex, where he had begun writing his first play, where he had gotten stuck on the third act. It was during the third act, one morning while he was sitting in his usual Village cafe drinking his usual morning espresso, writing his play by hand on a large pad of paper, that Carl had begun his first map: a character had just walked on- stage, opened his mouth, and nothing came out. Stumped for the right bit of dialogue, Carl sat staring at the espresso and pad of paper for an hour, and began to draw a map of the play, which he hoped would reveal to him what the character wanted to say. That led to another map and then another. "You're ob- sessed," Angie said simply, the first time she saw all the maps.

"Not at all," Carl answered, and she had to confess he didn't seem the obsessed sort Maxxi had told her about. "I'm not ob- sessed with my maps"—he smiled—"my maps are obsessed with me."

"Are they really."

"I have faith," he explained, "and faith transcends obsession."

"Mystification," Angie replied, "envy, too." A lapsed Jew,

Carl freely admitted that perhaps he put his faith in faith itself, also suggesting, however, that at bottom faith itself was the only thing anyone ever really had faith in. He was more idealistic about his desire than any man she had ever met, or would meet; forty years later, living in the penthouse of an abandoned old hotel in San Francisco, he would remember her telling him so. He rhapsodized about her smile more than her body, and seemed to mean it, and she was still too young to understand that men always love a woman's smile more than her body, even if they neither confess nor know it. Carl planned to retire someday to Provence and work in a vineyard—he had spent a couple of college years in Europe, and maps on the walls memorialized the autumn in London, the winter in Paris, the trip to Toulouse, the train to Vienna—and Angie had the feeling that, in his mind, he saw her working there in that vineyard with him.

She left Carl when she could bear to neither tell him her secrets nor keep them from him. She left when she suspected that a new pair of coordinates designated on his Manhattan map, right above the sink, marked where he had begun falling in love with her. She had come to fear her place on the one map that she found most fascinating, the Map of Mad Women, with its pins representing a series of deranged females, from a bartender in Dublin to a photographer in Brussels to a travel agent in Athens to a kibbutz counselor in Tel Aviv to a beautiful girl he saw in Madrid wearing nothing but the chaos in her eyes and a cocked red beret with a little red Soviet star stuck in it, standing in a plaza openly touching herself until the last vestiges of Franco's secret guard pulled up in a black car and took her away.

Angie couldn't stand the idea of becoming the small pin on the Map of Mad Women marked New York. She didn't really believe she deserved anyone's openheartedness, she didn't really believe she could accept anyone's emotional generosity under anything but false pretenses. Biting her nails, she called Carl from a pay phone on Forty-sixth one night several hours after standing him up, with the sound of the club where she used to dance right behind her; it was for this soundtrack in particular she had chosen this phone, as though the noise of the club in the background might explain everything to him. "Believe me, Carl, I'm doing you a favor," she told his uncomprehending silence on the other end, with as much conviction and as little melodrama as anyone had ever said it. "Unworthy," she summed it all up to herself, and to him, but only after hanging up the phone.

UPON turning eighteen, Angie got a job at a better escort service on the Upper East Side. Her first night one of the other girls, a young strawberry blonde, said to her, I'm the third of October 1980, the bombing of a synagogue in Paris killing four.

A lithe redhead, coolly blowing on her cigarette, said, I'm all music banned in Iran on 23 July 1979. When a voluptuous brunette took Angie under her wing, she introduced herself as the seventeenth of April 1979, the ordered execution of one hundred children for no reason whatsoever by the emperor of Bangui. Every gentleman who frequented the service had his pleasure, from the lawyer who loved to be dominated by the third of December 1979 (eleven teenagers crushed to death at a rock concert in Cincinnati) to the impotent oil executive who preferred a threesome—just so he could watch—with the cute little 1979 twins April 1 (seven hundred Jewish graves vandalized on Staten Island) and April 2 (one hundred Vietnamese boat refugees drowned off the coast of Malaysia). There was the shy raven-haired 3 August 1979 (two and a half million peasants starved to death in Cambodia), the giddy platinum 20 September 1980 (twenty women dead from toxic shock related to tampons), and the service's sad kind veteran who offered comfort to sad tired men, purring into their ears the partial meltdown of a Pennsylvania nuclear reactor on 28 March 1979. There was the most beautiful and exclusive prize whom every man wanted but few could afford: the exquisite and elegant eighth of December 1980, the murder by a crazed fan of one of the greatest songwriters of the century.

Angie's own place on the Apocalyptic Calendar came the third of October 1981, three years after first arriving in New York. By now she didn't spend a lot of time mourning the person she once had been, or her lost innocence; precocious in all matters except stuffed bears, she was precocious in her moral sense as well, refusing to see herself as either villain or victim. The only apparent casualty of her actions, besides her dreams, was a million detonated nerve endings in a thousand anonymous men, the vast majority of whom had only looked at her, she tried to reassure herself, only a few of whom had actually touched her. And if some part of her was mortified by what she had become, she wasn't on speaking terms with that part, but made a point of knowing its whereabouts at all times, and keeping it at arm's length; she didn't allow it to judge her. She did well enough with the service that she got by working three nights a week, and she had come to foresee a time she might be able to give it all up for something else, though by now she suspected a future as a Carnegie Hall pianist was probably not in the cards.

The furor within the industry over her underage film career had begun to die down when she decided that one or two more movies under her belt—so to speak—might make her enough money to break free for good. The going rate was $200 a scene, sometimes more; filming two scenes in the morning and two more in the afternoon, she could pull in eight hundred dollars a day, almost twenty-five hundred for a three-day gig. It was also true, as Maxxi Maraschino pointed out to her one night over beers in the now deserted club where she sang, that the business had gotten much stranger since Angie worked in it only a couple of years before, every sensation trying to trump the last in pursuit of some unspeakable ultimate; and when the downtown shoot that Angie had lined up for the next afternoon came up in conversation, even in the shadows of the bar Maxxi appeared to turn a little pale. The two women got into a fight. "If these are the guys I think they are," Maxxi told Angie, "you don't want to have anything to do with them."

"What do you mean if these are the guys you think they are?" said Angie.

"Guy named Mitch Christian. I know him really well. I know him *really* well. I did a movie once for him and his wife, who was almost as crazy as he was, before she dropped out of the whole thing. You should stay away from him."

Angie was annoyed. She had become cynical enough to suspect Maxxi's friendly little warning really had an ulterior motive—that with Maxxi's career as a punk singer having gone the way of the rest of the Scene, and her career as a dancer now going the way of her body, maybe she wanted this last gig for herself. Maybe she knew this Mitch guy even better than she said and she was paranoid Angie might move in on her action. "You want this shoot for yourself, don't you?" said Angie.

"That's not it," Maxxi insisted.

"You think I'm going to move in on whatever you've got going with this guy."

"Christ, Angie, that's not it." Angie wound up walking out; but though she kept telling herself she was onto Maxxi, the conversation stayed with her all night and the next morning and, if anything, grew louder and more persistent in her head the whole ride on the downtown subway the next afternoon, on the third of October 1981. Unable to completely dismiss Maxxi's warning, she was already anxious even before she ran into the strange woman at the warehouse where the film was being shot. Lurking in the shadows of the building across the street, the woman crossed the street in time to cut Angie off at the door.

Angie looked up at the number over the door to make sure it was the right address. Don't go in there, the woman said, very tough in an old, worn black-leather jacket with a cigarette dangling from her mouth; she had a slash of a mouth and hard eyes, dark hair chopped off just above the shoulders, and she looked vaguely familiar, like someone in the business Angie might have seen before, though not at all like an actress, not at all the type—are you the type? whispered that part of Angie she didn't speak to, but whose whereabouts she knew at all times—harsh, at least in her mid-thirties, perhaps older, which for this business was old.

"Who are you?" said Angie. Unconsciously she began to bite her thumbnail but stopped herself, reclaiming her cool. She had already cleared too many hurtles in her own mind to be dissuaded now. Casting aside her cigarette, the other woman appeared agitated; maybe she was on drugs. She *is* an actress, Angie decided, another has-been like Maxxi scoping out the competition before the director arrives. "Sorry," Angie said bluntly, "I wouldn't be here if I didn't need this job, believe me."

"Listen," the woman began, but Angie brushed past her, pushed open the door, and started up the long narrow stairway. Late-afternoon sunlight blasted the wall at the head of the stairs through an unseen window. When Angie reached the top, she turned to see if the woman in the black-leather jacket was behind her, but the stairwell was empty; turning the corner at the top of the stairs, Angie found herself on the second level of the warehouse, the sun hitting her in the eyes before she had a chance to shield them. The window framed the World Trade Center a few blocks away, and the sun was momentarily slipping through the sliver of daylight between the two towers. The warehouse space appeared empty; then a door in the far wall across the room opened, and a man holding an eight-millimeter camera stared out at her. He disappeared again into the back room, and through the open door Angie thought she heard him say to someone else, "It's here."

Another man came to the door. He was smoking a cigarette and looked at her for a moment. "We're waiting for Mitch," he finally said, "don't go anywhere." Then he vanished too. She could hear more discussion in the back room between the two men, and then the staccato monologue of someone on the telephone. Angie circled the open area of the warehouse, stopping from time to time in front of the window, watching the sun set behind the World Trade Center and the river beyond that. Every once in a while the man with the camera would look out the door to see if she was still there, and this would be followed by more conversation with the other man, in voices that grew quieter and more tense. She sensed a general concern that she might leave. After a couple more minutes of waiting and listening for the sound of the door downstairs and the arrival of the director, she made her way over toward the back room where she assumed the film was being shot.

Through the open door she could see a single light. There was no sign of the two men, though she could still hear them, occasionally talking but mostly just moving around. There was nothing else in the back room except a large black chair with a high back and black leather shackles bolted to the arms and legs and neck. Seeing it, Angie felt something she had never felt before, even in her worst moments; she felt the bottom fall out of her life, plummeting into dark.

It was evil. It was far beyond any quaint notions of mere depravity, far beyond anything even an apocalyptic age would comprehend, beyond a terrorist's bomb or a genocidal rampage or a nuclear holocaust, because it was clearly a chair for an execution, and an execution performed for no other reason than to give pleasure to someone, somewhere, watching it. It was an empty hole in the century where there had once been a soul. A whole new instinct screamed in Angie's ears, and in a flash she thought of all the other more familiar instincts she had been ignoring, she thought of Maxxi's warning and the woman down-stairs in the black-leather jacket. The moment Angie saw the chair she knew that if she didn't get herself out of there in the next minute, she would never see the sun hit the bottom of the World Trade Center, she would never see the fall of night, except for the longest night. The moment she saw it, the part of herself she thought she had so successfully kept at arm's length crept up behind her and whispered in her ear: Saki, go sit in the chair. Go sit in the chair, because it's been a long time since you were anyone's bright little star, and nothing matters, and there is honor in annihilation, but in God's disownment there is only the void.

She could hear one of the men coming and she pivoted where she stood, staring back out at the setting sun, slowly strolling back toward the window. Behind her she could feel the man with the camera standing in the doorway watching her again, and that whole new instinct told her that he was standing there trying to figure out what she might have seen in the back room, what she might have understood. She decided that if she heard him take a single step in her direction she would bolt; otherwise she paused, hoping he would disappear into the back room one more time, giving her escape a head start. When she looked over her shoulder he was gone, and she walked quickly toward the stairs. By the time she reached the top of the stairs, both men had reappeared.

The men didn't bother to call out to her to stop. They knew that she understood the situation and that everyone understood that everyone else understood the situation. Lurching down the stairs in her ludicrous stiletto heels, with the sound of the men right behind her, Angie wondered if she could stop just long enough to take off one of the shoes and use it as a weapon; she decided she would be overpowered before she had the chance. All the way down the narrow stairway she kept thinking the warehouse door at the bottom would open any moment and the man they had been waiting for would appear, and she would be trapped.

Just as Angie reached the bottom, the door did open. She drew back from it, but it wasn't another man, it was the woman in the black-leather jacket, who now grabbed Angie by the wrist and pulled her out of the stairwell and into the street, and then stepped back into the building, slamming the door shut behind her. For a moment, alone in the street, Angie actually stood there staring at the door, transfixed, out of some perverse curiosity to see who or what would eventually come through it, listening to the sounds of the scuffling and loud voices beyond it.

Then she kicked off both shoes and ran. Twenty-four hours later, she was on a plane to London, and nine months later, sitting in a café on the boulevard Saint-Germain in Paris, she met the Occupant.

THE woman in the black-leather jacket had been waiting there for some time. It certainly wasn't unlike Mitch to be late, but after an hour passed she began to relax a little, thinking maybe nothing was going to happen after all.

It was a warm fall day and the sky was full of helicopters, which seemed more lulling than ominous, as though the entire city was being fanned in the heat. This particular backstreet was a deserted one, of course, which was undoubtedly why Mitch had chosen it. There was no traffic except a single Ryder truck that wandered through, lost: *I fell into the arms,* a song from several years before played from the truck radio going by, *of Venus de Milo.* Then Louise saw Angie, a good-looking young Asian girl with that hard veneer all these girls acquired so quickly, and crossed the street to head her off. She had no idea what to say to her; she hadn't expected to have this conversation, instead she had expected Mitch.

There was no stopping her anyway. All these girls thought they knew how to take care of themselves. They all thought they were very tough, very cool. So Angie pushed her way past and disappeared into the warehouse, and Louise continued waiting for the man who had not so long before been her partner, her accomplice, her husband. About ten minutes later, when she heard the panicked steps inside the building coming down the stairs, she immediately knew the girl had grasped the situation and was making a run for it; Louise opened the door and Angie, at the bottom, recoiled for a moment. Then Louise pulled her out into the street and stepped into the warehouse to meet the men in pursuit.

They tried to push past her in the same way Angie had pushed past her ten minutes before. Louise didn't know either of them; they weren't regulars, but then this was the sort of thing where there were no real regulars. They knew who she was, however—everyone in the business did—and everyone knew she had once been married to Mitch; so, for the moment, at least until Mitch arrived, rough stuff was out of the question. At an impasse, cut off by Louise from the street, they just stood on the stairs looking at her until one said to the other, "We better get out of here," and then to Louise, "You better get out of here too."

"I got out," Louise replied, "a while ago. Besides, girls like that don't go to the cops."

"I'm so relieved to hear it," said the guy who had spoken.

"At this point she's terrified enough she'll probably be out of the country in twenty-four hours."

"That may be a good idea all the way around." The two men

turned and ran back up the stairs, the light at the top starting to fail. "Mitch is going to be unhappy," the one called back down to her.

Louise nodded at this information, unimpressed. "Mitch is a very dangerous man," she answered, "if you happen to be young, female, securely bound and gagged with duct tape." She opened the door and stepped back out into the darkening street, where there was no sign of the girl. There was also still no sign of Mitch. She waited a while longer, watching from her place in the shadows across the street as the two men exited the warehouse three minutes later, in a hurry, with only the camera in hand. Then she walked over to the World Trade Center, where she caught a cab to her flat in the Village.

That night she expected Mitch to either call or come by, if not to complain about her fucking everything up for him, then at least to get the things he had left the night before. She was sorry when he didn't; she wanted all traces of him out of there. She had no idea why she had let him spend the night; she hadn't seen him in almost three years and his appearance had been a surprise, and if there was one thing Louise had always hated in life, it was surprises. Put more exactly, she had no idea why she had slept with him, but that was a particularly depressing line of questioning because then she would have to ask herself why she'd ever married him in the first place, and the problem wasn't that she didn't have any answers, but that she did, and she had been trying to live down those answers for three years now. So the night before had been a brief lapse that she had succumbed to in a haze of wine, and it hadn't been over ten minutes before the phone rang and it was Mitch's current object of abuse, a punk singer and uptown stripper who called herself Maxxi Maraschino. Louise could hear her crying as Mitch hung up the phone laughing. "Crazy bitch," Mitch had chortled.

"I can't believe I was married to you," said Louise. "I can't believe I had sex with you again just now."

"Yeah, well," said Mitch, pulling on his clothes, "you and I know that's not the half of it, don't we."

"The next time I should just go down into the street and suck off the first guy who comes along. It would be a more elevating experience."

He finished dressing. "I'm going to do it tomorrow," he announced as he was leaving.

"Do what?"

"You know what."

"What are you talking about?"

"You know what I'm talking about." He was gone about five minutes when the phone rang again; it was now three-thirty in the morning. It was Maxxi. Not so many years before her somewhat successful but altogether brief career as a singer, Maxxi had been strapped naked to a table and sodomized by several faux-bikers in one of Louise and Mitch's earlier film ventures. Mitch isn't here anymore, Louise told her. Maxxi started crying again, until finally Louise said, Oh stop. He's not worth it.

He's a pig, said Maxxi.

He's worse than a pig, said Louise. He's a monster.

"I've heard the stories," said Maxxi.

"We've all heard the stories."

"I've heard them about you, too." There was a pause and Maxxi added, "I have a friend who's doing a shoot with him tomorrow. I'm worried."

"You should warn her."

"I tried but she wouldn't listen."

"Well, maybe next time she'll listen."

"Next time?" said Maxxi.

All right, Louise had sighed, and asked where the shoot was. Now, a little less than twenty-four hours later, back at her apartment, Louise expected she would at least hear from Maxxi if she didn't hear from Mitch, and looking at Mitch's stuff in the corner, she decided if he didn't show up by morning she would toss it. Finally around two o'clock she fell asleep and woke at eight, the night having passed quietly. She bundled up Mitch's things in a plastic garbage bag and took the bag downstairs to dump in the trash, stealing the neighbor's newspaper on the way back up. She made a cup of coffee, toasted a bagel, and took a shower while the paper sat on her bed at least two hours before she got around to it, and even then she almost missed the story on the front page of the city section. Many of the grisly details were omitted, the *New York Times* always being a very tasteful sort of paper, but over the days that followed she pieced together the rest of it, if that wasn't a rather tactless way of putting it, given the way the top of him had been sliced clean off as he stood in an open convertible trying to get a shot of God knows what—Mitch thought anything he committed to film was by definition brilliant—probably never seeing the low over-hang of the tunnel before it sent his head sailing through the display window of the PanAm ticket office. In the days after-ward, more than a few people wondered aloud why the driver of the car hadn't warned him the tunnel was coming, or perhaps she had tried and he didn't hear her over the traffic around him; as it happened, the impact of Mitch hitting the tunnel had sent the car spinning first into a concrete wall and then into a truck that crumpled the car like an accordion. Killed on impact, the driver had been identified in the paper as Nadine Sienkiewicz of Ludington, Michigan, sometime "dancer" and punk rocker known over the years to perform under the name Maxxi Maras-chino, long rumored to have been the exiled phantom member of the Shangri-Las.

DURING the Seventies, when Mitchell and Louise Blumenthal were making pornographic films, he had thought it quite witty and exceedingly subversive to employ the nom de cinema Mitch Christian. After all, he was a man ahead of his time, when cheap irony would come to be considered an artistic vision. Mitch "directed" the films and Louise "wrote" them; she called herself Lulu Blu.

Their most infamous collaboration was three movies known as the Virgin Trilogy: *Virgin White*, *Virgin Pink*, and *Virgin Black*. If they were remarkable at all, it was for two reasons. First, even in the annals of pornography they constituted some of the most spectacularly inept filmmaking anyone had ever seen. Second, in the last of the trilogy Mitch and Louise faked the murder of a young actress, thus gaining for *Virgin Black*, fakery or not, the distinction of being the first known "snuff" film. It was Louise's idea. All of the ideas were Louise's; she regarded herself in those days as an erotic terrorist, a one-woman sexual Baader-Meinhof doing whatever she could to create mass carnal confusion for the sheer chaos of it. As an intense young philosophy student of the Sixties attending college in New York City, she had never been sure whether she truly believed that the protests of the time missed some larger point, or that the self-righteousness of it all just bored the shit out of her. The notion of utopia held no allure. Whichever the case, she had been waiting twenty-two years for the One Big Defining Idea of her life when, at exactly 10:02 on the night of 6 May 1968, on the verge of what she anticipated would be her first orgasm, she heard something.

It came from outside, through the open window of her West Village apartment, from somewhere far away, so distant it was impossible to say for sure what it was, so ominous her pending climax was stillborn. "Did you hear something?" she said.

In his brilliantly uncomplicated way, Mitch continued fucking her, paying the question no mind whatsoever.

"Did you hear that?" she said again, propping herself up on her elbows, listening. "Oh, man," Mitch moaned in disbelief as Louise pushed him away. She got up and went to the window, leaning naked out into the night; Mitch sat in bed holding his head in his hands. "It sounded like a gunshot," Louise said. If there was anything in her life she hated, it was surprises, and the sound of that shot was a surprise in the night; but more than that, because she was an intense twenty-two-year-old philosophy student, she was inclined to think a gunshot in the night at the moment of her first orgasm was an epiphany of some sort. It was a season of gunshots: there had been a momentous one the month before in Memphis and there would be another a month later in Los Angeles; she drew herself back into her apartment and paced the room, considering the matter from all angles. Anxious, she lit a cigarette when she realized she wasn't figuring anything out. "Can we finish now?" said Mitch on the bed.

"Finish yourself," Louise answered.

"Christ," Mitch said, "I don't need this. I can do better than this somewhere else."

"So go do better somewhere else." Of course, at that particular time in his life he couldn't have done even remotely better anywhere else. He was unattractive and unpleasant, and he and Louise hadn't been together four months before she began wondering how she got mixed up with him in the first place. Even then, in the spring of 1968, she would have been astounded at the notion she could spend another year with him, let alone ten, let alone marrying him; his appeal, she decided sometime later, was his preposterous gall. Some part of her admired the way he offended everyone, even if it included her. She was attracted to how, with so little, he could somehow make himself larger than life; the sheer bravado of his lack of talent was mesmerizing. And the fact was, she would realize only much later, that if she knew he couldn't have done better than her, some self-loathing had convinced her she couldn't do better than him. Naked in a chair and smoking her cigarette, trying to think about the sound she had heard and realizing there wasn't any serious thinking to be done with Mitch around, she poured herself some wine and put on a record; like a gored animal, he bellowed at the first notes. *Strange days have found us*—"No," he cried, "no no no no no"—*strange days have tracked us down*. "You cannot possibly be listening to this record again. You've listened to noth-ing but this record for six months."

"We haven't known each other six months," Louise replied. "You have no idea what I was listening to six months ago."

"Tell me," Mitch said, "you weren't listening to this record six months ago."

She thought about it for a moment while smoking her ciga-rette. "You're right," she finally agreed, "I was listening to this record six months ago." Her brother, Billy Pagel, had met Mitch the year before in L.A., where the two were enrolled in film classes they never passed. At twenty-seven Billy was already three years older than the next oldest undergraduate in the uni-versity; not particularly interested in movies or an education or a degree, he had come to Los Angeles confident that the hippie girls he'd heard about wandering up and down the Sunset Strip were putting out at a pace so mind-boggling his only real con-cern, in those contemplative moments of deep doubt every man faces sooner or later, was whether he could keep up with them. For his part Mitch, having recently transferred from a college in the San Francisco area, chafed at the repressive notion that filmmaking might entail a certain discipline, perhaps even craft. He had seen all those French movies and knew better, and he hadn't come four hundred miles to sully brilliance with elitist aspirations of competence.

That was a time. But then Mitch and Billy got kicked out of the university and were running out of money, and the rainy season swept them off the green knolls of the campus sculpture garden—where they spent afternoons lying in the sun smoking dope and laughing at everyone—and right out onto Sunset Boulevard; and with the few funds they had left, they bought two tickets cross-country back to New York, where Louise lived. For seven days Mitch shot miles of film of everyone on the bus. The other passengers would wake in the dark to find his camera whirring in their faces: "Ignore me," Mitch would command, "I'm not here, act natural," while insulting them for their lack of screen presence, a motivational technique he would apply to various "actresses" over the years. By Philadelphia the driver kicked Mitch and Billy off the bus, and they hitched the rest of the way to Manhattan.

Mitch didn't have any particular aesthetic or prurient interest in filming people having sex, it was just the only interesting human activity readily available to someone who otherwise had nothing to say and cared nothing about anyone but himself and was unable or unwilling to interact with any other human being in any other fashion. Also in Mitch's favor were the times themselves, when the mere fact of actors penetrating one another explicitly on-screen was still enough of a novelty that any attempt at innovation would have just been a distraction. Get a bunch of people together in a cheap motel room and strap a poor-man's Bardot to a table and violate her with several male members at the same time for eighty minutes and everyone was happy. For Mitch and Louise it simply began one afternoon after they had been together for the better part of a year, when he began filming her in the middle of sex not because it excited him but because it was another direction in which to point his camera. The problem was getting himself into the scene; to do that he would have had to relinquish control of the camera to a third party, which was out of the question, so he began lining up other men to fuck Louise, including Billy. Louise, her identity as erotic terrorist already gestating at this point, wasn't sure which put her off more, that Billy was her brother or that Billy was Billy. She also suspected she was becoming a pawn in Mitch's ideas, and if there was anything more discouraging than being a pawn in someone else's ideas, it was being a pawn in the ideas of someone who didn't have any ideas.

So Louise began to write the scripts for Mitch's movies. Hearing in her ears the echo of a distant gunshot fired at the very moment of the only orgasm she ever came close to having, she extrapolated the French notion of the "little death" into something bigger, populating her screenplays with people who always expired just at the moment of climax. Sometimes the manner of demise was mundane, sometimes it was mysterious. Sometimes a lover would be seized by an unforeseen heart attack or abruptly choke to death, or succumb to some remarkably exotic ailment. Sometimes the end was murderous: one lover would ritualistically do in the other, or they would both do in each other at the same time; one would shoot the other or pull a knife out of nowhere, or slip the other poison. Sometimes some completely unknown and unidentified character would suddenly run into the scene and bash one or both of them over the head, sometimes the roof would fall in and sometimes the floor would collapse and sometimes something would come flying off the wall for no reason at all and fatally bean them. Sometimes it was almost mystical—though Louise would have been loath to consider herself a mystical person—the force of the moment's revelation in conjunction with the physiological explosion of the orgasm itself too much for a normal human being to survive.

Louise's scripts were filled with these characters who—at the moment of truth, rapt with the sort of vision Louise herself had come to believe she had at 10:02 on the evening of 6 May

1968—would cry out with their final breath some insight invoking Nietzsche or Camus or the street politics of the time. Grunting and moaning and heaving and thrashing, on the verge of ecstasy with grimaces frozen and eyes fixed, they would suddenly shout, "Life is a meaningless experience and thus the greatest heroism is to overcome absurdity!" or "Humanity will not be happy until the last capitalist is hung by the entrails of the last bureaucrat!" or, as declaimed to a skeptical female by some male aryan sort, the ever-popular "That which does not kill me makes me stronger!" at which point she usually killed him. The problem with Louise's scripts as far as Mitch was concerned was that scripts tended to have lots of scenes and narrative and dialogue and directions, and Mitch wasn't all that accomplished at dialogue and directions, they weren't his strengths as an artist. Directions and dialogue confined the natural ebb and flow of his creative vision. So Mitch devised a new way to make movies: he would shoot the film before the script was written. Every scene was filmed from the viewpoint of whoever might be speaking at the moment, which is to say that no one was ever actually seen saying anything in one of Mitch's films, rather the film was completely composed of shots of people listening to what was supposedly being said by other people, who usually had their backs to the camera or were out of the shot altogether. Or maybe Mitch didn't bother filming the people at all, instead he would linger for a while on a table or a window or a bowl of cereal, with the dialogue dubbed in afterward. Since these movies consisted of relatively few tables and windows and bowls of cereal but rather lots of people fucking and dying, the question of how to shoot the dialogue wasn't especially important anyway, compared to the incalculable advantage of being able to film an entire movie without having to worry about the tiresome business of a story until later.

This method of filmmaking struck Mitch as so obviously ingenious that it amused him no one else had thought of it. It was a wonder all movies weren't made this way, and as time went by he became more and more convinced he had inaugurated a new breakthrough in the art of the motion picture, along the lines of montage and moving the camera and Cinerama, like Godard and Peter Fonda and that guy in Russia with the baby carriage. For their part, audiences were inclined to view these quantum leaps in film art with distress. The crowds that went to grungy little theaters to see Mitch and Louise's movies were made up largely of lonely middle-aged men who as a rule were less enthusiastic about existential orgasms; they would come out of the theaters casting hurt looks of baffled betrayal at the box office, and the exhibitors began to notice they never came back, even when the marquee changed. A whole generation of pathetic masturbating creeps was being lost. A kind of panic hit the business. Distributors began refusing to handle any Mitch Christian/ Lulu Blu movies, and so Mitch and Louise set up their own distribution company, Blue Christian Productions, and over the course of the early Seventies drove up and down and across the country personally plying their wares from out of a used van that Billy had bought. Up and down stairs from one theater to the next, from one town to the next, the three trekked with film cans under their arms hoping their reputations hadn't preceded them, making sudden judgment calls according to the vibes of the town or the time of day or the situation in general as to who would do the talking, assuming they got in the front door or, more precisely, the back door. Though Louise was the brains of the operation—or perhaps because of it—she always wound up in endless confrontations with exhibitors over the fine points of the metaphysics of pornography. "Let me do the talking from now on," Mitch finally said, heatedly, one very cold night outside Cincinnati.

They were sitting in Billy's van just west of town on the Indiana side of the state line, Louise in the backseat staring south in the direction of Kentucky, Billy gazing northwest at Indiana, and Mitch mulling the black pockets of Ohio east of them. "Let me explain to you," Louise said slowly, licking her lips, "the principle of subversion."

"Please do," Mitch said.

The fog of their breaths filled the van. "The principle of sub-version," said Louise, "involves a particularly invisible kind of strategy, an unseen campaign of ruin, that one doesn't notice until it's too fucking late. It's different from an out-and-out inva-sion—you don't announce, Excuse me, if it's all the same to you, we're taking over your souls now. Kindly take note of the fact that we're armed and dangerous and coming to your town."

"I don't see your point."

"Ever look in a mirror, Mitch?"

"I'll see your point if I look in the mirror?"

Billy cracked the window on the driver's side; everything had gotten all fogged up. Through the fog on the glass, the flashing signal of a radio tower in the distance was a throbbing blotch. "What you'll see in the mirror," said Louise, "is a man who never shaves, never showers, who sweats a great deal, who in other words completely conforms to the sleaziest stereotype of a man who makes fuck films. You'll see exactly what people see in their minds when they picture a pornographer."

"I am a pornographer."

"But the guys we're dealing with who run these theaters don't want to deal with a pornographer who looks like a pornog-rapher. Jesus, Billy, will you roll up the window? The guys we're dealing with—"

"It's all fogged up," Billy explained.

"It's fucking freezing. The guys we're dealing with—"

"Roll up the window, Billy," said Mitch.

"The guys we're dealing with," Louise continued as Billy rolled up the window, "don't want to deal with someone whose very presence undoes their carefully constructed self-delusions of being respectable businessmen just like any other businessman. That's the principle of subversion. The principle of subversion operates on the assumption that those who are being subverted are happy to be subverted if someone just gives them reason to believe it's in their self-interest. By definition of what and who you are, you're not capable of subversion."

"As though they don't take one look at you and want to lock

the doors, Lu. They take one look at you and think you're going to blow up their theaters. Like you're really fooling anyone."

For some time after that they huddled in the van in silence until Louise finally said, "I guess we should let Billy do the talking." And so it fell to Billy, a bit dim but not altogether unamiable, to occasionally josh the theaters into taking a chance. These were one-shot opportunities. Booking a Blue Christian movie was the sort of mistake the theaters usually made only once, which didn't bode well for any grand schemes of a trilogy, even one so promisingly titled the Virgin Trilogy. Enough theaters were duped into *Virgin White* to raise the ten thousand dollars needed to shoot *Virgin Pink,* at which point the only theaters the film-makers could get into anymore were in the most dubious sections of the very largest cities, where there were always enough weird people to generate the requisite minimal interest in almost anything, including one of Mitch and Louise's movies. But Louise could see the writing on the wall. With *Virgin Black* they would have to raise the stakes, and that was when, one evening around Christmastime 1976 back in the West Village, after a distinctly discouraging trip around the country trying to sell *Virgin Pink,* she proposed that in the next film they murder an actress at the moment of climax. "That's fantastic," Mitch said.

There was something about the way he said it that made Louise quietly add, "I don't mean we really murder her. I mean we just make it look like we murder her."

"Oh," Mitch answered, and her blood froze at how disappointed he sounded. In the days that followed, she assured herself it had been her imagination, but in the years that followed, she would look back and wonder exactly where and when the great cosmic slapstick of their lives, based on nothing more terrible than their glorious and twisted incompetence, had crossed a depraved rubicon. If the terrorist in Louise had accepted, early on, the most basic premise of terrorism, that nothing is innocent, that in a corrupt world innocence is a luxury no one deserves, that it's justifiable to victimize the innocent not in spite of their innocence but because of it, then Louise and Mitch's incompetence would exact its price in innocence. Because they weren't good enough filmmakers to truly fake a murder through artifice, they could do it only with an unwilling and innocent accomplice, the actress herself who was to be the victim. The only way to fake the murder successfully—the only way to make the audience believe the woman had actually been murdered in the film—was to have the actress herself believe it, to have her believe, right up until the last moment, that she was actually going to die.

They had always been so incompetent at everything else, perhaps Louise believed deep down they would be incompetent at this as well. But in fact it was the only thing Mitch would ever be supremely competent at in his life; casting a particularly naive eighteen-year-old from Minneapolis named Marie, who had come to New York hoping to be in musicals, Mitch scheduled her to show up a day early at the deserted Brooklyn bus terminal where the filming was to take place, at which point she was tied, gagged, blindfolded and hung naked on a hook by her bound hands in a back storeroom for twenty-four hours while there swirled around her various discussions of what was to be done with her body once filming finished. After that, Marie was competent enough for all of them: she was more than compe-tent, she was *inspired*. The movie, or the rumors that came to surround it, flabbergasted everyone, exceeding Mitch's fondest dreams and fulfilling Louise's intentions all too perfectly; but perhaps it didn't flabbergast everyone enough. Perhaps any age that could produce such a phenomenon—and every age had pro-duced such phenomena, after all, going back to coliseums of spectators happily watching men and women torn apart by lions—wasn't capable of being fully flabbergasted. For a time Marie from Minneapolis just vanished, and when the police ar-rested Mitch and Louise on suspicion of murder, and the couple had to produce the girl in order to clear themselves, they won-dered if they had been competent to a fault.

They were in jail four days before the girl turned up. On the one hand she was such a complete emotional and psychological wreck that the couple faced a whole new battery of charges, not the least of which was kidnapping and torture; on the other hand the district attorney's office finally had to conclude the victim's account was too rattled and incoherent to build a case on, since there were no other witnesses. "I would ask what kind of animals you are," the detective who came to release them said, "but I suppose if you could answer that, you wouldn't be here and none of this would have happened." Mitch was beside himself with joy. On the subway back to the Village he went on and on about it; it was a coup; they were quite famous now, he assured Louise.

Louise smoked a cigarette and watched the black tunnel walls out the train window. Her hatred of the cop who had spoken to them that way kept rising in her throat like bile. For four days in jail she had convinced herself she was well and truly fed up with all this horseshit that included Mitch and cops and some little mouse from Minneapolis too stupid for life in the big city to even be in the big city in the first place. Over the course of the four days in jail Louise almost convinced herself that everything that had happened was everyone's fault except hers. When they got home she was exhausted; Mitch actually wanted to have sex and she pushed him away angrily. She wanted to sleep and sat staring at the bed, where Mitch went on fooling with his camera like always, and she kept thinking about lying down and going to sleep but instead just sat in the chair hypnotized by sleep's prospect until, in the light of the afternoon sun through the window, she did doze off for several seconds, before waking herself with a start.

She wanted desperately to sleep, but she also wanted to avoid sleep at all cost. She kept waking herself, until that evening she couldn't keep awake anymore. Then, asleep in the chair, she had the dream of Marie from Minneapolis that she had known all along was waiting for her outside jail, in the sleep of freedom where dreams are always unbound. She dreamed of Marie from Minneapolis and woke weeping; she continued to have the dreams on and off for the next year, until one morning in the

early fall of 1978, sitting in the same chair, with Mitch still on
the same bed still fooling with his camera, she read the newspaper and put it down and went into the bathroom and threw up,
and Lulu Blu's own private millennium had begun.

IMMEDIATELY Mitch assumed she was pregnant.
When she came out of the bathroom he just looked at her and
said with great irritation, "Fuck, you're pregnant." She returned
to the chair clammy and pale, and sat looking out the window
where ten years before she had heard the far-off sound of a
gunshot. Mitch's attention returned to his camera, and he said
offhandedly, "I know a place we can get rid of it."

"Maybe I don't want to get rid of it," she answered after
a while.

"What are you talking about?"

"Maybe I don't want to get rid of it. Maybe I'll have it."

Suddenly he didn't care about the camera so much. "You'll
have it?"

"Maybe."

"You'll have it?" He was incredulous. "You can't have it." He
began sputtering. "Listen, you go have a baby if you want, but
you'll have it by yourself, you understand? Don't expect me to
be there. I'm not ready yet to be father of any fucking baby."

"You're not ready *yet?*" Louise laughed, more weary than contemptuous.

"Oh, yeah, as though *you're* really ready. As though you're really ready to be a mother." He stopped. "Maybe it's not mine," and then he stopped again, confused as to whether this possibility relieved or enraged him. Louise laughed again. "Listen, Lu," he threatened again, "if you do this, you do it alone, you understand? It's up to you." When she didn't answer he said, "You can't just go have a baby without me saying it's all right."

"You just said it was up to me." The more apoplectic he became, the more she liked it. All day long his rant shifted strategies, becoming more and more one-sided as she became less and less responsive; she preferred instead to watch him writhe and squirm and twist in his predicament as he tried to bully, persuade, and reason with her, until finally, in the late afternoon, she got up from her chair where she had spent most of the day looking out the window, and on her way out the door she said, "Relax, Mitch. I wouldn't disgrace the planet with a child of yours." She went downstairs and down the street into the Village to a cafe on Bleecker.

That was the end of her and Mitch. On the one hand she had entirely enjoyed Mitch's consternation at her pregnancy, and on the other hand it made her sick, in the same way everything made her sick now. Of course, she firmly believed she would have aborted any child of his she might carry, not only because it would have been his but because a terrorist who targeted the world's false innocence wasn't worthy of anything as innocent as a child. Exactly when she had come to believe this about herself wasn't clear to her; maybe she had always believed it, and believing it was what had led her down the path of the past ten years that, in turn, had only confirmed what she believed, right up until this morning when she finally had to vomit up as much of the past ten years as could be expelled. She was not pregnant. She had thrown up in the bathroom because—unlike three years later with the story in the paper about Mitch's death—there had been another story in this morning's paper she had seen right away, even though it was buried deep in the front section, and when she read it the abyss opened up behind her, and she was standing on the other side.

Authorities in Hamburg, Buenos Aires, Mexico City, Tokyo and Los Angeles, said the newspaper, had confirmed the recent arrests of nearly two dozen people, in five separate pornography rings, for the murders of five different women tortured and executed on film, whose bodies had been found fastened to racks or bound in chairs or chained to walls or hung from hooks. The crimes were unrelated except by the similar circumstances and the way they "followed in the wake," the story went on, "of a controversy last year involving a New York husband-and-wife team of pornographers widely believed to have made the first known, so-called 'snuff' film. Sources close to at least several of the investigations say that while those under questioning appear to have been influenced by the New York case, they were apparently unaware, until being taken into custody, that in fact the earlier film was a hoax."

It was only a momentary relief to Louise that the name of Marie from Minneapolis was not in the story. It was only a momentary relief not to see her own name or Mitch's, or that of her brother, who had disappeared in his van after their arrest the year before, lighting out for a less intense America of laughing weed and room-temperature six-packs and aging hippie women, in order to forget New York, where he couldn't figure out anymore what was real. And not seeing Billy's name or Mitch's or Marie's or her own in the morning paper was only a momentary distraction from the fact that Louise was the Pandora of the story, and that all the ways over the years she had thought herself so tough now vanished, all the things over the years she had so bluntly denied now tormented her, and on this day in the early fall of 1978 she wasn't Lulu Blu anymore but Louise Blumenthal again, if not Louise Pagel, which would represent a turning back of the clock she didn't deserve.

After leaving Mitch, Louise took a job in a small bookstore

where she barely earned enough to pay the rent. She kept to herself. When she did go out at night, terrified she might run into Marie from Minneapolis, she was also looking for her, though what she could possibly say to her if she found her, she wasn't sure. She wasn't even sure, assuming Marie had pieced herself back together enough to be cognizant of anything, that the girl would still know who Louise was. For a while Louise had the dreams again, five murdered girls all looking like Marie, and then all the women in the streets of the Village looking like the five girls.

In the rumors that she heard about Mitch during these years, he transformed from a hopeless bungler into something of more consequence, in the way that evil always makes someone more consequential, always makes someone more serious. Who, Mitch might have well asked, wouldn't willingly become evil in order to make himself taken more seriously? He was now another embodiment, ludicrous and penny-ante though it was in comparison to more spectacular examples, of the Twentieth Century's most prevalent phenomenon: the failure and laughingstock who transcends penny-ante ludicrousness through evil genius of a distinctly audacious kind, the rejected art student who takes over half the world and in the process wipes out a few million here and a few million there on French battlefields and in Polish extermination factories, for the sheer sake of being taken seriously. Having perpetrated a pathetic fraud that led to the monstrous realization by others of an idea he didn't have the nerve for—conscience obviously having had nothing to do with his previous restraint—he was now as inspired by his own fraud as others had been.

So Louise became something more profound than tormented: she became haunted. Having trafficked in the sort of memories people had spent thousands of years trying to forget, and the sort of dreams they had spent thousands of years trying to awake from, she had wandered at will and without accountability on the apocalyptic landscape of the imagination. Now a stain spread from the darkest center of the unaccountable imagination, becoming only more confounding and unbearable with every moment, the question of when and where the imagination becomes accountable by and to whom, beginning with the one who imagines a nightmare simply for the thrill of its imagining, moving to the one who renders it an artifact to be experienced in common by others, eventually to the collective audience that chooses to watch, for the thrill of watching, a girl actually being murdered in a movie, to the individual man or woman who, before suppressing it in horror, entertains a fleeting curiosity, dallying with the temptation to look, then finally conforming to whatever sick social chic compels everyone at a cocktail party to watch, like they would watch the home movie of a summer vacation or a child getting his first bike. At what point, if any, in the exchange between the one who bears the fruit of the imagination and the one who devours it, does it all stop short of being beyond the pale, at what point is everyone complicit, at what point can one still consider himself unaccountable for what the imagination has wrought, right up until the moment that he's damned by it? Now in the years of the New York City zombielife, with the great punksurge of the late Seventies fading into the embalmed aftermath, all the girls in the clubs who reminded Louise of Marie from Minneapolis, every one of whom Louise believed she had betrayed, had the look of chaos in their eyes. They had been serviced by the chaos of the age. When Louise ran into Maxxi Maraschino down at Bleecker and Bowery, just a year or so before the "accident" that killed her, Louise could only hope the look of chaos in Maxxi's eyes wasn't answered by a look of murder in her own. Maxxi said a very strange thing to Louise. I'm the twentieth of November 1978, she said. I'm a thousand people desperate for salvation, poison Kool-Aid on our lips, dying together in the jungles of Guyana.

As it happened—the universe having a strange sense of humor—Louise did find Marie from Minneapolis, long after she ever expected to. When she finally got a card from Billy it was from a little town out west Louise had never heard of, and so after Mitch's death she set out on the bus to Sacramento, where she caught a couple of rides up to the delta. Billy was running a small bar he had taken over in a deserted chinatown on an island that could be reached only by ferry—about as much distance as he could put between himself and the stoned bonhomie of his early years now flooded by drink and a growing, uncomprehending terror for his mortal soul; in Davenhall he spent his time drinking up the profits he never made, and trying to forget what he had once been so awfully and complicitly part of, back when he was making movies with names like *Virgin Black* with his sister and his best friend. Louise got to Davenhall, walked into the bar, and found Marie from Minneapolis behind the counter drying whisky glasses. The girl appeared not the least surprised, as if she had been expecting her.

Then Louise went into the bathroom and threw up, not because she had finally found Marie but because she had been throwing up since a month or so after that last night she slept with Mitch, who presumably, even if he hadn't lost his head in New York traffic, still wouldn't have been ready to be a father. "God, I hate surprises," she muttered deep into the toilet of Billy's bar.

SHE went on throwing up for the next five weeks, until not only did it seem like nothing of her could possibly be left, but nothing of the child inside her either. Racked and depleted, she spent five weeks in bed in the room in back of the bar where Marie brought her soup and bread and juice. She felt alternately becalmed and beset by the stillness of the little chinatown, which was always silent except for an occasional tourist's voice or a transistor radio from the hotel across the street; sometimes she liked to imagine she heard the river beyond the trees, but it wasn't quite close enough that that was possible.

Marie had been with Billy for the past three years, scooped up by him in his van outside the police station the day before the cops released Louise and Mitch. "Jesus, little sister," was all Billy could exclaim now when he found Louise there in his bathroom, embracing the toilet bowl as Marie embraced her; from her bed Louise saw him look back and forth from her to Marie to her again, as Louise herself looked back and forth from Marie to Billy to Marie again, both of them looking for an answer in the air between them, Marie the only one not looking for it, maybe because she already knew it.

As well as the dull delta sunlight allowed, Marie appeared lit with a beatific kindness, from which Louise recoiled. Marie's reproach she was prepared to live with, but not her forgiveness, especially when it hadn't even been asked for. The weeks passed in which Marie continued to nurse Louise, who was dangerously drained and weak; she fed her and wiped her brow and changed her sheets and opened and closed the windows, as within Louise there grew a debilitating rage. "You don't have to do this," she muttered to whatever act of gratuitous tenderness Marie was performing at the moment. Often as Louise slept, Marie would sit in the room with her, quietly reading a book; when Louise was awake, the two women said nothing to each other, except for Marie's daily inquiries as to Louise's condition, and Louise's hateful protests to Marie's abject generosity. For his part Billy avoided the both of them, only occasionally peering around the edge of the door from the bar in front of the building before darting back out of sight. Finally one afternoon Louise woke from a nap and found Marie there in a chair by the bed; though she was sitting straight up, Marie's eyes were closed and her book lay open on her lap as the breeze through the window blew the pages. Not knowing if Marie was awake, Louise said, "I dream about it all the time."

Without opening her eyes Marie answered, "You don't have to dream about it anymore."

She smiled. By now she was barely twenty-one. She looked older and plainer than whatever tarted-up incarnation she had advanced so cautiously three years before in a deserted bus terminal in Brooklyn, right before she found herself hanging naked from a hook in the dark for twenty-four hours. "How's Billy?" said Louise.

"He drinks too much."

After a moment Louise said, "I've tried to stop the dreams but I can't."

"I haven't dreamed about it once," Marie told her, "that's rather strange, isn't it? In fact, I haven't had any dreams at all since it happened. It isn't like when I wake I've forgotten my dreams—even when you forget your dreams, you still have a feeling of having dreamed, don't you? You still know you've dreamed. You would have thought after it happened I would have had a lot of dreams."

Louise lay back into her pillow, staring at the ceiling.

"I had been hanging there in the dark," Marie went on, "all those hours, thinking I was going to die, and then something happened. Hanging there in the dark—or I guess it was dark, because I was blindfolded—I fell into a kind of huge light, and the terror passed. Billy said later that when I was let out of the storeroom I was hysterical. He said later that when the police came I was hysterical. I don't remember being hysterical. I don't remember anything about the police or much of anything, just a blur, maybe being in the back of a squad car and looking out the window at the street, maybe when the police took me to the station. I just don't remember." She saw the look on Louise's face. "I'm sorry."

"You're sorry?" Mortified and furious, Louise covered her face with her hands. "My God." She looked straight at the other woman. "I was there. I was there when we took you out of the storeroom. I was there when we shot the scene."

"I know."

"I was there when you were crying. I was there when you were screaming. It was all my idea. You can take my word for it that you were very hysterical. You can take my word for it that you were very terrified. We were very competent that day, believe me. If you have a soul—and I don't know that I believe you do, any more than I believe anyone does—but if you have a soul, we did a very competent job of reaching down far inside you and ripping it out and smearing it across the wall. We had a great time, believe me."

"I don't believe you," Marie answered evenly, with no anger, "and I don't need you to tell me this, though maybe you need to tell it. When you fall into a huge light like that, like I did hanging there in that storeroom, maybe there's a reason, maybe it's a passageway through all the things you don't need to have told to you later on. Something opened up and allowed me through, and sometimes maybe that's just what happens—so you don't need to tell me this, not for *my* sake anyway, and you don't need to try and convince me you're the monster that you've convinced yourself you are. You can believe that if you want to, but I don't believe it, and you trying to tell me so won't make me believe it." She said, "It was a Moment, there in the dark, hanging there on that hook."

"Like when you hear a gunshot in the night," Louise said, ashen, "far away."

"Maybe," said Marie, as though she knew exactly what Louise was referring to, "or maybe not. Maybe your mistake is having always believed the Moment was when you heard the shot. But maybe the Moment is when the sound of the shot has finally passed, and it's finally quiet again. Maybe that's the Moment."

In the downward spiral of what she believed to be her damnation, Louise couldn't decide which damned her more, to abort Mitch's child or inflict it upon the world. Or if she had been capable of believing in her redemption, she might have put it the other way around, wondering which redeemed her more, sparing the child or sparing the world. At first she had no doubt. Gathering her strength as best she could, the afternoon after their first conversation she got to her feet and was trying to put on her clothes when Marie came into the room: I can't have this baby, Louise tried to explain. Marie nodded. She took the clothes from Louise and put her back in bed. You need more rest, Marie said, and there's time. Next week, if you still want, I'll go with you into the city and we'll find a clinic. So early one morning a week later they took the little ferry across the river to where Billy's van was parked, and drove the two hours into Sacramento.

Sitting in the waiting room of the clinic with three other women, only minutes away from the nurse calling her name, Louise suddenly turned to Marie and said, stricken, "I don't know what to do."

"You can wait another day," Marie said, taking her hand, "if you need to think about it."

"I can't have this baby!" Louise cried. Her outburst rippled through the room. One of the other women just stared straight ahead, while the other two visibly started at the sound of Louise's voice; behind the desk, the nurses seemed to steel themselves. "There are these five girls I keep thinking about," Louise went on, in an agitated whisper; she didn't much care if she made sense or not, to Marie or anyone else. "There were these five girls and I'm accountable for all of them. Five girls like you and I had a hand in what happened to every one of them, and now I keep asking myself, what should I do for *them?* Do I have this baby for them, or do I stop it now, before it even becomes a baby? The sound of a gunshot hasn't faded yet. I haven't had that moment yet you talk about so much, that you believe in so much. I haven't had any magic moment that opens a passageway through my memories and dreams. All I've had is a gunshot in the night, so far away I wasn't even sure it was a gunshot. When will be the moment I don't hear it anymore? Is it the moment I have this baby, or is it the moment I kill it?" She became furious, her voice rising. "You tell me, Marie. You've become such a fucking saint, you tell me. You've figured it all out, right?" The nurses now appeared concerned; Marie remained calm. Louise said, "What are you even doing here with me? What's wrong with you? Why don't you want to take an ice pick or a knife or a barbecue skewer or something, or a pair of scissors, and stick it up inside me in the middle of the night while I'm sleeping and kill it? That's what I would want if I were you."

Oh dear, said one of the nurses. Two of the other women began to cry.

"That's what I would want! That's what I *do* want!" Louise pulled away from Marie, who was looking at her with great sadness. "Stop looking at me that way!" Louise said. "Stop looking at me with great sadness! What's the matter with you?" I'm having a breakdown, Louise told herself, with the first relief she had felt in years; then she collapsed into Marie's arms. We're going to go now, she heard Marie say, though whether to her or the others she wasn't sure. Maybe we'll come back. Helping Louise up from the waiting room couch, Marie led her outside where they sat in the van.

They didn't speak for half an hour. Then Louise said, Let's go back, and maybe she meant back to the clinic. But when Marie started the van and headed back to Davenhall, Louise didn't stop her.

AFTER that Louise didn't dream anymore. After that she had no dreams at all, the little chinatown where she spent the next six months hushing all the dances of her sleep, snuffing out every image of her subconscious, as though in the fitful hours of her nights, among the static blips of unconsciousness when her pregnancy made sustained sleep more and more difficult anyway, she was hurled out beyond all the color and noise of eternity into nothingness, until she landed hard and abruptly on terra consciousness.

She didn't dream anymore of the five girls in the newspaper article. She didn't dream of Marie from Minneapolis in the bus terminal. As spring approached, somewhere around the mystic fourth month of her pregnancy when the mass of tissue and light inside her hovered on the borderland of humanity, the blood coursing through Louise's body and into her child carried no nightmares to challenge the immune system of the soul: as the mother didn't dream, the child didn't dream. Through the genes and blood, the child was handed down no dreams of the past, no dreams of its own creation; it was handed down no dreams of its mother or father, or of itself.

Louise hadn't told anyone that Mitch was the father. Maybe Marie suspected; she never asked. Billy, altogether less perceptive or tactful, made some allusion to the matter a month or two after Louise had been there, wondering where the father was or whether he even knew, and Marie gently admonished him. On the banks of the island Louise lay under the trees staring out at the river, her womb rising on the horizon, swelling into her sight lines. As she didn't dream of her child in the unconsciousness of night, in the consciousness of day she felt no communion with it. She didn't speak to it inside her or hold it between her hands in the cocoon of her belly; she tried not to think about it at all, even as she could feel it sometimes try to crawl its way into her thoughts. She tried not to picture a son who looked like Mitch, or a daughter who looked like her, or some ghastly collusion of the two, a son with Louise's dark hair or a daughter with Mitch's light hair. When, in early March, the river rose from the rains and flooded much of the island including one end of the town's mainstreet, Louise thought of wading into the water in search of the perfect deadly current that would wash up into her and drown the child and carry it downstream and out into the delta, eventually to the sea. Some weeks later, when the spring came, the season was a perversion in her eyes, all its budding and blooming and growing and gushing; she yearned for a more forbidding autumn, of more funereal ambers, than the one in which the child had been conceived.

But as the child grew inside her, and as the spring flowed into summer, under the delta sky above, that glowed a hotter and hotter blue, the only thing that was dying was Marie. They were on the bus that early-July afternoon going into San Francisco to have the baby there, Billy having dropped them off that morning at the station in Sacramento in the midst of a hangover, and as Marie stared out the bus window, Louise said the thing that had been on her mind a while: Marie, she said; and Marie turned to her from the window. Will you take this baby? said Louise; and Marie turned back to the window, and for a moment Louise felt a mean kind of satisfaction. I've finally enraged her, she thought triumphantly. But then Marie said, "I can't," in the saddest way Louise had ever heard; despising herself as usual,

Louise realized that once again, as usual, she had underrated Marie's goodness. "I'm sorry," said Louise bitterly.

"No," Marie murmured to the window, "I'm sorry."

"Christ," Louise shook her head, "what made me think I could ask you? It's Mitch's, you know. It's the child of the man who destroyed your life."

"He didn't destroy my life," Marie lied. "Don't you see? This child deserves everything *because* it's Mitch's." And that was when Marie turned back to Louise from the window and said, "I'm dying."

The first impulse, as usual, was to say, What do you *mean*? But Marie had said it in a way so shorn of self-pity and with such a self-reconciled gravity, more profoundly regretful than anything, that Louise immediately resisted a trite response. Instantly, running down the litany of called-for responses, she rejected one after another: What do you mean? What are you saying? Are you really sure? Oh I'm so sorry—until rapidly descending the list to the basic "When?"

"I don't know."

"How?" No one knew that either. There was no tumor or malignancy, no forecast of a black biological rain on the x-rays, "the blood count's just been all wrong now for at least a year," Marie tried to explain, "and I just get weaker and weaker," and so, Louise said to herself with annoyance, it was going to be one of those coy and suspect deaths, where you never know what's killing you and you can go at any time, next month or next year; and if it occurred to Louise, then it must have occurred to Marie too: that almost four years before, in a vacant bus terminal, it entered Marie, the death no one knew, the death no one could find or name, defiling her in the dark on the altar of her own innocence. Hanging there, her hands bound, naked on a hook, she had stepped into the light of her own end and, in exchange, because she didn't deserve to die, and because the mystery malignancy could defile her body but not her spirit, she had been offered a small reprieve.

In San Francisco they checked into a small motel on Van

Ness not far from the hospital, and as the days passed there, Louise awaited her baby like doom. The two women didn't speak anymore of Mitch or Billy or Marie's dying; they hardly spoke at all, just waiting, until the fifth night, when Louise woke in a sweet pale-yellow red-streaked puddle, a flurry of theretofore clandestine contractions suddenly only minutes apart. Later, long after her daughter's birth, she would remain disturbed by the dream she had right before her water broke. In it, she and Marie made love. Even at the moment of waking, her memory of it wasn't clear: she couldn't remember whether it was she who approached Marie in the dream—and therefore it was a preda-tory act, a continuation of the way she had violated Marie in New York—or whether it was Marie who came to her, and therefore it was an act of forgiveness. At any rate, the two women had embraced and been swept by a tsunami of amniotic fluid to a far and foreign shore, where an orgasm ruptured the membrane in Louise's uterus and woke her to the beginning of labor.

Out of this orgasm—her body's expression of either violation or forgiveness, and the only orgasm Louise had ever had, long delayed since the night of 6 May 1968—the baby was born. Marie called a cab and helped Louise dress and waited out on the balcony until the taxi pulled into the parking lot, and then helped Louise down the stairs. What's wrong with her? the alarmed cab driver said, and Marie said, She's going to have a baby, and the driver said, Not in my cab she isn't, and Marie said to him very calmly, summoning a fierceness Louise hadn't seen or heard before, Now listen to me, you're going to take us to the hospital, and you're going to take us now. On the way up Nob Hill, as the night flew by, Louise said, Marie? and Marie said Yes, and Louise, for the first time, as though taking an oath, took firm hold of her belly and the baby inside and said to Marie: forgive me. "Forgive me, Marie," she whispered, "forgive me for four years ago."

Yes, Marie said.

"I've been wanting to say it," Louise whispered, "and I wouldn't let myself—because I knew you would. I wouldn't ask you to forgive me, because I knew you would and I had no right to take advantage of that."

I know, Marie said.

"I had no right to take advantage, because it's not something that can be forgiven."

It's all right now.

"Not even you can really forgive it," whispered Louise. "I mean, it's bigger than you, what we did to you. It's too big for anyone to forgive, even if you wanted to."

Shhh.

"I feel a little dizzy."

Cup your hands and breathe into them.

"I hope," Louise murmured in the dark, in the back of the cab, "it doesn't look like Mitch if it's a boy. I hope it doesn't look like me if it's a girl."

We're almost there now. Driver, there's the emergency entrance.

"I'm glad Mitch isn't here. Let's not ever tell the baby about him."

Shhh, we're here now.

"I hope it's all right," said Louise. "Marie? I hope the baby is all right."

The baby will be all right.

"But not like Mitch, and not like me. Like you."

They got out of the cab and Marie helped Louise into the waiting room, where they put Louise in a wheelchair and wheeled her away as Marie watched her disappear. Five hours later Louise delivered a daughter without dreams. When they brought the baby to Louise, she cowered from it at first, and then fell asleep with it in her arms; she was vaguely aware, before she slipped off into exhaustion, of Marie coming into the room and taking the baby from her arms and then a nurse coming in and taking it from Marie. The next day Louise finally made herself look at her daughter and study her, for a single trace of a single recognizable feature. The day after that, Louise was discharged from the maternity ward and they took a cab back to the motel on Van Ness, where she was perfectly willing to let the other woman hold onto the child while the new mother plummeted into a deep emotional stupor. She was now reasonably certain, even after the birth of the baby, that she hadn't had a Moment yet.

The last night that Louise saw her daughter, she once again fell asleep with the baby in her arms as she had in the hospital. Sometime the next morning she heard in her sleep the sound of the baby crying, growing more and more faint, until it disappeared altogether, and she woke to find the baby gone from her arms. In the first few moments of waking, she believed the baby had slipped from her arms into the bedding, becoming entangled and smothered; frantically in these first moments of semiconsciousness she searched the sheets and blankets for the little girl. But the baby wasn't there. Instead there was a note on the other bed. *I changed my mind,* it read. *If you change yours, you know where we are.*

SHE almost did. Immediately after the birth, to her own great shock, she almost went after the baby at once. To her own great shock, there tore through her heart a treacherous pang whenever she thought of her. Over the next year she suppressed every yearning for her, every feeling of loss.

She stayed in the Bay Area, living in the Haight and working as a teaching assistant at the local state college, mostly because it wasn't so far away from Davenhall, should she change her mind. She kept Marie's note as though it were a receipt.

Almost three years later, she came within a river of changing her mind. There were many reasons she hadn't gone back to Davenhall before, some of them selfish, none of them contradicting the very real conviction that the child was better off with Marie than she would have been with her own mother. On rare occasions, the two women exchanged letters that Louise often couldn't bear to open, let alone read. Then, almost three years after the baby was born, a letter came addressed not in Marie's writing but Billy's, and without reading that one either, knowing full well what it said, Louise sent word that she was coming, took the bus to Sacramento, and caught a ride out to the island ferry.

There she stood at the edge of the dock as the ferry approached. Far on the other side of the river she could see Billy waiting, with a tiny little person attached to his hand, looking back. Her little dress was a dot of blue fixed patiently on the shore. The ferry slowly made its way through the water and pulled up to the dock and lingered a little longer waiting for Louise to board, before setting sail back to the island without Louise on it. From the dock Louise thought she could see Billy hold out the hand that wasn't holding her daughter as if to say, Well? and all Louise could do was shake her head, turn, and go back to Sacramento, where she caught the next bus back to San Francisco. It was the twenty-ninth of April 1985.

NOW we drive deep into the heart of the former Lulu Blu. We drive a seemingly endless two-lane that never offers the long view, always disappearing just around the bend, over a hill, into the dark. But we have a sense that whatever is at the end of the two-lane, whatever city, whatever town, whatever resting stop, whatever clearing in the wilderness, is always a very long way away, with not so many motels to stop at in between.

Louise has always hated surprises in her life. They have always shaken her sense of possessing her own life. She can remember a surprise birthday party when she was seven, not long before her parents split up, her dim brother stunned at the very notion that a birthday could be a surprise: How could one's own birthday be a surprise? the boy had wondered; and his sister had spit out in contemptuous explanation, It's not the birthday that's a surprise, you toad, it's the party that's the surprise. Billy never understood the difference between the birthday and the party. So after little seven-year-old Louise picked up her birthday cake and hurled it across the living room of their tiny one-bedroom house outside North Platte, Nebraska, no one ever gave her a surprise party again; but now, years later, her own heart is a surprise to her, and all the bleak unknown stretches of its future journey. And as much as she hates surprises, she has nowhere to go but deep into her own heart, to follow the sound of a gunshot fired in the shadows of a distant aorta.

The day after she turned her back on her daughter at the edge of the river and walked away, she quit her job at the college and took off that weekend in a used Camaro heading east. Until she ran down the echo of that gunshot, there was no going back to get her daughter; and over the next twelve years she wandered the country from motel to motel and job to job, supporting herself just enough to revisit the scene of every city and every town and every movie house where she and Mitch and Billy had hawked their films out of the back of a van. What copies of the films she could buy, she bought; what copies she could haggle for, she haggled; what copies she could steal, she stole, breaking into theater vaults and collectors' basements and bondage shops and mail-order warehouses and the rare video store here and there that might have actually carried one of the films, from Atlanta to Denver to Dallas to Des Moines to Portland to Grand Rapids to Cleveland to Pittsburgh to Albuquerque to Salt Lake City (where her movies had a particularly dedicated cult) to St. George to Rawlins to Scottsbluff to Valentine to Mitchell to Albert Lea to Waukesha to Logansport to Haleyville to Dixons Mills. For a couple of months she scoured New York City from Times Square to the Lower East Side to the Bowery beyond.

With every copy of every film recovered, she transformed herself from erotic terrorist to erotic vigilante. She didn't suppose or presume she could undo what had transpired before. She didn't suppose or presume that from erotic vigilante she might transform herself into erotic redeemer; as she continued over the course of the twelve years to hunt out all the copies of Marie's murder—and in her own mind that was what it was, it was no longer Marie's "faked" murder or Marie's "staged" murder, or the "hoax" of Marie's murder—she came to accept she would never stop hearing the gunshot in her ears, that there was no undoing that either. Rather she accepted her wandering as a mission of the damned that could never make her worthy of her daughter, and she pursued that mission nonetheless until she convinced herself, twelve years later, it was finished.

Over the years as she drove around the country, she imagined her daughter growing up. She thought of her standing on the other side of the river that late-April afternoon in 1985 in her tiny blue dress. She wondered what she looked like even as there was no doubt whatsoever in her mind that should she ever happen to run into her, she would know her immediately. From time to time she would drop Billy a card asking about her, and from time to time she would stop long enough in one place to get a card back. She would note with expressed relief and forbidden disappointment that he never sent a letter from the little girl, or a photo. How is she? Louise would write, as though only casually interested; and years later, in the last response she ever received from him, written in a drunken slur, he answered, A little pain in the ass, if you want to know the truth. Nine going on nineteen. Really smart, though.

Well, God knows where she got that, Louise thought to herself, with a proud delight that, for once, she couldn't suppress. But then she didn't hear anything for years. She thought about Billy's drinking, and wished more than anything that Marie were still alive, and with her complicated sense of justice, she wondered if this was the price of what she had done to Marie—that Marie, whom Louise's child needed most, should be gone; and thus the child was paying for the deed of the mother. Of course this was unbearable to Louise. By such reasoning Louise was continually drawn west toward the child, only to be repelled east every time she drew near, and as more years went by, it became more and more impossible to bear, both the pull and the repulsion growing stronger and stronger, each in reaction to the other. And as more years went by, the prospect of actually seeing her daughter again, of being both reunited with and finally confronted by the child whose mother had abandoned her, became both more irresistible and terrifying.

Sleeping in the car—as she often did—she often woke as she had that morning in San Francisco when she had found the baby gone from her arms, momentarily believing that the baby had gotten lost in the sheets and blankets of the bed. Now she would wake believing the baby was lost somewhere in the car. For a few frantic, semiconscious moments, she would desperately search the oil rags and glove compartment and the passenger's seat next to her for the baby, before remembering that her daughter wasn't with her and wasn't a baby anymore anyway. One day Louise was driving outside Charleston in the early hours before dawn when she had a vision. It wasn't a dream, because she was driving, after all, and she hadn't had a dream in years, since she became pregnant; the vision was such an obvious one that it was strange she hadn't had it before. She was driving along the coast and there, in the paling early-morning hours, she saw her daughter in the storeroom of a deserted bus terminal, hanging on a hook. Though her daughter's face was in the shadows, though she could make out only the bare outline of the features, she knew for certain it was her daughter; and suddenly Louise lost control of the Camaro and ran it off the road, where fortunately there was nothing but the sand of the beach, and she opened the car door and ran out onto the sand, toward the water, where in the first slashing light of the sun rising above the sea, she wept. Her cries floated out above the sound of the waves. Gulls circling overhead broke pattern, fled her sobs in alarm; she walked farther and farther out into the water, not deliberate but dazed, until she finally finished crying and only then seemed to realize where she was, turning to struggle back against the tide.

It wasn't until one night in Los Angeles, in the immediate weeks after New Year's Eve 1999, that Louise finally decided it was time to go find her. That was the night she realized she didn't hear the gunshot anymore. It was maddening, the way the sound of the shot just faded, its lapse attached to no apparent epiphany or Moment at all. It wasn't really likely to have cut off exactly at the stroke of New Year's midnight; had it been at the stroke of midnight, it seemed to her she would have noticed immediately, like the sound of a distant siren that stops at precisely the moment one expects.

Louise had arrived in L.A. eighteen months before, having settled on it as a logical base of operations for the next phase of her mission. She drove into town with the trunk and backseat of her Camaro loaded down with hundreds of copies of her movies, and she took a room in a rundown Hollywood hotel called the Hamblin just off the Sunset Strip. For eighteen months every night thereafter, under cover of dark, she got in the Camaro and headed for the Hollywood Hills where she painted the satellite dishes black with the ashes of her films, into which she also mixed the cinders of other incontrovertibly evil mementos: torture films, murder manuals, autopsy photos, racist pamphlets, survivalist propaganda, soldier-of-fortune magazines, Nazi souvenirs.

On all the television sets in all the hillside homes, the regular transmission sputtered and gave way to images of cataclysmic memoir, a subjective newsreel of riots and murders and assassinations and bombings and hostages and demonstrations and killing fields and catastrophic accidents not simply as everyone had seen them in news footage over the years and decades, but as everyone had known and believed them. But mixed in with the images of collective memory were the confidential memories, the collapse of a marriage, the crash of a car, the passing of a parent, the death of a child, the discovery of a terminal illness: in the hills where Louise conducted her new crusade, from one house to the next, people were suddenly stopped frozen in their living rooms by the images coming over their television sets, jaws slowly falling, bodies slowly sinking into their chairs, transfixed by something on the television inexplicably familiar—an old movie they had forgotten? wait a minute, haven't I seen this one before?—until suddenly realizing it was the most profoundly hidden memory of all, tucked away so many years ago and now unleashing a personal millennium like a gunshot: a rumor one never should have started, a compromise one never should have made, a thing one witnessed about which he never should have remained silent, an illicit love affair one never should have had or never should have ended, a baby who died at birth never to be spoken or thought of again, so as to futilely try and make it something that never happened at all. The L.A. nights of 1999 were haywire with collective and personal memory. Into the dark of every home flickered a thousand soundless reckonings. Every morning people emerged stunned from their homes, cut loose from psychic moorings, panicked by the onslaught of all their lives' many meanings. In the light of dawn, their blackened satellite dishes left them feeling as if sometime during the hours of the previous night they had been marked by the angel of the Twentieth Century flying by overhead, though whether such a mark meant the angel would spare them or descend on them wasn't clear: had the blackened dishes been exorcised? or were they now rips in the fabric of a millennium that had nothing to do with the banal arithmetic of arbitrary calendars—gashes behind which marshaled, and through which rushed, a terrible invasion of the soul? With every morning, there came up the road that wound through the hills a truck full of new satellite dishes gleaming white, driven by a Japanese kid who replaced the disfigured black ones, which he then drove to a vandalized-satellite-dish dumping ground far outside the city that modern legend soon called cursed.

So on the night that Louise realized she didn't hear the sound of the gunshot anymore, its suspension wasn't like an incessant siren suddenly ceasing after all. She had no idea, for sure, when she had stopped hearing it; she didn't think it could have been long. She had just finished her last dish for the night, around ten-thirty, and with a little more effort than usual was pushing her fifty-four-year-old body up the hillside toward her Camaro parked in the shadows of a streetlamp, in the same leather jacket she had been wearing for almost twenty years now, when she stopped still in the dark, listening. The night was entirely quiet. There was nothing to be heard, either outside her memories or in, not the sound of a gunshot or traffic or television or coyotes in the canyons or voices in the foyers. The city had slipped off into the unconsciousness of the Twenty-First Century and there wasn't any sign of life at all, except of course for the girl standing naked in the window of that one house in the distance.

THE morning she left the Occupant, Kristin believed it was a sudden impulse that drove her from his bed out into the rain.

Thinking about it later, however, she realized the plan had been forming in her head for some time. It had been forming since before the night he had taken her out into the desert, since before he had made her the traveling center of his Calendar—since, in fact, the moment he had written the twenty-ninth of April 1985 on her body. When Kristin woke that last morning she realized that while she could be the vortex of pleasure, she could not go on being the vortex of chaos; so she took one last look at him sleeping in the bed, noting that his black beard had grown much whiter since the day they first met, grabbed the money that she had saved from the hundred-dollar weekly stipend he had been paying her, put on the long blue coat she stole from his closet since he had hidden away her clothes, and slipped out of the house at dawn just in time to hitch a ride with the Japanese boy driving by in his truck full of satellite dishes.

On that particular morning the weather was especially crazy and the sky was filled with lightning, which filled the dishes with little glowing white electric clouds. When Kristin came running out of the house in the rain, waving for him to stop, the first thing Yoshi did was wait to see who came running after her, and just how big he was and just how angry he was, and whether or not he had a weapon. It was cool, calm displays of judgment like this that made Yoshi, in his own estimation, such a dangerous customer, streetwise beyond his nineteen years. I like to appraise the situation and see what I'm getting into first, Yoshi told himself with some satisfaction. But more than once he had seen the girl standing naked in the window of the house, and so he slowed the truck and in the rearview mirror watched her leap into the back with the satellite dishes.

A few blocks away he pulled over. He didn't get out of the truck himself—it was fucking *pouring* now—but waited for the girl to get the message and climb down out of the back and come around to the passenger side.

She seemed to hesitate, perhaps afraid that as soon as she got off the truck he would hit the gas and strand her there. He turned and knocked on the back window, through which he could see her huddling under a dish; in the thunder, however, she didn't hear him. Soon, though, she figured out for herself that he was waiting for her and scrambled out from beneath the dishes and came around to the side, hoisting herself up into the seat next to him.

He just stared at her, somewhat more stunned than one would perhaps expect of such a streetwise and dangerous customer. "Where are you going?" he said.

"Anywhere you're taking me," Kristin answered, far more breathlessly suggestive than she had intended, but not looking at him anyway, instead gazing up through the windshield at the weather. Well, Yoshi certainly liked that answer. In that extremely discerning streetwise way of his, he wondered whether underneath the blue coat the girl was wearing anything at all. "Why don't you take off that wet coat?" he said, and she said, "I'll leave it on," and he said, "Oh, boy."

"What does oh boy mean?" said Kristin.

"Nothing." Yoshi flushed. All right, he's a jerk, Kristin said to herself, like every other teenage guy. You can't even call him a point-misser—he doesn't know there's a point to be missed. He seemed about sixteen to her, but since he had a regular job she decided he was probably older. They sat for a while in the rain and didn't say much more, though he kept trying to strike up a conversation, asking questions she wasn't inclined to answer: You running away? You that guy's daughter? Where you going now? or, What are you going to do now? or the recurring favorite, Why don't you take off that wet coat? When the rain let up a little he started the truck again and drove on to the next address listed on his clipboard, where she watched him unload a dish and haul it down the slope behind the house and then haul the black one back up; as Yoshi worked, she kept her eye out for the Occupant, possibly searching the neighborhood for her at this very moment.

Beyond the windshield there fell harder and harder an amnesia rain, washing the L.A. sky clean. Hungry, Kristin stole one of Yoshi's cigarettes. Yoshi got back in the truck and looked at the cigarette with great disapproval. "I only took one," she said, but he didn't care about that, he just didn't like it when girls smoked. He didn't say anything. "What do they paint them black for?" she asked as they drove on to the next house.

"Who?"

"Whoever's painting them."

"Got me," said Yoshi, still disgruntled about the smoking.

"Don't they work when they're black?"

"What?"

"The *dishes*," she said. Jesus, what a numbskull.

"Sure, they work fine," he answered, almost a little contemptuously, his stated certainty belied only by a furrowed brow. The truth was, he had no idea whether the dishes worked or not, or how they worked; he just delivered them. "People get fucking weird about them when they're painted black," he tried to explain to her, "they keep thinking they see weird shit on their TVs." He didn't want to pursue it because he wanted to make sure this girl understood that delivering satellite dishes was small potatoes in the larger scheme of his general plans.

Over the course of the next few hours, after he finally gave up on hauling satellite dishes up and down increasingly muddy embankments in the rain, he explained to Kristin—trying to suggest a kind of mysterious criminal glamour in the process—his larger involvement in the Japanese memory black-market. Digging up graves in Black Clock Park that afternoon, Yoshi elaborated, as best he understood it himself, since he was really less Japanese than American, how over the years the capacity for memory in his home country had withered like a genetic trait rendered obsolete by time and history and evolution; it had been going on ever since 1946, when the Emperor had announced he was not God. Now memories were smuggled into Tokyo every day, bought and sold on the memory black-market at a healthy profit. Yoshi would raid time-capsule cemeteries in the West, usually in the dead of night but also sometimes on days like this, when the weather was so bad no one else was likely to be around and the rain softened the ground into mud, and then he sent the capsules back to Tokyo, where customers adopted them as their own.

Picking which grave to dig up was always a matter of random chance. One could be a mother lode of forlornness and sentimentality, another the paltry pickings of some repressed sort who might as well have not bothered. Over the many months that Yoshi had been digging up memory graves, he had found the capsules to include everything from the rather obvious family photos and lovers' letters and favorite books and travel brochures and video recordings and military medals and cassettes of songs and passages of scripture and prized pieces of jewelry to trinkets of meaning so personal they defied speculation, from a piece of rock covered with unreadable graffiti to a wristwatch broken at a particular hour to a postcard of a showgirl in a Las Vegas casino, to a prescription bottle with nothing inside it but a red paper clip, to a small solid silver ball that didn't open and had nothing written on its surface, to an occasional tarot card—usually the Fool or the Moon, the cards of faith and madness—to a tiny black coffin that held a tooth and a piece of charcoal and a single long scrolled strip torn from a picture of a naked woman having sex. In one capsule had been a used condom.

It was always difficult to know how much value these more esoteric bits of memorial archaeology would have in Tokyo, as opposed to diaries, for instance, a predictably popular item, or a locket with a picture of a pretty young girl or a handsome young boy. It did seem to Yoshi that the flow of Western memory had been tainted lately, the pure grade-A stuff being cut with something unidentifiable but particularly toxic; recently reports came back from Tokyo of violent reactions and even overdoses in extreme cases, all of which, unless it was completely Yoshi's imagination, seemed to coincide with the rising incidents of vandalized satellite dishes in the Hollywood Hills. Increasingly bizarre items were being found in the capsules shipped over from L.A.: doorstops, clothes hangers, cockroach baits, rotting hamburger meat, broken light bulbs, the amputated knobs of microwave ovens. It frankly concerned him because it threatened the future of his business and made the arbitrary crapshoot of precisely which time-capsule graves to target all the more consequential.

Standing with Yoshi among the knolls of Black Clock Park trying to choose, Kristin said, "How about this one?"

As they dug up the time-capsule, Yoshi got a look in his eyes that reminded Kristin of when the Occupant had written the twenty-ninth of April 1985 on her body. Yoshi had no sooner unearthed the large metal cylinder than he pounced on Kristin, having finally concluded in his dangerous streetwise fashion that if he just got past the long blue coat, there was indeed nothing underneath to stop him. She was fighting him off when he suddenly flew into the air and landed a few feet away from her with a thud that was audible even in the thunder. Lying on the ground in the drizzle beneath the flashing afternoon, panting and marshaling her resistance for his next assault, she realized he wasn't making a sound; and when she turned to look at him, he appeared very peculiar. He was lying on his back very still, staring straight up, exposed and very erect, with a little line of smoke rising from where a dream should be. Either he had just had the greatest sex of his very inexperienced life, Kristin figured, or something altogether untoward had happened, and once she realized what it was, she sat on the lawn of the cemetery staring for several minutes at the cylinder that had been touching his thigh when the lightning hit. She wondered if it was still somehow conducting electricity. Physics—or was it chemistry?—had never been her strong suit.

Finally, she decided that just leaving the Occupant's capsule behind on the ground or in the open grave was unacceptable. So she gripped it with both hands, found herself quite unelectrified, and then grimly and delicately took the key to the truck from Yoshi's shirt pocket before rolling him into the nearby hole.

THE lightning that hit the Occupant's time-capsule left a mark part black scorch and part livid scar. It was a rorschach blot in which Kristin saw an ashen one-winged bird plummeting to earth. She put the capsule in Yoshi's truck and went through the glove compartment, finding not only Yoshi's wallet with a driver's license but a one-way ticket to Tokyo. Naked in her wet coat, she sat in the truck becoming colder and colder, finally starting the truck and driving just to get warm.

She still really didn't know Los Angeles at all—having spent most of the past two months in the Occupant's house—and she was still a less-than-proficient driver. So she spent the afternoon shuddering up and down city streets at fifteen miles an hour, constantly stalling out as passing drivers shouted at her. It took her the rest of the day to locate Yoshi's loft downtown, on the other side of a black wasteland of railroad tracks and junk where a flaming train car had once jumped the track and set the landscape around it on fire. Four floors up a fire escape, Yoshi's loft was barren and gray except for a small television and a map on the wall in which Tokyo coiled like a snake; there was a bed on an upper half-level that looked down on the rest of the space, a refrigerator with nothing in it but beer, and several huge freezers lining the walls in which Kristin found more than a dozen other time-capsules all sealed and carefully preserved. There was also dry ice and packing crates for shipping the capsules to Tokyo. The freezers made the loft cold, and a puddle of water seeped out at the bottom, slowly widening across the floor.

She stayed in the loft a couple of days since she had nowhere else to go. But she didn't like it and was all the more uncomfortable that it was Yoshi's, and while she had left the truck with the satellite dishes on the next block over rather than in the parking lot of the building, she knew that sooner or later someone would find it and report it and it would be traced back to Yoshi and then back to the loft. With the little money she had and the little money that had been in Yoshi's wallet, she would slip across the street for a meal at a Mexican restaurant. She supposed she should try and buy some clothes; Yoshi was thinner than she was and his didn't fit. The rest of the time she sat in the loft, staring at the Occupant's time-capsule marked with the black lightning-scorched one-winged bird on it. She was consumed by curiosity to open it, but resisted; several times she ran her hands along the metal surface, picking up the capsule once or twice and shaking it.

On her second night in the loft, asleep in the bed on the upper level, she was awakened around one o'clock by angry rapping on the door. There was more rapping and then voices she recognized as Asian, if not necessarily the Chinese she had grown up with in Davenhall; she could make out Yoshi's name. When those on the other side of the door broke through, she lay absolutely still, terror-stricken. Yoshi! one called up to the bed. It sounded as if there were four or five of them. I'm going to be raped and murdered by Japanese gangsters all because this stupid boy was struck by lightning while trying to fuck me, she thought to herself with great annoyance; it certainly seemed in the general spirit of the rest of her life lately. Yoshi! the one called again. Kristin didn't answer. The beam of a flashlight flitted around her and across the ceiling above her. She waited for the sound of their footsteps coming up the stairs; instead there was some mumbled discussion among them, and then she heard them moving around in the loft below as flashlights continued to dart along the walls. There was some determined activity in what sounded like the corner of the loft that went on for nearly twenty minutes. With a minimum of talk people came and went; she could hear their shoes in the puddle of water from the freezers, wet footsteps slapping back and forth across the floor.

For nearly an hour after they left she didn't move, and then when the adrenaline wore off she was exhausted and fell back to sleep. At dawn she woke with a start, and sat up listening for the sound of anyone else in the loft. Carefully she got out of bed and went to the rail of the landing and peered over, down to the space below; it took her a moment, following the smear of water from the puddle of the freezers across the room, to notice that the freezers were open and empty. All of the capsules were gone. Then it took her another moment to remember the Occupant's capsule, which had been sitting at the foot of the stairs.

IT was gone too. At the top of the stairs she just stood staring down at the bottom steps and their awful vacancy. Slowly she descended and gazed around at the surrounding floor, as if in hopes that the capsule had somehow rolled out of view by itself.

But it was absolutely, unmistakably gone. And then finally, certainly for the first time since leaving Davenhall, maybe for the first time ever, everything about Kristin collapsed, every wall she had erected around herself, every piece of psychic armor she had worn around her, every one of the seventeen years during which she had been so tough, so self-sufficient, shattered and fell away from her, leaving the girl in nothing but her long-lived sense of abandonment, leaving her more completely and utterly the twenty-ninth of April 1985 than she knew; and she sat at the foot of the stairs where the capsule had been and sobbed into her hands. Everything finally shattered and fell away from her for the first time since one afternoon when she could remember, as a small girl of three or four, running from out of the Davenhall mainstreet into the town bar and stopping dead still in the middle of the room and asking her astounded and half-sodden uncle, What's missing from the world?

What? Billy had choked in disbelief.

What's missing from the world? she asked again, and for years afterward she thought she had said something wrong, the way Billy had recoiled from the little girl's question. Billy wasn't quite bright enough, of course, to know it would have been an impossible question for even an intelligent person to answer, certainly to the satisfaction of a four-year-old; he assumed it was his failing that he was struck so dumb by it, and hated her for it. By this point he had done the only thing he figured any reasonable man could or would have done in his situation, stuck with a small girl to raise alone: he had thrown up his hands and left her to raise herself. But for years afterward Kristin assumed she had said something indiscreet, that her question was taken for an accusation, as though she could possibly know that the answer to the question of what was missing from the world might be: her mother. For years Kristin assumed she had asked something bad, and then made the conscious choice anyway not to be ashamed, no matter how bad it was, no matter that she had no idea what it was she had said or done that warranted shame.

Now the Occupant's time-capsule was missing, and it would have been bare consolation, if it had occurred to her at all, to think the capsule might have distracted the intruders from coming up the stairs where she had slept, thus saving her. She was too devastated to think of that. Like a midnight tide, abandonment rushed in, loneliness rushed in, terror rushed in, a childhood without love rushed in, and swept her away for a while, dashing her on this memory and casting her adrift on that, until she was beached on her own nature: it wasn't her nature, in the end, to go under. It was her nature to swim; so after she had cried for a long time, she composed herself, put on the Occupant's blue coat, took her money and Yoshi's plane ticket and the key to the truck and a beer from the refrigerator, and left the loft, pulling closed behind her the door that, splintered around the latch from being broken open the night before, now didn't quite shut.

She was half surprised to find the truck still parked where she had left it, though a few satellite dishes had been pilfered. For the rest of the morning she lurched around the city in an aimless panic. She ate in drive-thru places so she wouldn't have to get out of the truck or stop for very long. At one point she parked on a side street to sleep, but these days she never slept well, always waking to sounds that were all the more ominous in her dreamlessness, seventeen years of black empty dreamlessness beginning to leave her feeling more fitful, slightly crazed, pushed to the brink of something.

She returned to the Occupant's house for several reasons. The first was that there was nowhere else she knew to go. The second was that she felt compelled to somehow try and explain to him that, at this moment, his time-capsule was on its way to Tokyo in the hands of black-marketeers. The third and perhaps most compelling reason was sheer accident; wandering the city in a truck full of satellite dishes, from the beach to the hills, as twilight fell, Kristin just happened to find herself at a somewhat familiar intersection passing a somewhat familiar hill, then on a somewhat familiar street passing a somewhat familiar house.

Since she had never really seen the house very often from the outside, she wasn't sure it was even the right house—dark, unlit, with no sign of life. His car wasn't there. She rolled the truck a little farther down the block and parked.

She found the front door standing wide open, exhaling the house's black breath. Inside, she called and no one answered. Her heart was beating and she called again, and when no one answered again, she turned on the light switch of a lamp near the old piano, next to the sofa where the Occupant would lie tormented by headaches, and then she moved from room to room, from the library to the kitchen, where she found a package of luncheon meat on the counter torn open as though by an animal, and bread scattered in pieces across the counter and floor. In the sink sat a juice bottle without the top, and her bare foot stepped in something sticky which turned out to be more juice. She wasn't sure what to make of these small signs of upheaval. Even in the frenzy of his headaches, the Occupant wasn't the sort to leave packages of food ripped apart on the counter. But except for the kitchen, nothing else about the house appeared particularly disturbed from how it had been several days before, and so Kristin went downstairs. She went into the Occupant's bedroom and turned on the light, half expecting to find him still in bed, in the same position that she had last seen him sleeping, his once black beard now the color of ice. But his bed was empty, and then she went down to the bottom level of the house, breaching the sanctuary of the four-walled Calendar. He wasn't there either.

She went back up to what had been her room. The first thing she noticed was that the bed was unmade; and remembering that she had slept in the Occupant's bed the last night before she left, and the night before that, she was more and more sure that her own bed had been made the last time she saw it. Still on the shelf by the bed were the books she had taken from the library, and still on the wall were the various news clippings she had tacked there. Then she saw a dress—in a shade of light blue that might have been chosen to match the color of someone's eyes, though certainly not hers—hanging in the closet. She was damned sure there hadn't been any damned blue dress there before. Had the Occupant already found someone to replace her? Had his wife returned? Immediately Kristin dropped his coat she had been wearing and slipped on the dress, which was too tight.

She found her own clothes about an hour later, underneath the mattress of the Occupant's bed, cleaned and pressed and folded. She went back up to the kitchen and found a fully stocked refrigerator and cabinets, as though he had stored up for some long siege with his demons, which made the fact that he wasn't there all the more curious, and suggested to her that wherever he had gone had been in a hurry, and that he would be back at any moment. Now she wasn't sure she wanted to be there after all, her guilt about the time-capsule notwithstanding. It occurred to her maybe he had gotten a phone call about the capsule being disinterred and that was why he had taken off so quickly, but when she checked the phone that he had yanked out of the wall that one night, it was still dead. The other possibility was that he had torn out of the house immediately upon discovering she had escaped—if that was the right word—in order to find her, and hadn't come back since. But that really didn't make sense either: he would have returned at some point, if not to sleep or shower or do what normal people do, or people more normal than he was, then at least to confirm she hadn't shown up; and besides, there was all this new food and a strange dress in the closet that had materialized in the meantime.

Every answer she came up with seemed contradicted by other questions, and all the answers to those questions seemed contradicted by other answers. Kristin's main concern now was exactly when the Occupant was going to reappear, and whether she really wanted to be there when he did; but finding somewhere else to spend the night just didn't seem like an option at this point. She would bathe and read and get some sleep, and whatever happened when the Occupant showed up, she would deal with. She got the key to the truck from out of the pocket of the coat and in her too-tight blue dress went back out into the night, because if and when someone came looking for the truck, whether it was cops or Japanese gangsters, she didn't want it near the house. The night was very quiet except for the sound of someone down the street trying, without success, to start their car. At first, walking down the street, from a distance Kristin thought someone had taken the truck, and then when she finally made it out in the dark, she thought someone had taken all the satellite dishes from the back, until she realized the dishes were still there, but now painted black: every single one.

THEY were still wet. She touched one and felt with her thumb the gritty moist black spot on the end of her finger. Across the street, the sound of the old Camaro trying to start became more frantic.

Kristin walked over to the Camaro and knocked on the window that was cracked open at the top. All she could see inside was the dark form of the driver and the hovering red glow of the end of a cigarette. She knocked on the glass again and the grinding of the ignition stopped, and finally the woman in the car rolled down the window; a cloud of cigarette smoke floated out. "If you have any jumper cables," Kristin said, "you can hook it up to that truck."

Louise stared at the girl and stubbed out her cigarette in the Camaro ashtray. "I don't have any cables."

"Oh." Kristin shrugged. "I'd let you use the phone in the house, but it doesn't work."

Louise said, "You live around here?"

"It's not really my house. The truck isn't really mine either." Kristin explained, "I'm in that phase of life when nothing's really mine."

"Lucky you," answered Louise.

"Maybe there's a service station down the hill."

"There is, but it's closed by now."

"Well," said Kristin, pointing at the homes along the hillside, "I'm in the third one down, if you need anything." She didn't know what else to say. She was a little sorry she had said anything, since the woman didn't seem very friendly. She went back to the house, and a few minutes later Louise was at the door, smoking another cigarette in her leather jacket and appearing ill at ease. Kristin let her in, but the older woman unsettled her so much that she warned her right off, "The guy who owns this place will be back any minute."

Louise nodded, looking around the living room. She sat down in silence, gazing out the windows at the lights of the city below her, and after a few minutes she finally said, "When did you say this guy's coming back?"

"Any time now," Kristin insisted.

She doesn't have any idea when he's coming back, Louise thought. "You're sure the phone doesn't work?"

"Yes," Kristin answered. For a moment she wondered if that was such a good thing to tell her, but given the circumstances there was no way to tell her anything else. "He pulled it out of the wall," she offered, at this point evaluating the tactical advantage of everything she said; she kept hoping Louise would decide to leave, taking her chances on the streets of Hollywood. "He's kind of a psycho," she assured Louise emphatically.

Well, that makes three of us then, doesn't it? Louise smiled
to herself ruefully, remembering the girl from one night some
weeks before, standing naked in the window. She lay her head
back against the sofa and closed her eyes; when she opened
them, Kristin was still looking at her.

"You live near here?" said Kristin.

"About five miles." Louise added, "Too far to walk."

"I didn't mean it that way."

Louise looked around at the fireplace and piano.

"I just stay here once in a while," explained Kristin, "off and
on. Now and then."

"You from L.A.?"

"Let's say it's the only place I've ever lived worth men-
tioning. You?"

"Passing through." Louise closed her eyes again, brow furrowed. "Before this I was in . . . Albuquerque. No. Yes. From
here I go to San Francisco."

"I was there," said Kristin, "a couple of months ago."

"Albuquerque?"

"San Francisco. I lived in a hotel. Been traveling long?"

"Well," said Louise, "if you want to look at it a certain way.
If you want to look at it a certain way, I haven't done anything
but travel."

"I would like to travel. I haven't been anywhere. I haven't
even been out of California. Have you been to a lot of places?"

"A lot of places," Louise agreed.

"In that car?"

"In that car."

"Are you a salesperson or something?"

"No." Louise laughed. "Well, actually . . . no, I'm not a
salesperson."

"What do you do? Going around to all those places." I'm
asking too many questions, Kristin thought.

Louise didn't want to sound melodramatic. "I undo things. I
spent the first half of my life doing things and I'm spending the
second half undoing them."

"What are you going to San Francisco for?"

"To find someone I haven't seen in a long time."

"To undo something?"

"Yes." Louise didn't want to talk about it. Talking about it filled her with terror; she glanced impatiently at the front door.

Kristin chewed the inside of her cheek. "Want to see something?"

"All right," Louise finally answered. Kristin got up and started down the stairs, and Louise followed her, lighting another cigarette. They got to the bottom, where Kristin and Louise stood in the middle of the room looking around at the Blue Calendar. Louise said, "What is it?"

"See, it has all these dates of various events that have happened over the years," Kristin said. Louise stared at the Calendar, smoking her cigarette. "Now, the man who made this calendar has a certain way of looking at things," Kristin went on. "He believes things that happened for important reasons are not important, and things that happened for unimportant reasons are very important. Also, you'll notice something different about this calendar. You know how, on most calendars, the first of August tends to be followed by the second of August? And after that usually comes the third of August? People have always tended to be very conventional that way. On this calendar, the first of August may be followed by the twenty-third of May, while the twenty-third of May is followed by the eleventh of October. Also, have you ever noticed how, on most calendars, if you get three hundred and sixty-five dates in one place, they all tend to fall in the same year? That's just way too much of a coincidence for this guy. I mean, how likely is that, that three hundred and sixty-five consecutive days would all happen to fall in the same year?"

Louise studied the Calendar and continued to smoke her cigarette. "You're right," she finally concluded. "He's a mental case."

"Check this out," said Kristin. She undid the tight blue dress she was wearing that was already straining the buttons. On the side of her bare body was a now fading *29.4.85*.

"What's it mean?" said Louise.

"It means," Kristin replied, "*nothing*. Not a single thing. Nothing happened on this date of any importance to anyone, least of all me, since I wasn't even three years old at the time. It means I *am* this date: I'm a date in time, a date on this calendar, of paramount importance because absolutely nothing important whatsoever took place on it."

"Maybe something important happened to him."

"If it did, he's forgotten."

"Maybe it's something nobody wants to remember."

"Yes, well, you can pursue that line of conversation with him when he shows up."

Looking at her intently, Louise said, "Does he do things to you?"

"What do you mean?"

"I mean does he do things to you when you stay with him."

"He's never hurt me," Kristin said.

"Does he frighten you?"

"Sometimes."

"You shouldn't let him frighten you."

Actually, Louise frightened her, truth be told. But Kristin didn't say that. "I'm not really planning to stick around much longer."

"What's this?" said Louise, something on the Calendar catching her eye.

"Very perceptive of you." Kristin walked over to the date in the corner. "This is the other thing he's figured out that the rest of us are all just very confused about. That last December thirty-first that everyone thought was the beginning of something, or the end? That wasn't the beginning or end of anything. This was where everything really began, in Paris, right here"—she pointed at the place on the Calendar where it read *2.3.7.5.68.19*—"at two minutes past three o'clock on the seventh day of the fifth month, in the sixty-eighth year of the 1900s. May 7, 1968. That was the real beginning of everything."

"The beginning of everything?" said Louise.

"Or, looked at another way, the real beginning of nothing."

"In Paris?"

For a while the two women stood watching the Calendar in silence. After a moment Kristin said, "So why do you paint them black?"

Louise was trying to figure out a place to put out her cigarette, and finally dropped the butt in the pocket of her leather jacket. "To purge the evil airwaves," she answered.

"Ah," Kristin nodded, thinking, Oh yeah, and the Occupant's a mental case. She led Louise back upstairs. On the second level she gave Louise a small tour, showing her the Occupant's bedroom and then what had been her room—as though to make it clear, Louise said to herself, that the girl in fact slept in her own bed and not his. Louise noted the clippings that Kristin had tacked to the wall above the bed, as well as the books on the shelf. By now it was getting late, and when they got back up to the living room Louise said to Kristin, "Maybe this guy's not coming back tonight."

"I don't know," Kristin admitted.

"Maybe," said the older woman, "I could sleep here on the sofa."

"All right."

Louise took off her leather jacket and lay down on the sofa, pulling the jacket up around her. "Thanks."

"Do you want me to turn out the light?"

"I'll get it. Thanks."

"I would say sweet dreams, but I wouldn't know."

"Me neither," said Louise. Half an hour later, after the girl had disappeared down the stairs, Louise found Kristin's last comment as curious as Kristin had found Louise's answer. Lying in the dark with the lights of the city coming through the window, Louise didn't fall asleep until she had given up on sleep, resigning herself to waiting impatiently for daybreak; when she woke, sunlight having replaced the window's city lights, it was to a realization that slipped from her mind as quickly as it had entered, not unlike a dream. For some time, thinking about the girl, she lay there trying to recapture it. On the small table next to the sofa were the keys to the truck.

THEY hadn't been there before, had they? Picking them up, Louise discovered that in fact only one of the keys was to the truck, and presumed the other was to the house, until upon closer scrutiny she read on the key *Hotel Poseidon San Francisco*, and then, under that, P—for the parking garage, she guessed. What else would P stand for?

Louise got up from the sofa slowly, feeling old. But it was better than spending the night in the Camaro, she thought. She assumed the guy who lived here had not returned in the night or she would have awakened. "Hello?" she called out at the top of the stairs. She went downstairs to use the bathroom. When she came out of the bathroom she looked into the main bedroom to see the bed still empty, and then into the other small bedroom across the way, which was also empty. She now had the feeling the girl was gone.

She went down the stairs to the bottom floor, and looked in the room with the Calendar. No one was there either. For a few minutes she stood in the middle of the room trying to read the Calendar and then went back upstairs. She tried the telephone on the off chance it really did work after all. In the meantime she kept trying to figure out what to make of the keys, whether the girl had left them there for her on purpose, and what exactly it meant if she had, or if in fact it was purely by chance. She went back to the main bedroom searching for some kind of clue, and then to the other bedroom, where the only thing that struck her was that most of the news clippings that had been tacked to the wall above the bed were gone. She thought maybe some of the books were gone too.

This is a house, Louise said to herself, where everything disappears.

The last thing she did before leaving was go back down to the bottom floor, into its lone room, and tear off from the Blue Calendar the date in the farthest corner that read *2.3.7.5.68.19.* She folded it into a square and put it in her pocket.

Then she went back upstairs and pulled on her leather jacket and went outside. Looking over her shoulder, she quickly walked down the street to her Camaro, noting the truck still parked with the black dishes, though there seemed to her perhaps fewer dishes than there had been the evening before. She tried to start the Camaro, more dead than ever. I can drive the truck down to the service station at the bottom of the hill, she thought, and get someone to come up and start the Camaro; then I can leave the truck and the keys where I found them.

She got in the truck and started it up, and rolled down the hill with her cargo of black satellite dishes. She was quite sure people stared at her as she descended the hill, though in fact the residents of the neighborhood had gotten used to seeing the truck take the ruined dishes away every morning, if not so many at one time. She was so paranoid by the time she got to the bottom of the hill that she kept on driving past the service station, and then found herself heading west on Sunset Boulevard toward the hotel where she lived. As she drove on, her paranoia grew rather than diminished; she wanted to stop the truck in the street and run from it, and at the same time she felt like she didn't dare stop, and so kept on going. When she reached the hotel she drove right on by, hit Santa Monica Boulevard and continued west until she reached the beach, then turned north on Pacific Coast Highway.

She drove up Pacific Coast Highway through Malibu and then on to Ventura. An hour later she was hungry and stopped at a Mexican stand in Oxnard and had a fish taco. After lunch she got back in the truck and continued north, passing the turnoff back to Los Angeles and heading on to Santa Barbara. Past Santa Barbara, the highway cut inland before picking up the coast again outside San Luis Obispo where, after five hours of driving, Louise now realized she was exhausted from not sleeping much the night before. Thirty miles past San Luis Obispo, she stopped for the night at a beachside motel south of San Simeon. By the time she paid for a room she was already low on money, having filled up the truck twice since leaving L.A., where she had also left everything she owned behind at her hotel. The next day she continued on up what had become Highway 1, through Big Sur, where the winding road along the seaside cliffs—treacherous even in the best of conditions—was partially fogged in and slowed her progress to ten miles an hour. With every perilous turn she could hear satellite dishes rolling around in the back; she expected them to go tumbling out of the truck altogether, crashing to the ocean below. By the time she got through Big Sur it was dark, and in Monterey she slept in the truck.

From Monterey she assumed she would take the San Jose route into San Francisco, which was mainly eight-lane highway, but a service-station attendant advised her that traffic was always so bad she might want to consider just continuing up the coast instead, through Santa Cruz and past the lighthouse. As she got farther and farther up the coast, people seemed to find her satellite dishes both generally less interesting on the one hand, barely noticing at all, and more individually interesting on the other hand, since each time she stopped, either to sleep for the night or get a bite to eat or pick up something at a market, she would return to one or two fewer dishes in the back. By the morning she woke in Monterey, there were only three left. While she certainly didn't miss the dishes, their disappearance didn't particularly alleviate her paranoia since, she noted to herself, a trail of stolen black satellite dishes up and down the entire West Coast seemed rather conspicuous for anyone who wanted to follow it.

She decided to ditch the truck in San Francisco, from where she would catch a bus to Sacramento and then a ride from Sacramento to Davenhall to find her daughter. She now realized how fate had forced her hand in its own mysterious way, conspiring to pull her to her daughter beyond all resistance. Many times she had wondered if she would have the courage to take that final ferry across the water to the island, as she hadn't that afternoon many years before when her daughter was just a little girl standing on the other side of the river in her little blue dress. In such moments Louise both felt herself pulling away from this meeting and, in response, driving herself toward it all the more ruthlessly; and so, driving herself ruthlessly, upon entering the city she went directly to the bus station, parked the truck, and went into the station to buy a ticket.

There were no more buses to Sacramento that afternoon, however. The next wasn't scheduled until ten-thirty the following morning. Louise sat in the station prepared to spend the night there, and for a while sat calmly looking at the torn blue corner of the Calendar she had taken from the house in Los Angeles, and the date on it. But it made her nervous to have the truck sitting right outside with the last of the telltale dishes, and so she decided she should move it; then she had an idea: she would leave the truck in the parking garage of the hotel for which she had the key. The girl from L.A. might be more likely to find it there, assuming she wanted it back. So Louise folded the piece of Blue Calendar and put it back in the pocket of her leather jacket and looked up the address of the hotel in the phone book, and vaguely remembered from her time living in San Francisco right after her daughter was born that Grant was the main street running through Chinatown. She went back out to the truck and got in. It was night when she got to the hotel.

But there was no parking garage that she could find, only a valet in front. If a valet parked and unparked all the cars, why would there be a key for the parking garage? She kept looking at the key to make sure it was the right hotel, and then, as she gazed at the sign of the hotel over the outside of the lobby, her eyes rising up the side of the building, it occurred to her maybe P didn't stand for "parking" after all. She kept watching the windows on the top floor, trying to determine if it was a light she saw there, or if the place was perhaps vacant, and then she kept thinking about something odd Kristin had said, about sweet dreams she wouldn't know, somehow so portentous a non sequitur it was almost a code, and she thought about waking that morning in the house in the Hollywood Hills to the keys sitting right there on the table next to her, and to a realization—a knowledge she had forgotten as soon as she knew it. But maybe more than anything else she thought about how old she had felt sleeping on a sofa, and how old she would feel sleeping in the truck again or the bus station.

And then after thinking all that, she didn't think at all. She just followed an impulse, and left the truck where it sat, and strolled past the Dragon Gate that opened up into Chinatown, past old Chinese dreams and Chinese jabber and the clamor of gongs, through the doors of the hotel and across the lobby and into the elevator, where the key fit perfectly into the lock that read "Penthouse." She turned it and the doors closed. She leaned against the back of the elevator and closed her eyes, and didn't open them until she heard the doors open first.

TWENTY years later, in a decade that lives in its own hindsight, an old man opens his eyes and—his brain making one last inexplicable calculation—sees all his coordinates collapse to zero.

He's surrounded by maps tacked up to the walls of the old condemned penthouse. Maps of the world, maps of every continent, maps of oceans and maps of mountain ranges. Maps he's collected for more than sixty years, since he was a boy, maps he's worked with for more than forty years, since he became a professional mapmaker. Almost all of them are old maps, more than a few outdated, brown at the edges and coming apart at the seams, where they've been folded and unfolded, again and again, as maps always are. Maps are really the only thing he has left, kept in a shoe box, dragged around with him his whole life.

As well as by the maps, the old man is also now surrounded by scraps of paper on which he's made endless calculations for what seems like days, though in fact it's been only a little less than forty-eight hours. The calculations have been translated on the maps into coordinates. The mystery of the coordinates has so gripped him he hasn't slept at all, until he now feels slightly delirious; he hasn't gone out for food today, and is finally feeling hungry. He's done nothing but sit in the shambles of the penthouse at the top of the old condemned hotel, staring at maps and plotting coordinates, and then sometimes staring out the window, and then back at the maps in a growing rage over what the coordinates mean.

The maps surround a window before which sits an old wooden table covered with all of old Carl's calculations. The window overlooks the dark and desolate Dragon Gate of what's now more ghost town than chinatown. As twilight falls and the small desk lamp burns brighter, it becomes harder to make out the graffiti of the building across the street, though Carl has read it a thousand times if he's read it once; when and how someone wrote this particular graffiti isn't entirely clear, since it didn't reveal itself until the building in front of it fell. All the buildings of San Francisco are destined to fall sooner or later, including presumably this destitute old hotel in which this destitute old man has taken up residence in the penthouse. If you're going to be a squatter, Carl says to himself, you might as well squat in a penthouse. But he wonders what scrawled manifesto will materialize on a hidden wall when this hotel comes down, taking him with it.

AS though in response, the hotel shakes a little. The old man braces himself.

Not this time. Well, actually this might be a good time, Carl thinks, it might make me forget the business with the coordinates. But do I really want to die in rubble with their riddle still in my head, expiring in frustration? So let me just figure this one out, Carl asks whatever god or fate is listening, before you bring everything down.

Once he had told someone, what was it? that he wasn't obsessed with maps, that maps were obsessed with him. "I have faith," he had said, "and faith transcends obsession." He had hoped to be a playwright then, and had begun the maps one morning while sitting in a Village cafe back in New York City drinking his morning espresso and working on his play—when sometime during the third act a character walked onstage, opened his mouth, and nothing came out. Now, years later, looking again at the building across the street, Carl remembers he made a map of graffiti once, back in the Eighties. Was that the one the city fired him over? No, they wouldn't have fired him for that: a map of graffiti in a city like New York almost made a kind of sense; a map of graffiti would barely be crazy at all, it would hardly even qualify as eccentric.

No, there had been odder maps to come. Having mapped the city streets and having mapped the city bridges, having mapped the sewers and having mapped the subways, having mapped the power grids and having mapped the water ducts, having mapped the sound currents and having mapped the wind tunnels, Carl had eventually begun mapping the true heart of the city, until there was nothing left to map and until his superiors, trying to run things as reasonably as possible, trying to get a grip on things in a time that already seemed to be slipping from their grip, didn't want to see another map from him, not his maps of graffiti or his maps of sexual rendezvous or his maps of mad women or his maps of runaway children or his maps of dead bodies—not, in short, his Maps of Real Life, not to even mention the later maps, the Maps of the Subconscious City: the maps of nervous breakdowns and the maps of psychotic episodes and the maps of religious hallucinations.

Now that Carl thinks about it, it was the Map of Unrequited Love that got him fired. It was his most subjectively conceived and tenaciously rendered cartographic triumph, inspired by a pretty, secretive Asian girl who dumped him at the time; he was around twenty-five or -six; he can't even remember her name now. But while he can't remember her name, he's thought of her every so often, every once in a while, since it was she who inspired him to make the Map of Unrequited Love that provoked the city to fire him, that changed the direction of his life, though he can't honestly say it was for the worst, even if now he's a slightly addled old man without a dime to his name or a single human contact of any significance, with nothing but his maps. In the past few days he's been thinking of the girl a lot, ever since a few mornings ago when he passed a small kite shop in Chinatown and saw another young girl who reminded him of her. Now he thinks about both girls as he stares at the mysterious coordinates tacked to the penthouse wall in front of him, the coordinates he's been trying to decode for days and which are finally starting to drive him crazy.

More out of instinct than any analysis, he knew immediately, the moment he saw them, that the final numbers in the series were coordinates. Jesus, he's been making maps more than forty years so he God damned well knows coordinates when he sees them. But by any latitude or longitude he chooses, north or south or east or west, 68 and 19 wind up in the middle of nowhere—the Sargasso Sea, the Arabian Sea, off the coast of Iceland, deep in the jungles of Chile. Maybe a treasure is buried in one of those places. I hope to God, Carl growls to himself, it's not a God damned buried treasure. I'm too old to go search for a buried treasure. No, it's obvious the answer is in the code that precedes the coordinates, written on the small crinkled square of old blue paper tacked to the wall: you're mocking me! he yells at it, but the truth is, it's not mocking him so much as haunting him, it's commanding him to solve the equation from somewhere beyond the grave. Because splattered across the series of numbers, and across the rest of the old blue paper, is a very deep purplish-brown stain that, as soon as he saw it, Carl knew instantly was a burst of blood. Not the thin streak of a single cut or the trickle of an accident, but the splash of a glee-fully violent wound, delivered to someone who wore the map a little too close to the heart.

He found the map several mornings ago, the same morning he saw the girl in the kite shop in Chinatown. It was buried in a wall in his penthouse that had been separated by another tremor. He had been out on his errands when the tremor hit, the paper lanterns that hung in the little Chinese eatery he was visiting dancing to something obviously stronger than a wind or a fog, fishball soup sloshing over the sides of the large black urn in which it simmered. Every morning before ten o'clock Carl had been making his way down the precarious stairs of the hotel to Grant Avenue and then up Bush Street to the little bakery where he buys bread, then returning to the Dragon Gate of Chinatown with its once grand monster perched above the entrance now as shabby and toothless as Carl himself, and walking through the gate up past the long-closed bazaar and stopping to gaze in the window of the old kite shop, its own monsters of wood and paper and nylon slowly disintegrating behind the glass. It's a neighborhood of dead monsters.

At the little Chinese restaurant, one of the few in Chinatown still open, the cook always sends Carl home with some leftovers from the night before. Soup and bamboo shoots, sometimes a little piece of garlic chicken or moo shu pork or a "pot sticker" or two—a dumpling that sticks to the pot in which it's fried. This one particular morning that the ground shook, it stopped Carl and the Chinese cook still in their tracks, and they held their breath, slowly peering around them to see if anything came crashing down; and it was on his way back to the old hotel that he stopped again to look in the kite-shop window, and saw the pretty Asian girl carefully and patiently painting one of the kites.

She looked up at him as he stood there gazing in the window, and she had the most blazing blue eyes he'd ever seen. He couldn't remember ever seeing such blue eyes, certainly not in an Asian face, and he was so startled by them that it was only a few minutes later he realized how much the rest of her reminded him of that other girl from forty years ago—though he was quite sure the earlier girl had not had such blue eyes. The girl in the kite shop was probably about the same age as the other girl had been when he knew her, perhaps a little older, and this girl working in the kite shop looked right back at him for as long as half a minute, and then returned to her work.

It was a couple of hours later, after the old man made his uneasy way back up the hotel stairs to the penthouse and sat at the table eating his day's one and only meal, that he noticed the wall on the other side of the room had separated from the tremor that morning. Just beyond the breach in the wall he could see the glint of the old blue paper, as blue as the Asian girl's eyes. When he saw the blood on the blue paper, his first horrified thought was that there might also be a body behind the wall; and that night, from his bedding on the floor, he kept staring at the wall, until the next morning, after a sleepless night, he made himself pull part of it away to see what else was there. If there was a body, he kept reasoning with himself, surely he would have known about it before now—these walls weren't that thick, after all—though on the other hand it was likely to have been there a long time, since this building had been abandoned for a long time. He wondered if he would find a weapon. He most dreaded finding a bloody knife.

But there was nothing else behind the wall. There were no other signs of whatever had happened here, or how the blood-stained paper with the numbers had ever gotten behind the wall in the first place. Maybe, he thought at first, the coordinates themselves held the answer. Maybe someone had been after the code that preceded the coordinates; maybe it was a secret formula of some sort. But if it was a secret formula, it didn't seem likely it would have been stuck inside a wall; either it would have been taken or destroyed altogether. As a man whose life had been a grid, as a man who had lived his life by coordinates, Carl accepted a more personal meaning in the numbers, an amazing grace: they once were lost and now were found; and had been found by him.

It was possible, he supposed, they weren't coordinates. But then what were they? A bank account, or a phone number? Upon investigation, the only possible place he found on the planet that might have such a phone number was Cameroon. At first he wasn't even certain where Cameroon was. Just because maps were his specialty—he said to himself with irritation, in one of those arguments old men are always having with no one—didn't mean geography was. Studying one of his maps of Africa, he eventually found Cameroon next to Nigeria, above the Congo. On another geological map, he discovered in Cameroon what looked to be a large volcano; that was interesting, but not an answer, or not one he could use; there wasn't a buried treasure in a volcano in Cameroon, was there? And if so, would there be a phone booth next to it? Did one place a long-distance person-to-person call to a volcano in Cameroon?

It's not a phone number or bank account, he decided. *2.3.7.5.68.19.* The 68 and 19 were coordinates; the 2, 3, 7 and 5, the code to which latitude and longitude, and what they meant. But then, in spite of himself, his thinking took a slightly more mystical turn; the first thing he noticed, the thing he realized right away, was how every single integer from 1 to 9 was represented in the series, with a single conspicuous exception, or at least conspicuous to anyone who spent any time at all contemplating the meaning of numbers. The truth was that Carl didn't actually spend a lot of time contemplating the meaning of numbers, he was just a God damned mapmaker, so numbers were always just a means of measurement. But then he noted that all the numbers of the code that preceded the coordinates were prime ones, which is to say numbers that could be divided only by themselves. He was sorry the 5 came *after* the 7; it threw off the progression, and what did *that* mean? Since he wasn't a numerologist, he couldn't bring much expertise to the numbers' meaning beyond the obvious: 2 was the basic division of life, of course, the bipolarity of earth and sky, day and night, male and female. 3, well, there were three physical dimensions, and the gestation period of the human fetus was divided into trimesters. 3 was the most explosive of numbers; it always challenged the 2 that preceded it, threatening to disrupt the 2, until it finally either tore the 2 apart or bound it together forever. Where there were two lovers, for instance, or even two close friends, the intrusion of a third upset the balance—unless the third was the child of the two. So 3 was the number of both unity and chaos, the holy trinity and the three-ring circus. 7: seven days of the week, the time in which God created the Earth and heavens and then rested; and in the Bible, if you were trying to scratch an existence out of the Egyptian dust, 7 was the number that made you run for cover or kick up your heels, depending on whether it was about to attach itself to years of feast or years of famine. 5 was the most primitive unit of higher mathematics, Carl reasoned, cavemen counting their five fingers, until eventually they evolved to joining one hand to the other, in the applause of ten.

But the number that caught Carl's attention was the only integer between 1 and 9 that wasn't in the series, in either the coordinates or the code. To begin with the obvious, 4 was the first integer that wasn't a prime number. But more important, 4 was the number that space and time had in common. In time there were four major points on the clock, four seasons in the year. In space there were four directions, four quadrants. Of course, this translated into larger cosmic terms, if anything could be larger or more cosmic than space and time: four weeks in which the moon circled the earth, four weeks in a woman's menstrual cycle, four weeks, in other words, in which the human race is constantly offered the chance to perpetuate itself. So 4 was the number of supreme order in space and time, composed as it was by the 2—the number of day/night and earth/sky— doubling itself, with 2 and 4 separated only by the anarchic and unpredictable 3. The absence of 4 from this particular series on this blue bloodstained page, with every other integer present and never repeated, struck Carl as so momentous that it bypassed mere significance and veered into the territory of the ominous. The blue bloodstained page was a map, in other words, in which the single most important numerical component of space and time and life *was missing*.

And he still had no idea what it meant. He kept trying to read the formula as a hieroglyphic, trying to impart some symbolic value to each component; but he felt flummoxed from the beginning, almost before he ever got started, in his attempts to interpret the 2. Up or down? Day or night? He never had much consciousness of time anyway, the poetics of time always seemed banal to him compared to those of space; a mapmaker who cared more about time than space should be a watchmaker instead, and in his life Carl had hardly owned a clock, let alone a calendar. Computing figures, adding them, subtracting them, multiplying them, dividing them, adding some and dividing others, subtracting some and multiplying others, he searched for whatever formula would shift the cross-coordinates of the small blue map to a point on his larger maps of some obvious relevance, to a topography of some spectacular familiarity, as inevitably as crosshairs falling on a target.

HIS last and most deranged adventure in cartography had been more than fifteen years ago, when he was hired by the city of Los Angeles to map the city's missing dreams. Over the months immediately following the thirty-first of December 1999, the residents of L.A. began to realize their sleep was now utterly drained of dreams, a phenomenon that coincided with a wholesale ransacking of time-capsules from the city's Black Clock Park over on the west side of town. Gradually the city's populace sank into a state of insomniacal fitfulness and then a kind of functional madness.

Of course, by any logical consideration Carl's assignment was absurd. It would be difficult enough to map dreams that existed, let alone those that didn't: what's missing from the world? a four-year-old girl had once run from the dusty mainstreet of a small Chinese ghost town to ask her bewildered uncle—and years later Carl was being commissioned to not only answer the question, but diagram it. While the leaders of the city were at a loss to account for why the dreams were missing, they were determined to track them down at any rate, because the life of the city depended on it. Though Carl had never been to L.A. before, he understood it was nothing if not the city of vicarious dreams, and that this was why the city leaders had had the urbanscape literally transformed into one vast projection room, where old movies were constantly screened night and day on the sides of buildings, on the walls of rooms, on the concrete slabs of sidewalks and the asphalt plains of streets.

A city of synthetic dreams flickered in the place between consciousness and unconsciousness where the collective subconscious had fallen through a schism. In his room at the dilapidated Hotel Hamblin, Carl slept as these hysterical dreams sputtered endlessly on his ceiling: a writer, watching a demonically beautiful woman ride the New Mexico mesas on horseback scattering the ashes of her father from an urn, falls madly in love with her; the most beautiful man ever filmed goes to the gas chamber not for a murder he committed but for a murder he *contemplated* committing, out of love for the most beautiful woman ever filmed; the manager of a casino in postwar Argentina marries the woman he loves solely for the purpose of destroying her for once rejecting him; a wealthy socialite walks into the sea so that the concert violinist she loves won't give up his music for her; two lovers, an outlaw and a half-breed, crawl wounded and bleeding toward each other over harsh Western plains, beckoning each other with entreaties and unable to resist, though each knows the other is bent on murder. By the time that Carl, gathering together the information from all of his dream maps, had determined the missing dreams were located in the back room of a twenty-four-hour convenience store down at the corner of Adams and Crenshaw, amid the cigarettes and beer and sex magazines, he didn't care that the city leaders fired him. One last dream convinced him he had had enough anyway.

The mystery of where this last bit of old film came from, and what subversive act introduced it into the dreamloop projected onto the city, was almost incidental to the horror. A young actress hung naked on a hook in a deserted bus terminal, in the throes of a terror nothing less than mortal, before her audition turned fatal. The scene had barely played itself out on his ceiling before Carl hastily packed his bag, ran from the hotel, and hailed a cab on the Strip; he took the cab to the Hollywood bus station and caught a bus north. He wound up in San Francisco, where he thought he might at least eventually get his own dreams back. After that Carl lost his faith in maps for a while, and sank into a destitution that eventually led him to the abandoned Hotel Poseidon next to the Dragon Gate of San Francisco's Chinatown.

But now, after having found the small bloody blue map in the wall of his suite, he's become consumed again with the logic of maps. All through the day and night he's been charting coordinates, maps surrounding him on the floor beneath his feet as well as on the walls around his head, until his mind is swirling. Now, day and night, he's been doing calculations in his head, racking his brain trying to figure out what algebraic strategy will illuminate the equation in question, what crucial x factor will provide the answer. By the end of this evening, ravenous with hunger since he hadn't made his usual trek this morning to the bakery and the Chinese eatery, Carl had worked himself into a myriad of postulations involving deranged charts and courses and plots and crisscrossing latitudes and plummeting longitudes, his brain mad with equations, mad with coordinates, mad with x factors, exhausted by increasingly absurd results until he simply couldn't turn his old brain off. Even when he sank into the chair at the desk and turned off the lamp and closed his eyes, he couldn't stop the calculations from tumbling through his head. If anything it was worse in the dark, nothing but codes and coordinates rolling up and down the cylinders of his eyes, until even the insides of his closed eyelids became little maps.

He sat with the light off for a while, wishing he had gotten something to eat. In the dark the penthouse was frightening; he found himself listening for strange sounds of other intruders. With a terrible hush, a dark shadow opened up where the elevator used to be, now an empty shaft with only a single board nailed across the space where doors had once closed and opened; he's always afraid to move around the room in the dark, afraid he'll topple down the elevator shaft. Outside in the dark he could make out the fog of the bay rolling up Grant, obscuring the mystery graffiti on the building across the street, though he's read it a thousand times if he's read it once: it says I FELL INTO THE ARMS OF VENUS DE MILO. He turned the lamp back on and started plotting again a new computation on yet another map, and then again dropped the pencil in fatigue, his body hating the chair, his mind hating this obsession. I'm not obsessed with my maps, my maps are obsessed with me, he had said, years before; but now he was certainly obsessed with them, and he wondered if this meant faith was gone for good. He had never truly known what his faith was, he had once said that at bottom all faith was only in faith itself. His eyes felt weak, losing their focus, though he'd always had very good eyes, for which he'd become more grateful over the years, when glasses had become more difficult for him to afford; but once again, though he lay down the pencil, he couldn't stop the calculating in his head, and in his exhaustion his brain descended into chaos, all the day's denials and the night's beliefs converging, the 2 and the 3 and the 7 and the 5 and the 68 and the 19 and the black gasp of the elevator shaft and the graffiti on the wall across the street, and her name.

It flashed through his mind so quickly he instantly forgot it again. But in its aftermath, his brain made one last inexplicable calculation and, when he opened his eyes, all the coordinates collapsed to zero.

Now he stares at the map on which he's been working, frowning. Zero? Zero and zero, maybe? Zero degrees latitude and zero degrees longitude, somewhere at the edge of the Bay of Guinea? But it wasn't zero and zero that his mind had sputtered, just zero, and now he starts figuring again, only to become confused; and the more he tries to re-create whatever calculation his brain made in that fleeting moment, the more entangled he becomes in other calculations instead. He closes his eyes again and tries to calmly rethink how he possibly came up with zero. He's certainly never come up with zero before, he's never been aware of any point on any map he's ever worked on that was just, simply, zero; and now, no matter how he tries, he can't re-create it. What did I do to come up with zero, he says to himself out loud, how did I do it? Now he thinks he really will go mad, and begins poring frantically over the earlier calculations for an answer. But he can't find it.

He doesn't want to find it. That's the maddest part. He doesn't want to find an answer that's zero. In the moment he arrived at zero, a Moment opened up before him, and beyond that moment a terrible sense of the abyss, and he shrank from it, perhaps explaining why he can't find it again now, perhaps explaining why he hasn't been able to find it at all until now. He hopes it's simply a wrong answer that his brain, now so tired it's babbling to itself, arrived at in error. But what makes it seem so unlikely is also what makes it feel so true: the perfect emptiness of zero, the perfect collapse of every coordinate—determined by a code that omits the 4 that gives order to space and time and life—to nothingness. Now, after hours and days of being consumed with trying to prove an answer, he's consumed with trying to disprove one, investigating every possible combination of calculations in order to assure himself that no matter what, no matter how, the blue map on the wall never adds up, or subtracts down, to zero.

Finally, when he can't stand any more, he sets his old body down on the floor, pulling his maps up around him like a sheet and covering himself, maps across his chest and beneath his head, strewn around him like bedding where he sleeps, so that even in the dark he can immediately crisscross two lines into a point. With pencil still in hand, he slips into a turbulent sleep. Though he dreams often, he almost never dreams of the past; but recently he's dreamed of Provence, where as a young man he thought of retiring to work in a vineyard, and now in tonight's fitful sleep he dreams of her, he can see her face quite clearly, can see her on the streets of the East Village in the afternoons or on the occasional night when she would get away from whatever it was she did at night. He wasn't so completely naive he hadn't wondered what it was, but that was a time when he was still young enough to forgive anything, assuming she would allow him to forgive her; and when they lay in his tiny St. Marks apartment looking at the maps of London and Paris and Vienna that papered the walls, he knew he came closest to delivering her from the secrets she refused to tell. A small stuffed bear sat in the corner. We'll take him too, Carl promised her. You are more idealistic about your desire, she said to him—or something like it—than any guy I've ever known, you talk about my smile and not my breasts, and I almost believe you mean it.

After that he could only try and live up to that idealism, which often meant choosing idealism over desire, a choice that marks both the end and the beginning of love. For a while, he barely resisted the urge to follow her at night to where she lived, where she worked, to all the places that he knew she didn't want him to know. At the time he thought that perhaps if he confronted her, if he said to her, *I know about this, and it doesn't matter*, all her secrets would decompose into powerlessness. But he did resist the urge to follow her, and was never sure it was because she would consider his following her a betrayal, or because no matter what they were, just by their very revelation those secrets were bound to open a chasm between the two of them, or mostly because he feared that he would find out he was a smaller man than he wanted to know, and having learned her secrets would instead confront her and say, *I know about this: and I can't stand it*. He didn't trust the possibility that she might be more right about his heart than he was. Now, forty years later, her name has become the greatest secret of all.

Then the dream whispers the secret in his ear.

He wakes in the dark to her name. Once again it vanishes immediately from his memory. Fog from the bay drifts through the window and fills the penthouse. He sits up from his bed, still holding the pencil in one hand, still holding in the other hand the map he's plotted in his sleep; hobbling over to the table where he turns on the small desk lamp, he sees, written a split moment before waking, coordinates spiraling off into space before reducing themselves to a single point, located—if one could blow this map up to the size of life—in a ramshackle penthouse at Grant and Bush in the city of San Francisco. He doesn't turn out the light for the rest of the night, in the certain and unshakable conviction that he's disappearing.

Still, it has to happen one more time before he actually understands. It's the next morning when, more exhausted than ever, but with his exhaustion now locked in a bitter duel with hunger, Carl gets up to make his way down to the street and then to the bakery and Chinatown—only to find that rather inconveniently, during the night, the hotel stairs have collapsed. Several of the steps leading down from the penthouse hang in midair, and far below him he can see several steps rising and stopping in midair, with no particular sign of ruin between the two, as though all the other flights of stairs just vanished in the dark. He stands at the top peering down at the bottom, stunned and trying to remember if he heard the collapse of the stairs in his sleep, wondering how the steps could disintegrate so completely and silently, stranding him here. Wondering if he's going deaf or numb, or has just become so submerged in exhaustion and obsession that he's completely unaware of everything else happening around him, Carl feels more baffled than panicked by the fact that he now has no way to get down to the street. He stumbles back into his penthouse in a daze and over to his window, looking out over the city and wondering if there's anyone he can call, if there's anything he can say that anyone can hear, if there's anything anyone can do anyway, even if they heard.

He's staring out the window like this when he happens to see in the street below the girl from the kite shop, who some days ago reminded him so much of the girl whose name he can't remember. Then, in the arch of the Dragon Gate, she actually looks right back up at him; even from the distance, Carl can make out her electric blue eyes.

He's about to try and call out to her when, as though it's floated in on the fog, he remembers the other girl's name for a split second, and the lightning-fast calculation of zero occurs once more in his mind—and he finally realizes it's the memory itself that's the elusive x factor of his demented geography. Triggering and exploding every possible meaning of his life, reducing him to a void, the small blue map hanging on the wall fixes him fast on the terrain of his memory; though it's not, the blood that stains it might as well be his own. To a man whose life has been a grid, to a man who has lived by coordinates, these are numbers of a grace more perverse than amazing: he once was found but now is lost, his own personal coordinates traveling with him, corresponding not to any common map but rather to an ever-fluid, ever-transforming map that's only his. These coordinates are a reference point for everything and everyone else but him. He's the north pole of unrequited love, and all around him, with the tide of memory rising from the street to the top of the arched gate of the dead dragon to his penthouse window, swallowing up the girl below, the zero of the fog closes in.

ONE night in the late months of 1998, the Occupant woke to a terror as old as time. It was a terror of death's presence, if not its presence in his bedroom, if not its presence in his house, if not its presence in his city, then its presence in a chaos now known for sure and glimpsed for real rather than conceived abstractly. He had been vaguely aware recently of crossing into that realm of life when the memory of a thing is more magical than the thing itself, when the memory of the dream that didn't come true is more powerful than the life that did.

It could have been any dream. It could have been an architect's dream or a movie star's or a politician's, its death more devastating than the death of life, because one must live with the death of a dream afterward in a way that one never has to live with the death of one's own life. The Occupant woke one night in 1998 and then the next night and then the next to this most important of deaths, the death of a reason for living, knowing his Calendar was a failure, that the meaning of the age had eluded him, that the great huge mesh of crossing timelines—in which he had hoped to catch the truth, at the center of which he had hoped to build a door, through the portal of which he had hoped to step back to the moment thirty years before, when as an eleven-year-old boy in the streets of Paris his childhood was lost forever—that great web of crossing timelines was broken, only a gossamer of his imagination all along, and that moreover it had been a quest made in bad faith, pursued not for truth but for glory, for the most vainglorious of reasons that undermined not only the integrity of his life but any chance of success the quest might have had. He had failed in his pursuit because, he now knew in the dark, he deserved to fail.

He had recently taken out a life insurance policy. Over the course of the Eighties and early Nineties he had survived by— and he and Angie had lived on—support for his work from academic and historic circles, and the modest and moderate grants they gave him to pursue the apocalypse. But finally in the late Nineties everyone just got fed up with him. He came to be seen not as a visionary but as a minor crackpot who had nothing to say of interest to anyone. Soon his resources began drying up and then his prospects with them, until there was no convincing anyone anymore and he knew he was irrevocably caught in the downward spiral of life's end. Late in 1998 he had a dream one night in which he coughed up his own heart. In this dream he caught his heart in his hands after dislodging it from his throat and spitting it out. For a while he stood there in his dream looking at the still-beating heart in his hands, and then he took the organ and was about to nail it to the Calendar on his wall, to the date marked the seventh of May 1968, when he heard someone behind him say, What are you doing? He had been about to strike the first blow with his hammer when he turned and saw a small infant with black Asian hair and Angie's features, but with his own startling blue eyes.

 ARE you my daughter? he said.

Yes, she answered; and he woke.

Let's say I'm a monster. But let's say the night my child was conceived I heard the first murmur of possible redemption. I dreamed of her before Angie even knew she existed, a newborn talking up a storm, erudite and provocative. Let's say, the little girl said to me, I'm the god you want to pretend you don't believe in.

When I woke from the dream, I was sleeping between Angie's thighs, my ear to her belly.

The next night the infant was already growing into a person, with the black Asian hair of her mother and the blue eyes of her father, and the night after that she was a year old, and a week later she was a toddler, beset by primal calm, a sanguine visitor from outer space. With each night and week she grew older into childhood till Angie deduced a presence. . . . More and more, Little Saki looked like Angie except for the blue eyes, all the more unnerving in her Asian face. In the dreams, she spoke in the voice of the cosmic reason I had always insisted time had swallowed. We debated life and she beat me every round, my defeats not crushed humiliations but joyous realizations, their clarity and force evaporating only with the first light of waking.

One night not so long ago, in an interview on television, a very famous actress, a legend in her own time, flinty and New English and "indomitable," now well into her eighties and looking back over what she clearly considered the grand drama of her days, said the sort of thing you hear from such people who are constantly reading from the script they've come to call a life. "If I had it to do all over again," she declaimed with quivering pride, "I wouldn't change a thing." Of course the world loves this. It's so flinty and indomitable and legendary. The world receives it as evidence of a survivor's hard-earned wisdom, a triumphant valediction, a granitic testament to the human spirit, rather than what it is, the final expression of narcissism, the last gesture of self-congratulation, a humble parting homage to one's own myth . . . my life has been so legendary, who could want to change it? Even my fuckups have been so legendary, who could want to change them? I am so legendary and indomitable and flinty, who could want to have wasted such a fabulous life actually *learning* something? Given the chance to relive such a mythic existence, who could bother wanting to do a hundred things I didn't have the passion or courage to do before, who could bother wanting to undo a hundred things I didn't have the good sense or strength of character not to do before? My life has simply been too perfectly extraordinary—and really, could it have been anything else, given that *I* lived it?—for me to now have anything resembling a single human regret, to feel anything resembling a single pang of remorse, to spend anything resembling a single reflective moment acknowledging and reconciling myself to a thousand missed opportunities to have done, or not done, one single thing better, stronger, braver. . . .

We spent so much of the Eighties trying to make ourselves be together, Angie and I, for a reason we never understood. . . . Spent so much of the Eighties trying to overcome the emotional wasteland between us that we stared out over from opposite horizons. By the beginning of the Nineties, we finally met in the middle of that wasteland, crossing from opposite ends with great effort, overcoming everything our lives set in our paths. But of course our meeting in the middle didn't change the landscape. While she and I were in closer proximity to each other, the landscape was still all around us, its proximity to us not having changed at all. We had believed that each of us crossing the landscape in the direction of the other might somehow make the terrain disappear, when in fact upon reaching each other we looked around us only to see wasteland everywhere. Maybe going the direction of each other, we'd each been going the wrong direction all along. Married fifteen months after I reached L.A., in another fifteen months I had an affair with an "executive producer," one of those witty titles L.A. bestows on people to make them think their lives mean something. Couple of years later I had a brief fling with an office receptionist, so in one sense I was moving up.

More corrosive than the feeling of guilt over infidelity was the feeling of bad faith, assuming there's a difference between the two. Both are betrayals but one seems more routine, something in the course of day-to-day life and love, the other more fundamental, a corruption of not just a sexual agreement but a mutual understanding of shared life. I cheated on more than Angie's body. Can't say for sure I cheated on Angie's love, the question of love as mysterious to us ten years later as it was when we first met. But I cheated on everything we'd gone through together, I cheated on the price we paid together, even as we each paid it in our own way. Bad faith lay in the realization that my cheating might not tear us apart at all but rather keep us together, and that if she cheated as well, that was also likelier to keep us together. We got to a point where, if I suspected her of cheating too, it was a relief. That was what our marriage was based on, mutual relief at our common corruption. Maybe some marriages are based on even worse. But that wouldn't change the bad faith of it and, as the years went by, I woke at night in terror of my whole life being an act of bad faith, where everything was self-interest and nothing more, where every human interaction was driven by a silent, even subconscious calculation of some ulterior motive, where at the point that a sea of bad faith has taken over your whole life, there's no small island left from which you can even try to build a bridge of good faith, because even that effort becomes suspect, even good faith is nothing but self-interested, even altruism is nothing but solipsistic, even this professed agonizing right here right now is nothing but a gesture, made to the conscience in order to assure it that it exists.

In the midst of this, neither of us ever talked about having a child. By the time Angie got pregnant she was thirty-six, and I'd known her nearly half her life. Having in the age of chaos kissed women awake from their own private millennia, which was also bad faith, given the reason I kissed them—to own them—I now faced a void of meaning in my life because Angie had the temerity, if you can believe this, to save her own life. She saved it just by living it, saved it just by surviving the bad dreams of New York, by growing beyond the one-word reductions of everything she felt and believed, even if the surviving and growing was in a wasteland. I think I'm pregnant, she said, and I nodded—and she was surprised I wasn't surprised. We talked about the steps we would take to end the pregnancy, till finally I said, "What if we had her?"

Angie looked at me in confusion. "Her?"

"The baby."

"It's a her?"

"Whatever," I said. "The baby."

"You want to have the baby?" Part of her was moved, part

of her angry. Most of her was more shaken than I'd ever seen her, more shaken than by a hundred New York nightmares. None of her various adopted personae over the years, not the little girl with the stuffed bear or the sleek tough sophisticate, was prepared for this development. We're talking, I told Little Saki in my dream that night, of ending the pregnancy. The child seemed unfazed. Let's say, I said to her, you're the god you say you are . . . what divine mission will it terminate, to terminate you?

There's no divine mission, the little girl said patiently. If you don't give me birth, the god in me just moves on, to be born somewhere else to someone else. "We have to decide," Angie said a couple of days later, "do you want to have this baby?"

Why couldn't I have just said yes? I didn't believe the yes, I didn't believe the no. In a life of bad faith, every answer was suspect. I left it to Angie, who needed to hear me believe something out loud, or at least believe in this one thing, of all things. So I said nothing and later, after she was gone, concluded that in my silence I betrayed my child. Having saved lives I never cared about just for the thrill of it, I couldn't say a simple yes to save this one for the love of it.

So Angie saved it. She didn't have an abortion, for reasons that, given my passivity, she decided were none of my business. In my life of bad faith I got through my faithless days just to be with my daughter at night. Down through the weeks and then the months, Angie swelling toward deliverance, I slept each night with my ear to her belly. One night several weeks after we confirmed the pregnancy, Little Saki was nowhere to be found. I wandered my sleep looking for her, was awakened in the dark by a rip in the unconscious universe . . . Angie lay in bed next to me in terrible pain. For three hours she had writhed, uterus slithering, sure she was losing the baby, and to my astonishment I found myself praying, to any dubious god who listened, Don't lose the baby. It was a plea beyond rationale or even emotion, speaking from a part of me I didn't know. Don't lose the baby.

Angie didn't lose the baby. It wasn't a response, on either

her part or any god's, to my prayer, just happenstance. The next night when I saw the little girl again, I said to her, Something happened last night—and she only answered, We won't speak of it. As she grew older into adolescence and then young womanhood and then full maturity and middle age, we spent many hours in which I taught her nothing and she taught me everything. We traveled endless railroads and witnessed the vast night's errant shooting stars. What do you see? I asked her. I see the shadows of my mother's ribs crossing the dome of the sky, she said. What do you hear? I asked her. I hear the rapids of my mother's blood roaring through capillary ravines, she said. All I could offer in return was the Blue Calendar, stretching down a long narrow hall. . . . This, I told her, vain with a father's hope to finally impart something of significance to his child, is what I've spent my whole life learning. This is the passage of chaos I've spent my whole life walking.

She followed me patiently down the narrow hall to the farthest corner at the very end, where she'd found me in the first dream about to nail my heart to the wall. I pointed out to her the second minute of the third hour of the seventh day of the fifth month of the sixty-eighth year of the final century, "when it all began," I explained—and she said, It? She must have seen the panic in my face, because immediately she rushed to reassure me, Oh, yes, of course, Father, I understand. The apocalypse, I said. The apoca*lapse*, she answered, and laughed—she was making a joke. As I did every morning, I woke to doubt and faithlessness. As I did every evening, I returned to her inexplicable wisdom. In the dark of the bedroom, before falling asleep, I would lie in the terror of death, as I had for a lot of nights now. I would think about how the meaning of my life had run out along with the money, and I would will my heart to stop beating while I slept. . . .

It didn't seem so self-indulgent. There was a $400,000 life insurance policy, after all, that Angie and Little Saki could survive on a lot longer than they could survive on my terror and self-loathing. But then I'd fall asleep and see her, and sense with the growing movement in Angie's belly the birth of a faith I couldn't name, a faith no more or less complicated than the simple fact that there was finally something in my life that wasn't about me, that there was something in my life of more value than myself, that the solar system of my life had acquired another sun.

Thirty-eight weeks after my first dream of her, she came to me and shook my arm. Asleep in my bed, I woke to her touching me; by now she was an old woman. Her bright blue eyes were wet in her old Asian face and she smiled sadly at me. "Goodbye," she said.

"Goodbye?" I asked, alarmed.

"Goodbye," she whispered again, and closed her eyes, and the tears ran from them.

I had no idea what she meant, but I cried, "Wait!" before she faded from view, so loudly I woke myself. I sat straight up from my nightmare, burying my head in my hands, waiting for Angie to reach over and touch me. But she didn't, because she wasn't there.

lay in bed waiting for her to return from the bathroom, but she didn't return. I went upstairs looking to find her sitting in the window drinking tea, but she wasn't to be found. I worried she had strayed off for a moment in the night, only to collapse suddenly in labor, but there was no sign of her. I waited for her to reappear from her morning walk, but she never showed up. I looked for signs of foul play—fingernail marks along the wall, forced lock on the front door, an ominous splash of blood—but there were no signs. I looked for signs she had packed and left—a suitcase missing, clothes and makeup gone, the nursery stripped of baby things—but everything was in its place. I noted the car still in the driveway and the car keys still on the bookshelf where we kept them. I found her little stuffed bear still sitting on top of the piano where she always kept it, the most telltale sign of all—except I didn't know what it told. She hadn't come back by noon, and I went walking the neighborhood to find her. She hadn't come back by midafternoon, and I went driving the hills looking for her. She hadn't come back by evening, and I called the police and the nearby hospitals. She hadn't come back the next morning, and I went driving the city; I drove to the beach, I drove through the valleys, I drove to Black Clock Park. I came home so I might find her mysteriously back in place, like she never left, sitting at the piano playing a Chopin nocturne or a Jerome Kern tune, with a forbidding air about her suggesting these past twenty-four hours must just be one of those mysteries of her life that remain a mystery, no questions asked; but the house was still empty. I waited for her the next day and the day after that, and the day after that . . . I drove to the desert, I drove to the sea, I drove to Mexico. I drove to the Mojave, I drove to Las Vegas, I drove to Monument Valley. I drove from Santa Fe to the Continental Divide, I drove from the Rockies to dormant Canadian volcanoes. I assumed that, like Mama, she was taken by the apocalypse I so arrogantly came to believe was mine to master. I drove to all coordinates of my Apocalyptic Calendar, from one date to another, from one pulsing source of anarchy to every outpost of chaos within my reach, all over the country looking for her. I drove from thoughtless sites of toxic-waste dumps to wrecking grounds of pointless air disasters to conspiratorial hotbeds of senseless terrorism. I drove from furious Mormon metropolises to half-deserted California chinatowns.

AT a blackjack table in Reno, the Occupant heard a guy say he thought he'd seen a pretty Asian girl carrying a baby walking with two thousand other women and children in the Nevada desert, before disappearing into the Sierras.

The Occupant caught up with the migration at Lake Tahoe. Circling them clockwise in his car, then parking several miles down the shore of the lake, he trudged back to meet them, falling in with them and mingling. He checked every woman's face and listened for the sound of every baby crying. Every woman he asked shook her head. After searching for an hour, he found himself surrounded by half a dozen men in white robes who, without saying a word or answering any of his questions, escorted him back to his car. Before leaving Tahoe, he bought a pair of binoculars at a sporting-goods store and followed the exodus in his car, watching them through the glasses from an adjacent ridge as they descended from the Sierras into a delta plain that was half field and half marsh; for hours from the ridge he pored over all the faces of the women through the binoculars, searching for hers, the white-robed priests watching him back, the glint of his old silver car caught by the blue winter sun. After three days of searching the same faces over and over, he gave up.

A couple of days later, hearing of a Chinese woman that a pair of Western eyes had taken for Japanese, he took a river ferry over to an island in the delta where he spent the night in a small ghost town. In the mainstreet bar where he had dinner, the only people were himself and the bartender; he also seemed to be the only guest of the old hotel across the street. That night the bare branches of the trees outside his window scraped the moonlight, the dark hummed with the buzz of mosquitoes; and he had a dream in which Angie came to him, moving soundlessly down the street past the houses to the hotel, through the old wooden lobby up the stairs to his room—to make another daughter, she said. Another? he asked. Through the shadows of the room she glided to his side. She dropped her clothes, touched herself until she was wet, and then straddled him, slipping him inside her. Impatient for the flash of his dream in her mind, she had him faster and faster until, stirred from his sleep, his erection collapsing in confusion before climax, he woke, half desperate and half mad with hope, to a strange girl on top of him in the dark. Angie? he murmured; and she vanished.

LET'S say she knew. After seventeen years with me, married for nine, with our first and only child in her belly, she woke one morning, looked at me asleep in our bed, and saw the monster. Maybe she never saw it before, so she must be held as accountable for her blindness as I am for my monstrousness. Maybe she saw it in glimpses and turned away, so she must be held as accountable for her denials. But in the first case, what was her worst crime, except to have been innocent? And in the second case, what was her worst crime, except to have given me the benefit of the doubt?

Now, on the verge of bringing our child into the world, she could no longer afford innocence, she could no longer afford denial. Let's say she woke that last morning, looked over at the father of her child sleeping next to her and, aghast at the sight of the monster, left. . . . Or: the apocalypse that was my plaything took her. In the form of an intruder or kidnapper, chaos stealthily broke into our house, made his way down to the second floor, put his hand over her mouth as she woke, and dragged her from the bed and up the stairs and out the front door. Either way she vanished from the face of the earth, the price paid for my flirting with apocalypse so romantically. All along I had been vain enough to believe chaos was my plaything. All along I had been the plaything of chaos.

On New Year's Day the Occupant came home. He drove to Black Clock Park and bought a plot and time-capsule. He stood staring at the grave for an hour and returned the following day, and returned the day after that. Each day he returned at the same time to visit the grave.

He took out the ad in the newspaper that Kristin would read a week and a half later. The ad was both a fiction and a confession. It was a confession because it was what he truly wanted at that moment, unvarnished, and it was a fiction because he didn't really expect anyone to answer it, and might not have even printed it at all if he had thought someone would. He intended the ad as a kind of erotic virus unleashed on the world, just to see who would catch it; at best—or at worst—he expected women to read and recoil from it, and then, perhaps, the carnal immune system not quite being what they thought, find themselves swept up in the virus' irresistible contagion, unsettled by day, sleepless by night. He not only put the ad in the newspaper but sent it in response to the personal ads of select women, the shy ones mostly, privately looking "to be put in my place," or "to be made shameless," by someone who would nonetheless also save their lives. Not the ones who signed themselves "HornyGirl" or "Slut4U," but rather "Dreamer," or "Amethyst." In his original ad the Occupant wrote *I'm more interested in the look in your eyes than how perfect your body is. The only thing I ask of you, other than that you be available however I want you whenever I want you, is that you be true to who you are*, two lines he wound up not merely deleting but slashing out with his pen as though with a knife. He had no way of knowing that of all the lines he wrote, those two in particular would best describe the girl who answered.

That week and a half he spent every night out by the beach in the strip joints and brothels of Baghdadville. In single-minded pursuit he went looking for its saddest girls in particular. If a girl onstage or at his table gave him one of her practiced frozen smiles, he left immediately. He wasn't looking to save anyone, he wasn't looking to deliver to anyone the Kiss of Chaos. Constantly wracked by an increasingly spellbinding headache, he administered to himself ever larger doses of fiorinal and vodka. Picking up plump fortyish women in bars and driving them out across the desert where he would take Kristin a couple of months later, he would pull over and have the women over the hood of the car with fleeting joyless exhilaration, their breasts bobbing in the Mojave dust on the chrome. Then he would drop them off at the airport on the way into Vegas, check into a hotel alone for the night, and drive back the next day.

For three nights he didn't leave Baghdadville at all, sleeping in his car and virtually living at a brothel called The Angel Eyes where, every few hours, he returned to Room 7. A Turk sat inside the front door of the brothel watching soccer games on an Italian television station, along with a big German blond hired as security guard and enforcer. The Turk would greet the Occupant with a cold amused charm, as a pusher greets a customer who is obviously and rapidly in the process of becoming addicted: Ah, the gentleman for Angel 7, he would smile, and lead the Occupant up the stairs, down the hall, and around the corner of a dark L-shaped corridor to Room 7, where the door locked from the outside. The Turk would turn the lock on the door, open it, and the Occupant would give him some money and step inside Room 7, where a young girl, no more than sixteen years old, blond with long legs and small breasts, hung by her bound hands from the ceiling, naked and blindfolded on a hook at the end of a rope. The rope attached to the hook ran down along the side of the wall so that one could raise the girl to her feet or lower her to her knees. Next to a single bare burning bulb on the wall behind her was a sign written in black marker ink, like the sign a father might hang on his daughter's bedroom door, that read YOU CAN STICK IT IN ANY HOLE. I WANT YOU TO CUM NOW. It was always the same girl, no matter when the Occupant visited Room 7, whatever the hour of the day or night, and it would have been difficult for him to be certain, with the blindfold across her eyes, whether she was awake or asleep, alive or dead, except for the slight resistance of her body when he put himself inside her. She never made a sound, she never responded to the door opening or closing, she never stirred when he was inside her, except for the way her body slightly tensed; when he was inside her, at the moment of climax there opened up in his head, in the midst of the pain of the searing headache, a light into which he could almost fall, as though it was a Moment into which he could almost step, a passageway through his memories. It was only much later that it occurred to him maybe the light was for the girl, not him. Of course he meant to obliterate the memory of his wife and daughter. Of course he meant to obliterate the landscape of his life around him and the end of his dreams and the terror of death as old as time. Humiliation couldn't have mattered less to him; he had no interest one way or another in whether the naked blonde hanging from the hook felt anything or not. The girl on the hook didn't respond in any way to his being there, or in any way to his white moan inside her. She was his favorite. Sometimes, inside her, he was sure he loved her.

HE doesn't return to Room 7 for a couple of months, until after Kristin leaves. He sleeps late that morning, awakened by a particularly vicious crack of thunder, and the moment he wakes he knows instantly Kristin has become one more vanished woman in his life. She isn't in his bed, where she was sleeping; when he gets up from bed and goes to her room, she isn't there either.

As he stands in the doorway of her room staring at her empty bed, it doesn't occur to him even for a moment that she might have gone for a walk, or upstairs to make tea. He's altogether familiar with the aura of this kind of absence. It's a female absence, of someone who's come to take on a particular importance to him beyond what he can possess or control. She has in recent weeks gone from being the device of his sensual satisfaction to something more, the missing piece of his Apocalyptic Calendar by which he believed he could solve the inconsistencies of modern time's terrain and thereby track down the mother of his child. Now the girl is loose, wandering the city with the vortex of the Apocalyptic Age marked on her bare body, setting into motion pending cataclysm like an alien presence that makes all the monitors and compasses go haywire.

He can only hope that, as when he first found her, she has nowhere else to go, and will return.

But she doesn't return, and the Occupant just sits in his house watching the hills sink into dusk. He waits all the next day. On the morning of the third day he drives out to Black Clock Park to visit the grave of the time-capsule he buried upon returning to Los Angeles. All the way there he keeps his eyes peeled for her hitching a ride or loitering at a bus stop. When he gets to the park he leaves the car and walks out across the knolls of the cemetery, passing the other graves toward his own.

A hundred feet away, he can already see it. A hundred feet away, he can already see the rude gash in the ground. The grave is open. The capsule has been dug up and taken. The hole is empty except for the unmistakable print of a hand in the mud. Trailing off from the hole, the grass is matted, as though something was very recently dragged from it, though exactly what, the Occupant can't begin to guess, since the capsule itself isn't that big or heavy. Stunned, he just stands staring at the hole where the capsule was, feeling a deeply fundamental kind of shock. It's the kind of violation one waits for his whole life, without knowing he's been waiting for it.

Standing there on the mound, under the clearing storm, he has no doubts about who's taken the capsule. All he can wonder is when she first got the idea to steal it, whether it was a sudden impulse or something she had planned for a while, a retributive bit of vandalism by which something is taken not because it has any value whatsoever to the thief, but because it has value to the victim. The only thing he knows for sure, staring at the slash in the earth in an amazement that is at once disbelieving and knowing, is that there's no point in waiting anymore for her to come back, there's no point in waiting anymore for anyone to come back. The only thing he knows for sure, staring at the open grave, is that if there's to be a Moment in his life that is a passageway through his memories, it isn't a light but a black gaping pit.

HE drives back home and goes down into the room at the bottom of the house, where he stands for half an hour looking at the Calendar, which has constituted the magnum opus of his past twenty years.

He can't make any sense of it now. No matter how closely or carefully he studies it, none of the timelines are as he remembers them, or as he has drawn them, and none of the dates correspond to anything of meaning. Not the apocalypse but the apocalapse, his daughter had laughed in his dreams; he thought it was a joke.

He goes back upstairs and lies down on his bed again and sleeps. When he wakes, he looks over next to him to see if anyone has returned; but the bed is still empty, and he gets up and goes back upstairs and gets in his car and drives back into town. It's now late afternoon. He gets to the bank in time to close out his account, and then drives to a dress shop down on Melrose Avenue and buys two blue cotton dresses, one dark and one light, that he supposes might match a certain girl's eyes, if he had any idea at all what color her eyes are. Of course, he can't be entirely sure of the size. The young sales clerk watches him a while and finally says, For your wife? A girlfriend? And then, hoping she won't insult him, Your daughter? My daughter, he agrees. She helps him pick out some underwear. He asks her what an average size is for women's shoes and she says seven and he picks out a pair of size-six sandals. He drives to the market and buys a couple of weeks' worth of food, and loads the bags of groceries in the trunk of his car, and then drives west on Sunset Boulevard.

Just before Black Clock Park he cuts down Beverly Glen under the canopy of trees now showing the signs of spring. Then he drives out Pico toward Baghdadville. Above him the sky is darkening blue, completely windswept of the huge storm that woke him a couple of mornings ago. The Los Angeles he drives through now routinely anticipates apocalypse the way other cities routinely anticipate nightfall; no one is a citizen of Los Angeles, in Los Angeles everyone is a citizen of his dreams, and if he doesn't have any dreams he's a nomad. As night falls, he parks across the street from The Angel Eyes and waits. He can hear the moaning of dogs that run through the streets in wild packs, and every once in a while he sees in the shadows the flitting figures of reguibat pleasure-girls, naked except for their heels and jewelry and black burnooses, muttering to the passing men in bastardized Maghrebi. Even in the night a white silted light seems to lie like a filter over the braying palm trees.

He sits for almost forty minutes before he sees a guy come walking along, passing back and forth in front of the brothel several times, constantly and furtively peering over his shoulder trying to muster up the nerve to go in. The Occupant gets out of his car and, without hurrying, strolls across the street. The man is startled when the Occupant speaks to him; he thinks he's a cop.

I'm not a cop, says the Occupant. I want you to do me a favor.

The man keeps looking over his shoulder. You're not a cop?

The Occupant takes out his wallet and gives the man a hundred dollars. I'm going to go in there now, he says, gesturing at the front door, and in ten minutes I want you to go in and ask for Room 8. If Room 8 is taken, ask for Room 6.

The man waits for the Occupant to finish. You're giving me a hundred dollars to get a room?

Room 8 or 6.

The man thinks for a moment. You're not a cop.

No.

How do you know after you go in I don't just take the hundred and split?

Well, I don't, of course, the Occupant answers. Just before he enters the brothel, he thinks of something and turns back to the man: it's a leap of faith, he explains. Inside, the same Turk who was there a couple of months before vaguely acknowledges him. The same big blond German enforcer sits just within the door, half dozing, half watching a movie on television. Ah, the Turk says, trying to place the Occupant, the gentleman for Angel . . .

7.

The Turk nods, his eyes narrow: haven't seen you in a while. Everyone seems suspicious tonight, or perhaps it's just the Occupant's imagination. The Turk's demeanor shifts to a false cordiality. Well then, he smiles, and leads the Occupant up the stairs and down the hall, around the corner to the other hallway that leads to Room 7 before it disappears into shadow. At Room 7 the Turk unbolts the door and the Occupant gives him a hundred dollars and goes inside. The same naked young blonde is hanging from the same hook as two months ago. It's hard to be sure in the light from the bulb that burns on the wall behind her, but her pallor seems grayer, and her body seems to slump on the hook even more than usual; she's thinner than before, and in the dank light the Occupant can almost count her ribs. She's still blindfolded, and drools slightly from the corner of her dazed, parted mouth.

He's relieved when she lifts her head slightly at his entrance, as though struggling for some kind of consciousness. He loosens the rope that runs down along the wall, lowering her to her knees and then to the floor where she collapses. He takes her blindfold off. She's semiconscious and her eyelids barely flutter.

He takes off his coat and puts it around her shoulders, and then puts his arm beneath her, lifting and supporting her, and opens the door of the room with some struggle. He carries her not in the direction of the stairs but rather into the shadows at the end of the hall, where he lies her down against the wall.

From the door of Room 7 one can almost see her in the shadows at the end of the hall if one looks closely enough, a faint figure in the dark on the floor against the wall. From the door to Room 6 the Occupant is afraid the girl will almost certainly be noticed. But maybe not from the door to Room 8. He goes back into Room 7, closes the door, unscrews the bulb so the light can't be turned on, and waits in the pitch black.

Five minutes pass, then ten, then fifteen. He's in the middle of trying to devise what can only be a very unsatisfactory and highly confrontational alternative to his original plan when he finally hears the sound of footsteps in the hall, though it's impossible to be certain exactly where or whose they are. He's wondering what he will do if the Turk notices the girl lying in the dark end of the hall a few feet away. Then he hears the door of Room 8 open, a brief exchange between the Turk and the man to whom the Occupant spoke outside, and then the door close followed by the footsteps of the Turk starting back down the corridor toward the stairs.

As the footsteps pass Room 7, the Occupant loudly raps twice on the wall next to the door. The footsteps stop. The Occupant pounds more violently; outside in the hall the Turk says something through the door, and the Occupant answers only with more pounding until the door opens and the Turk comes in. As the Turk stands stupefied in the dark of the room, blinking in confusion, the Occupant steps from behind the door and out into the hall, closing the door behind him. He's turning the lock just as the Turk, with an outburst of outraged Turkish, finally understands what's happening.

The Turk begins banging on the door. The Occupant lifts the naked girl from the shadows and carries her down the hall. Behind him the Turk is making quite a racket, and halfway down the stairs with the girl, the Occupant meets the German security guard. You better see what's happening, he shakes his head to the German, while I get her out of here. For a moment the German looks at the girl in confusion, and then up the stairs in the direction of the Turk's voice; fortunately he doesn't appear to fully grasp outraged Turkish. He pushes past the Occupant, who now knows he doesn't have much time. He hoped the snoozing German might be a bit slower in his response.

The Occupant carries the girl down the stairs and out through the lobby. He carries her out the building as the sound of the crashing sea a block away fills the night. He's barely gotten across the street, setting the girl against his car and trying to hold her up as she keeps slumping while he unlocks the door, when he hears the faint shouts of the Turk inside the building suddenly become louder. He knows the German has just let the Turk out of the room. He opens the car and puts the girl inside. He's getting into the driver's seat when they come running out into the street, the Turk shouting and the German scooping up a pipe from the gutter; swinging wildly, the German catches the back window of the car with the pipe and shatters it just as the Occupant is pulling away.

THE Occupant drives the girl back to his house and carries her inside, down to the room that was Kristin's. He lays her on the bed and pulls the sheets up around her and gets her a glass of water and tries to make her drink. Then he goes back out to the car and brings in the groceries he got at the market, some of which have spilled all over the trunk in his lurching getaway from Baghdadville. He puts away the groceries and then hangs the two blue dresses he bought on Melrose in the closet of Kristin's room, where he also leaves the shoes and underwear, and for several minutes stands looking at the bassinet that Kristin put away there. For a while he sits in the dark of the room watching the blonde in bed and soon it seems to him her breathing has gotten easier and she's resting more comfortably, and then he goes back into his own room and packs a simple overnight bag with some clothes, as if he's going to be gone for only a couple of days. He goes downstairs and stands there for a while studying the Calendar again, as though perhaps he will now understand it better and be able to read it with more clarity; finally, however, he assures himself it remains incomprehensible to him. If there were something meaningful to be done with it, if some ritual bonfire would change anything, he would do it, but he leaves the Calendar on the walls and goes back up to where the girl is sleeping, and there in the dark he might ask her to forgive him if he was entirely sure she was really still all that unconscious now, and if he didn't believe it would only be the worst faith of all. He goes back upstairs with his overnight bag, leaves the house, gets back in his car with the shattered back window, and, heading down the hillside in the night, nearly hits some fool driving a Camaro with its lights off.

TWO days later he's in Paris. He checks into the same hotel on the rue Jacob near Odéon where he lived for a while almost eighteen years ago. He walks down the boulevard Saint-Germain to the rue Saint-Jacques where the rue Dante converges, only to find that the apartment building in which he lived with his mother and father in 1968 is now a hotel as well.

He talks with the concierge for a while and explains how the flat on the top floor was once his home. It's difficult to be sure just how fascinating she finds this disclosure. But she agrees to show him the flat, or rather what used to be the flat; it's since been divided into three separate units, one of which was once his bedroom, the second his parents' room and the third the living room. All three are vacant. The Occupant pays for a two-night stay in the room where his mother and father once slept, and then goes back and checks out of the hotel on the rue Jacob.

He walks into the Quartier latin and gets a sandwich, then over to the river where he leans on the low stone wall gazing out at the water. Finally he makes himself turn back up the boulevard Saint-Michel, walking to the Sorbonne, sitting for three hours in the enclosed courtyard where more than thirty years ago time became a ghost and history became an equation that disproved itself. I am 7 May 1968 he says to himself. I am students sitting in the windows smoking, I am songs being sung and wine being passed, I am a low drone rattling the walls of the courtyard. I am the yellow lights of the Sorbonne in the dark and, in the amphitheater from the lectern to the galleries, students and professors talking themselves into exhaustion. I am strategies proposed and rejected. I am the train workers on strike, I am two thousand workers on strike at Nantes, I am Renault on strike then Citroen, then the chemical plants of Rhône Poulenc, I am the post offices closed, I am the newspapers closed, I am the airports closed. I am the power plants on strike, I am the strippers of the Folies Bergère seizing the premises, I am Nanterre closed. I am Berlitz closed. I am the Sorbonne closed. I am many angry hands raised against the sun, I am an outcry against the dull bourgeois spectacle, against the matinees of affluent matrons and fat balding doctors, I am the chant of *Métro boulot dodo*, I am Sartre saying something silly, I am history pretending to be a science now crumbling into absurdity, I am the gaslamps of Odéon and the blond colonnades of the theater fastened with red and black flags in the archways, I am cops with fiberglass stares and poreless faces, I am a girl's heedless murmur *Pas de provocation* and then the response of pandemonium, I am the snarling of the trees in the gardens, I am the last time the garden pools will ever stand still and shimmering, I am murder beyond the intimidation of witnesses, I am children caught in fences, caught in the hedge of roses, pink bloody petals strewn across the grass, I am café tables spilled and overturned, wineglasses hurtling through the air, I am window shutters splintered from their hinges and old men roasting chestnuts flung from their stools on the street corners, I am the quotation boards of the Bourse going up in flames, I am a dull red smoke in the night, I am the exodus of the riot from the Luxembourg Gardens into the mouth of the Métro at Gay Lussac, I am panic trapped in the turnstiles, smashing the exit gates, tumbling down the steps into the tunnels where the trains rumble in, except there are no trains; I am a cul-de-sac of melee. I am the moment in which explodes the Twentieth Century's great ménage à trois between chaos and faith and memory. I am the moment when everyone turns to everyone else, student to student, cop to cop, student to cop, cop to student, thrilled beyond comprehension, faces shining, mouths trembling, eyes ecstatic, and says: we are all out of our minds.

He spends the rest of the afternoon making the rounds of Parisian cemeteries. He goes from Père Lachaise, where Proust and Chopin and Bernhardt and Piaf lie among the vandalized remains of L.A. rock singers, to the Montparnasse Cemetery, where Baudelaire and Beckett and Saint-Saëns rest in the arms of Hollywood-starlet-turned-radical-activist suicides, to the Montmartre Cemetery, where Berlioz and Nijinsky and Truffaut hear no rock and sleep with no blondes that anyone knows of, to the little Saint-Vincent cemetery where no one of any note at all is buried, to the catacombs where the millions of bones have no names, let alone celebrity. The Occupant isn't looking for starlets or rock singers or immortals. He's looking for the grave of his father.

But the body of a man isn't as immutable as a time-capsule. Finally he gives up, and around seven o'clock strolls back down the boulevard Saint-Germain to the Lipp, where he has dinner of chicken and potatoes and spinach and red wine. At that time of evening the Lipp is uncrowded and he's the only one in the restaurant. Then he walks back to the hotel and up to his room and lies on the bed staring at the ceiling.

OF course it isn't the same bed his parents slept in. It's a different bed, probably two or three or half a dozen beds removed from that earlier bed, and not even in the same place but against a different wall altogether.

Actually the room doesn't look anything like he remembers it. It's been entirely repainted and redecorated. If not for the general layout of the room and its relationship to the outer hallway—which used to be the hallway that ran from this room to his own, the hallway into which he rushed when he heard the gunshot and where his mother grabbed him in time to stop him from seeing the body—it would be difficult to be sure this was the right room at all. Lying on the bed thinking about this, he gets up and starts searching the room. There's a dresser against the wall where the bed had been, and after inspecting the wall around it and moving the dresser away to look at the wall behind it, he gives up. There's no telling for sure that there was ever a bullet hole in the first place, since the bullet would have had to go through the girl, and perhaps through the headboard of the bed, to lodge in the wall. And if there was ever a bullet hole in the wall, in more than thirty years the chances are pretty excellent someone patched it up and painted over it. Obviously the actual bullet itself would have been recovered by the police.

He lies back down and turns off the light by the bed and goes to sleep. An hour and a half later he wakes in the dark with a start, to the presence of someone in the room. Angie? he whispers. In the moment that he wakes he's certain she's there; when he turns on the light and there's no one, he might conclude it was only a dream, except for the fact that since the night that Kristin left, he hasn't had any dreams. He doesn't sleep again for the rest of the night. Exhausted in the morning, he shaves and takes a long shower. Though he feels as if one of his headaches is coming on, by the time he's gotten to the Gare Montparnasse, the headache has passed. In one of the shops at the train station he buys a large leather billfold and stuffs it with most of the money he got when he closed out his bank account on his way over to The Angel Eyes that last night in L.A. He rents a locker in the train station and puts the billfold in the locker. He doesn't much like the idea of leaving the money in the locker, but he doesn't want to open a bank account and he doesn't want to keep it in his room or anywhere on his person. He isn't going to be staying in the room much longer anyway, or in Paris, for that matter.

This is the day he begins his campaign to save the whores of Paris. Clockwise he scours the city searching; he finds the first in Pigalle. She's fifty-something years old, with once black hair going white and most of her teeth gone, and can barely stand against the shop window where she plants herself whenever the shopkeeper doesn't chase her away. Seeing her ravaged face flashing black circles and black lines and a flesh the color of marble, the Occupant knows immediately she's dying. When she musters everything in her being to give him a smile, it's so awful and heartbreaking he recoils; backing away from her in a horror he can't disguise, he turns on his heels and runs, and when he finally gets up the nerve to look back over his shoulder, he sees her slumped back into her place on the ledge of the shop window. A few minutes later he returns and, propping her up, waves down a cab that drops them off ten minutes later at a small right-bank hotel. The concierge of the hotel takes one look at the woman and turns them away. They go to several more hotels of ever-diminishing reputation until one gives them a room. He takes the woman upstairs to the room and undresses her and bathes her as best he can at the bidet and puts her in bed. He goes back downstairs and pays for the room and catches the last Métro down to the river, where he walks down to the quay below the Pont Neuf and hides the train-station locker key between two stones in the wall a hundred feet away from where he sleeps beneath the bridge. A few hours later in the night, he's awakened by a couple of thugs who roll him, and by dawn he's pummeled over most of his body, his mouth dried with blood, but the locker key is still in its place.

The second whore is a terrified fourteen-year-old he meets in Les Halles. He buys her dinner and puts her up in a hotel and that night under the Pont des Arts he's accosted again. The third whore is a sad plain junkie he picks up on the rue Saint-Denis after she's been viciously beaten by her pimp. He gets her a hotel and nurses her wounds and leaves some food for her on the small table by the bed where she sleeps. He isn't interested in the good-looking whores or the healthy ones or the girls on the avenue Foch who can take care of themselves. Rather it's the ones with the chaos in their eyes who are each adrift in their own millennia where memory has no beginning or end.

After a couple of weeks, word gets around about him and the whores and he isn't attacked anymore in the night except by an indignant pimp or two. Generally the thieves and beggars stay clear of him because they assume he's demented, a cracked deviant saint of futile gestures who goes around rescuing old diseased hookers from the street and checking them into hotels, though more than a few wonder where he gets the money that he never seems to have when they roll him. The whores themselves don't know what to make of him except that he obviously has an angle, even if they can't figure out what it is, because every man has an angle and they're inclined anyway to feel contempt for any man who doesn't. A few conclude it's in fact the ultimate perversion, a man who gives a whore money and buys her a meal and a hotel room *and then expects nothing*: what kind of sick psychological shit is that? As for the Occupant, he doesn't for a moment think he's really saving anyone. He doesn't for a moment think any of these women will wind up anywhere except back on the street or perhaps dead in the hotel beds where he leaves them. But now, far beyond the question of his own good or bad faith, he does it because somehow, when the meaning of apocalypse fled him, faced with a Moment that wasn't a light but a black hole, as much to his own surprise as it would have been to anyone else's, he found himself filled with not guilt, not remorse, not torment, not the heavy burden of being monstrous, but rather a new and inexplicable and unendurable capacity for pity that his heart simply cannot hold in.

Lying on the quay of the river in the afternoon, staring up into the blue French sky, he thinks back on his life. He remembers almost twenty years ago, the last time he was in France, lying in a field outside Paris staring at the same blue sky, a month or so before he moved into the hotel on the rue Jacob and met Angie. It was a rootless and potentially dangerous time of his life . . . twenty-five years old, the chaotic punk soundtrack of the Scene behind him, he had been fired from his job with a New York research firm and returned to Paris, where he fell in for a while with a group of bohemian revolutionaries who kept a flat near the rue de Vaugirard, south of the Eiffel Tower. There everyone fought constantly, crazed ex-boyfriends bursting through windows in rampages of lover's revenge that proved more ridiculous than consequential, until soon they had all gotten so completely on each other's nerves that when spring came, they fled Paris for the countryside. Lying on the quay of the Seine now, the Occupant tries to remember the names of the old couple who owned the little farm and vineyard in the country where the whole entourage stayed; he assumes by now both have long since passed on. Nearing the end of their lives, they had little to show for themselves but the farm and vineyard and a garden and a wine cellar that wasn't much more than a hole beneath the house . . . and—as is often the case with people who have so little—they couldn't have been more generous. He remembers now how there was nothing they wouldn't do for him, how they seemed to view every moment as an opportunity to refill his glass, as though they lived to do nothing else, how there wasn't a need or wish they wouldn't attend to.

There was something revelrous about their graciousness. In the day they worked the vineyard and garden, cooked the meals and cleaned the house and washed everyone's clothes. At night they sat around watching American TV shows badly dubbed in French on their little black-and-white TV. Caught in this peaceful pastoral in that spring of '82, the Occupant had gotten one of his worst headaches, exploding in nausea and shooting up his spine and radiating behind his eyes with such intensity he wanted to tear them out of his head. So the others had hustled him into an ancient concrete guest house where they boarded up the windows and barricaded the door and locked him away like a wild animal.

When he rose the next morning, his headache had lifted and the door was unlocked. On the outside of the door had been written, in black letters, OCCUPÉ.

The old woman of the house was cooking the first of two grand feasts. Around eleven o'clock, everyone sat down to eat in the French garden with the blue sky above, the white table-cloth lapping in the breeze, flies buzzing languorously around their heads. She started bringing out the food and the old man started hauling up bottles of wine from the cellar and at some moment during this, a wind shifted perhaps, a cloud drifted dreamily across the sun, and all the havoc of the Occupant's life settled like dust, until by the time the old man brought up the last bottle, four hours and many bottles after the meal had begun, the Occupant thought to himself, Oh, this is what life is supposed to be about. Everyone was in love with everyone else, ex-boyfriends who had been fighting with ex-girlfriends, revolu-tionaries who had been fighting with decadent Americans, there was something about the red wine on the white tablecloth under the blue sky that brought out the humanity in everyone, flirting and joking in a tangle of languages no one understood, laughing in a common language everyone understood perfectly until, when the meal was over, it was all they could do to push themselves away from the table and stumble down the road to a clearing in the high grass and lie down. Now, years later, lying on the quay of the Seine looking up at the sky, the Occupant remembers lying in the high grass and closing his eyes and falling into the sky above him, his head as light as air, as though it was a balloon that would float away from the rest of him and leave him in peace, and he wonders, as he supposes probably everyone who's ever had such a moment wonders, why such moments are so fleeting, why all moments can't be like that one. Sleeping in the grass, he had awakened a couple of hours later to Madame Mao or Miss World Revolution 1982 or whoever she was—actually her name was Sylvie, and she had never looked so beautiful—gently touching his shoulder and calling his name, and telling him it was time for dinner.

SOON he's almost out of money. After a few weeks in Paris, as April turns to May, he returns one morning to the Gare Montparnasse to make a withdrawal from his train locker and buy a ticket on the French bullet train to the Breton coast. Waiting for his train, he buys a shirt and an inexpensive pair of pants in one of the station shops, because his old clothes are now nearly in tatters. He would like to buy some new shoes too, but can't afford them. He spends a few francs on the public shower.

Though he's now showered and shaved and in clean clothes, and though he sleeps for most of the train ride, the other passengers steer clear of him. By now he's tired and sick from nights of sleeping under the bridges of the Seine and being mugged. From Paris to Chartres to Le Mans to Laval to Rennes, he sleeps better than he has in a while; and seven hours after leaving Paris, at the old fortified seaport of Wyndeaux, he transfers from the bullet to a local train which takes him to the Breton village of Sur-les-Bateaux. Here all the original houses still stand built from the overturned hulls of boats that mysteriously beached themselves on the land a thousand years ago, twelve kilometers from the sea. Getting off the train at the hilltop station in the middle of the night, he can see the bleached white bottoms of the hulls in the valley below him, gleaming in the light of the moon.

This is the town whose postmark was borne by the letter the Occupant found from his mother years ago, though he still can't remember ever receiving it. Arriving this first night in Sur-les-Bateaux, he sleeps in the train station and when he wakes doesn't feel so great; he walks down the hill into town and has a bowl of stew and a glass of wine at the Café Pissarro. The bartender and cook explain that Pissarro spent one night there in the village a hundred and some years ago and many of the townspeople are still in quite a tizzy about it. Besides the Café Pissarro there's the Restaurant Pissarro, the Hôtel Pissarro, the Boulangerie Pissarro, the Patisserie Pissarro, the Crêperie Pissarro, the Supermarché Pissarro, the Pissarro laundromat, the rue Pissarro, a small patch of water where the river collects called the Lac de Pissarro, the Bois de Pissarro, and two or three hundred villagers who claim to be direct descendants of Pissarro, apparently a very busy man on his one night passing through. Other artists come to Sur-les-Bateaux to paint in its magical light, which the residents of the town point out so obviously infused everything that Pissarro ever painted afterward, though since the painter spent the *night* in Sur-les-Bateaux, exactly when and how he experienced this profoundly transformative glow is unclear. At any rate, the bartender explains, the town feels quite proprietary about both the light and Pissarro.

When it's time to settle the bill and the Occupant comes up short, the bartender pays for the glass of wine himself. He takes the American stranger into town, where he sets him up for the night with Nathalie, an old woman in her mid-seventies who's lived in Sur-les-Bateaux her whole life. Widowed at the age of twenty-three when she was eight months pregnant, and never remarried, Nathalie has been running the small Pissarro Inn that her father handed down to her; she makes up a room for the Occupant on the top floor from where he can see, through his window, the town square below, with its cafés and markets and tourist shops and the small cobbled pedestrian way that leads up to the art school on top of the hill. Beyond the square is the river. What conversation the American stranger and the old woman have is very brief, cordialities surrounding his single question: *non*, she lies when asked if she remembers an American woman passing through years before. It's only afterward, when the innkeeper has gone back downstairs, that the Occupant feels a little foolish, even addled, to realize that his mother wasn't, after all, actually American, that a French person would have considered her French.

The room he sleeps in is very plain for an old European bedroom in an old house, even one used as an inn or hotel. Besides the bed, there's a simple dresser with a mirror, no clock; and on the wall, other than one small watercolor painted, no doubt, with Pissarro light, there's only an old fragment of a page from what the Occupant presumes was once a diary. On the fragment of paper is a date, *2.2.79.*

He's been a maker of calendars too long not to know a date when he sees one. He takes the date down from the wall and, for much of the night, in the light of the small lamp that sits on top of the dresser, he lies on his bed staring at it, wracking his brain trying to place it. Having studied nothing but such dates his whole life now, he would have thought he could instantly identify any date and its significance in the scheme of chaos; for a long time, however, as hard as he thinks about it, he has no idea what happened on the second day of February in the year 1979. He goes over all the dates of that month and that year in his head; he goes over all the corresponding events; his brain zeroes in on the second of February 1979 and then expands, a widening circle, to take in all the dates around it. On the *first* day of February 1979, an old and vengeful ayatollah, who spent many years of exile in Paris, returned to his homeland in the Middle East and a hero's welcome, so the Occupant wonders if perhaps an ecstatic Shiite Moslem, possibly even one of the ayatollah's Parisian disciples, was passing through Sur-les-Bateaux at that time and commemorated the moment by pinning the date to this wall. But would he have gotten such an important date wrong even by a single day? And would the old innkeeper have then left it pinned to the wall for twenty years? It's only after he's closed his eyes for a moment that the Occupant remembers the second of February 1979 was the day that the most infamous of all punk rockers, suspected of having murdered his girlfriend, was found dead in New York's West Village, and consequently also the day that Maxxi Maraschino locked the Occupant in a room on the Lower East Side where he spent the next seven months. Suddenly realizing this, he's astonished, but exactly what it means in this place and at this moment, and exactly why it should appear here and now in this remote room in this remote village at this remote time, he has no idea.

Somewhere between consciousness and sleep, he has a vision of his daughter being born. He and Angie are lying together on a high cliff on the coast of Northern California, just below Mendocino; and just before the stroke of midnight, in the light from the stars in the night sky above them, he touches his wife's face like he's never touched it. They look at each other terror-stricken by this tenderness. Perhaps it was the very prospect of such an unbearable tenderness that led her to flee him. Perhaps fate believed he was neither capable nor deserving of such tenderness, and so took her from him. But now in Sur-les-Bateaux he remembers it, though in fact it never happened; and there bubbles up in him an overwhelming longing for his little daughter, a longing accompanied by everything he would have felt if he had been there to see her born in that burst of blood and afterbirth, which is to say the realization of an immense new talent for self-sacrifice, the exquisite new instinct by which a father suddenly, without a second thought, knows he might not step off the edge of a cliff for faith, but would immediately and thoughtlessly hurl himself to the sea below for his child.

With Angie at his side, he walks away from the cliff carrying his daughter. There explodes in his heart a bomb of love where only chaos used to be. He looks down at the newborn's face and, already world-weary, she yawns: that was a very big yawn, Little Saki, he says to her. That was a very big yawn for such a tiny girl. That yawn was bigger than you; you almost fell into that yawn. For the first time in his life, he finds the most irrefutable evidence of chaos to be not the prospect of his own death, but of his child's. Where the prospect of his own death filled him with a dread almost too huge to be truly comprehensible, the thought that his own little girl, so small and new, will someday grow and die is bigger than huge, it's infinite; it's more mind-boggling than merely incomprehensible, it's almost literally inconceivable.

But if the fact of his child's death seems, in one way, the greatest and cruelest evidence of chaos, then in another way, in some paradoxical fashion that's finally beyond him, its cruelty is also the very refutation of chaos. Because he has never before assigned a moral property to chaos. He has always before believed chaos eluded either morality or judgment, in the way a hurricane eludes morality or judgment. But now the chaos of his child's death, in a way he never considered true about his own death, looms in his heart as incontestably cruel, cruel in a way that can't be denied by chaos' empiricism, cruel not only in his own heart but in the heart of the universe too, which means that the universe has a heart after all, that the universe has a sense of good and evil after all, before which chaos is finally accountable after all. He's shocked now, lying on this bed in this little room, the tears streaming down his face, by the universe of his heart, by the way his own heart explodes beyond every dimension he's ever been capable of feeling before, by the vision of a bomb of love not only in his own heart but in the heart of the universe. That he would walk off a cliff for his child without thought or calculation is a body-blow to chaos, the first thing in his life he's ever seen or felt against which he knows chaos could never survive; that instinct that would immediately send him off that cliff supersedes any other impulse or thought, of survival or anything else. Now the Occupant realizes that for the past several weeks, since Kristin left, all that's mattered to him was to try and be a father who measured up to the worth of his daughter, even if it's a daughter he'll never know.

When he wakes the next day, wondering if—for the first time since leaving Los Angeles—he's had a dream, he almost expects the small mysterious scrap of paper with the date *2.2.79* to have vanished from his fingers.

But the date still lies on his chest, in what he now surmises to be afternoon light. He doesn't know exactly what time it is, since there's no clock in the room; he only knows he's slept very late. There's a bowl of soup and a sandwich left for him on the dresser. The soup is cold, so he knows it's been sitting there a while. He doesn't feel rested from his long sleep; he feels as though his life tried to slip away from him in the night. It's now the seventh of May: New Year's Day 33 by the Apocalyptic Calendar. He rises slow and weak and aching, and washes and dresses. He goes downstairs to say goodbye to the old woman but she's nowhere to be found. By the time he winds his way through town, among the skull-white hulls of the ancient boats, he has no expectation of finding anyone from the past. By twilight he's walked down the road that leads in the direction of the sea, through the woods to the crumbling ancient tower in the northwest—condemned, a villager explains to him, not only for its eroding foundation but also for the legend that haunts it. When he reaches the tower he sits among the tall grass looking at the trees rustling above him in the dark Celtic wind. Then he finally gets up from the grass and goes into the tower to lie against the cool stone, where a farmer will find his body the next morning.

He closes his eyes for a moment, and opens them to see a young girl about seventeen years old standing in front of him.

**ARE** you my daughter? he says.

Of course not, she replies. I'm not your wife either, or your lover.

Who are you then, he says.

I'm the occupant of this place, she answers.

He closes his eyes again, and when he opens them a few moments later, she's still there. Everyone is his own millennium, he says.

Yes.

Everyone is his own age of chaos. Everyone is his own age of apocalypse.

No, she says, there is no age of apocalypse. Everyone, she says, is his own age of meaning.

Thinking about this, he asks, What was my meaning?

She smiles; at that moment, upstairs back at the Pissarro Inn, Nathalie can't help hoping the Occupant is gone for good, and that he's not to return this night. She doesn't want him to ask any more questions about his mother, whom she met only briefly anyway, many years before, and she doesn't understand why the old piece of map that her daughter once tore from a navigational journal long ago has been taken down from the wall and lies on the bed where the Occupant slept. It always disturbed her, tacked to the wall like that, even as it also disturbed her to remove it, which she could never bring herself to do, even as it now disturbs her that the Occupant removed it. She picks it up off his bed and looks at it in the light of the lamp from the dresser: *2.2.49*, not 79 as the Occupant thought, having mistaken the French 4 for a 7. Nor is it a date. They are coordinates, 2.2 degrees longitude and exactly 49 degrees latitude, that marked the place in the English Channel where, in the last days of summer in the year 1950, her young husband was blown up on a French weather ship by a long-dormant World War II sea mine. The difference between the generation of the young pregnant widow and that of her daughter, who would be born three weeks later, could be marked by how reasonably tragic the mother considered such an event, as opposed to how infuriatingly irrational her daughter considered it.

When the Occupant's mother had come to her, many years before in 1968, to try and tell her about what had happened to Christina in her own bedroom in Paris, Nathalie didn't really want to speak of lost daughters any more than she wanted to speak with the Occupant of lost mothers. By that point Nathalie's life seemed so defined by loss that just trying to understand it was a risky, perhaps even life-and-death proposition: what if she failed? What if, after trying so hard to understand it, her loss made even less sense? If loss was all her life was to be about, then the utter failure to understand it would render life unlivable. So it was a matter of her own sheer survival for Nathalie to leave undisturbed the meaning of loss. When the Occupant's mother came to Sur-les-Bateaux more than three decades ago, at which time the two women met for no more than ten minutes, each was at such a loss for words that they finally just ran from each other, bursting from each other's presence so combustively it was hard to be sure who bolted first; and for all the years after that, for all the ways in which it was such a tiny town, they avoided each other. They learned each other's schedules, ascertaining that their individual timelines never need cross, until the day came when the Occupant's mother suddenly vanished forever. In the meantime Nathalie consigned the mystery of her daughter to the same universal mystery that had consumed her husband, even as she knew it was exactly this sort of resignation that had driven her daughter from Sur-les-Bateaux in the first place.

Christina had become obsessed with the chaos that took the father she never knew. A bomb from a war five years over, not even an evil Nazi bomb but a good Churchillian bomb, a bomb of obsolete political function but still completely functional destruction, bobbing and drifting in the channel waters off Saint-Malo, waiting to collide with the stupidity of life in a bright flash of stalemate. . . . As an adolescent in the early Sixties, the girl would stare in cold fury at the map coordinates that she tore from a navigational journal and tacked to the wall of her bedroom; she would talk lust-struck village boys into driving her to the coast, where she stood on the shore staring hatefully at the channel waters waiting for some scrap from fourteen years before to come floating up on the sand, a piece of shrapnel maybe, or a body part, or a ship's errant deadly compass cracked and stuck on whatever southwest or northeast direction had pointed the way to oblivion, or a bottle with a presciently written note inside, written by her father the night before his death. Of course, nothing like that ever washed up on shore. "It was fourteen years ago," some lunkhead of a boy would plead, "what's going to suddenly wash up after fourteen years?"

"What bomb," she coolly answered, "suddenly explodes after five?"

The bomb of love. The bomb of chaos. The bomb of faith. The bomb of memory. The bomb of the missing number. The bomb of the forgotten letter. The bomb of the locked door. The bomb of the penthouse key. The bomb of the fallen stairs. The bomb of the free-floating day. The bomb of the desert night. The bomb of the empty grave. The bomb of the hanging girl. The bomb of the taken child. The bomb of the saved whore, of the redeemed man. The bomb of the broken heart, of the desolate soul. The bomb of Christina's smile, not to be confused with the bomb of beauty, because she wasn't really beautiful, but God the guys loved her; freckled and redheaded, she had a smile that not only broke through the rage, it was somehow lit by her rage. The bomb of rage: if rage ever smiles, it was Christina's smile.

If rage ever laughs, it was Christina's laugh, heard across the square from her bedroom window. Until she was fifteen, it didn't even occur to her there was any place she would rather be than Sur-les-Bateaux. Like any other young romantic girl, she was charmed by the Celtic legends of Arthur sleeping in the nearby grottos, waiting for his stony tomb to crack open and release him from the previous millennium so he would reunite Breton with the homeland that lay across a channel since riddled with bombs. Christina was in love with such a promise of deliverance from chaos. For a thousand years the countryside had hummed with the legend of a king who would rise from the ground and cut down chaos with a sword. But by the time she was fifteen she was laughing at the village and its legends, out of not only the natural cynicism of adolescence but a more personal disenchantment; she was laughing at the villagers with all their silly nonsense about Pissarro and the light—"as if," she cracked, "they don't have the same light in the next village over"—and then one night, to the alarm of her mother, she slept in the condemned, crumbling ancient tower outside town where she woke around two in the morning, quite unstartled, to meet another girl, about seventeen years old, whom Christina had never seen before. For the next several hours the two girls lay together in the dark discussing the betrayal of fathers and, by extension, of ancient kings, who promise to return and never do. When Christina woke again at dawn, she went back home and, completely ignoring her mother's pleading and scolding, packed and left for Saint-Malo, where she caught a ferry across the Channel to Portsmouth, half expecting and half hoping it would blow up on the way. When it didn't, she believed herself released from something. From Portsmouth she took the train to London, a very lively and modern place in those days. Nathalie never saw her again.

In London, Christina was one of the wildest girls in a time and town of wild girls, riding motor scooters in miniskirts on Carnaby Street. Her favorite song was a dirty smudge on the airwaves called "Over Under Sideways Down," its recurring question, *When will it end?* swathed by a druggy, orgiastic Middle Eastern guitar riff; fifteen years later and five thousand miles away, in a club on Forty-sixth Street in Manhattan, Angie would strip to an entirely different song called "Day of the Lords" that asked almost exactly the same question. Christina had been living in Earls Court for a year when she began to have the dreams. At first there was only a flicker of red in the far dark distance, like a cigarette lighter being lit; and then in the ensuing dreams the small red flash grew closer and larger, until it even had a sound. By the time she left London for Paris in the fall of 1967, the dreams were coming to her one after another, not just every night but several times every night, and then all night, each dream picking up where the last one left off, the small burst of flame growing nearer and noisier as though it was on the far horizon of a vast veldt she was crossing; and with each new dream Christina moved ever more inevitably toward it.

Eventually she was having literally hundreds of dreams a night. She barely had to shut her eyes, as though the dreams were too impatient to even wait for unconsciousness. By now she had determined this explosion in the distance was a mine going off in the Channel, and that she was dreaming over and over of her father's death. But on the night she took the ferry from Dover back to Calais and France, from where she would take the train to Paris, the crack of the ever-repeating flash finally revealed itself to be not a bomb—it was too sharp and abrupt—but a gunshot, its source and reason incomprehensible.

Soon she could hardly bear to blink, dreading the vision of this gunshot that had come to frighten her far more than when she thought it was a mere bomb. Because she was desperate to release herself from this dream, before the red gunshot got too close and too loud, she moved through the cabin in the early-morning hours of the ferry ride, looking for another dream into which she might escape. She understood, after all, that a dream is a memory of the future. The Channel was rough as usual, and though there was more than half a moon, most of the night weather blotted out the light. The cabin was filled with the slumping figures of other passengers, fitfully asleep in their seats or sprawled out across several vacant seats. Though she had heard a man has an erection when he dreams, it was difficult to read either the bodies or the clothing of the men around her, particularly in the dark, except for those moments when the clouds parted overhead and the moonlight slashed through. Pulling off her jeans and touching herself until she was wet, she straddled and slipped one man after another inside her, so as to leave the detonation of her own dream inside all the dreams around her, blowing up all the dreams that sailed that night on the Dover-to-Calais ferry, the heads of all the male passengers exploding with a gunshot from the future, until she hoped she would finally close her eyes and see only darkness, until she hoped she might go to sleep and slip into a quiet dreamlessness.

It was to no avail. By the first light of dawn and the sight of the Norman beaches, exhausted, she had delivered herself from nothing, the light and report of her recurring dream just that much closer; and finally, by the time she stepped back onto French soil, she had just resigned herself to it.

Having resisted the dream for so long, she finally embraced it in her reckless way. From her nights in the small hotel attic where she lived near the Opéra, to her afternoons at the Sorbonne where she enrolled as a literature student, if she couldn't leave her dream behind in the dreams of the men she had sex with, she would find another way to blow up their dreams: if chaos was coming for her, she would take everyone down with her. This was the thought that occurred to her the afternoon she sat at the Deux Magots near the Saint-Germain-des-Prés, looking at the American couple with their young son several tables over. The father was a poet; Christina had seen him at the university.

The mother was a prodigal daughter of France, on the edge of rebellion. The man looked at Christina, the woman looked at Christina, and Christina looked back, a brilliant red in the golden Paris spring, and flashed at both them, like a burst of gunfire, the smile of rage.

PEOPLE make maps on the corners of Tokyo. Kristin sees this her first full day in the city. She doesn't yet understand how Tokyo is the most epic and confounding expression of chaos by a national soul otherwise famous for its love of order. Tokyo is a city of no order that Kristin's alien eye can discern; the streets have no names, the houses no addresses of any sequence that makes sense in space. Rather it is a sequence of time, structures numbered by their age and memories.

In Tokyo, Kristin is never really sure which way is east and which way is west. Everyone constantly circles Tokyo looking for a place to land, commuters riding the Yamanote subway line in a never-ending loop, cabbies in taxis wandering pell-mell the spiraling boulevards, students driving freeways around and around in search of phantom exits. On the back of every hand in Tokyo is tattooed a small piece of one huge moving map of the city, and in their perpetual confusion people constantly gather in circles on street corners thrusting their hands palms-down into the center, the backs of their hands joined like the reunited fragments of a letter torn to shreds. The whole map can be formed finally and completely only by all fifteen million Tokyoites joining hands. Everywhere she goes Kristin sees congregations of lost people gathering on street corners trying to read directions from their assembled fragments of the larger map.

But for the plane ticket in Yoshi's truck, it never would have occurred to Kristin to go to Tokyo. For the first few days she lives in the small ryokan near the wharf, her window looking out toward Tokyo Bay. She sleeps on her tatami mat behind the sliding paper door and leaves her shoes at the inn door. Every morning at ten o'clock the maid chases her out of her room, every night at ten o'clock the innkeeper summons her to the lobby downstairs to watch his son perform a traditional lion dance, complete with ferocious growls and coiled attacks. It seems to Kristin that the son saves his most hair-raising antics for her in particular, and bows a little lower to her when he finishes, upon emerging from underneath the lion mask.

In Ueno Park the trees shed their cherry blossoms. Teenagers sit drinking on the wet ground, under the white rain, mourning the passing of the blossoms almost before they have been born, the bloom immediately scattered in the collision of seasons. For a few days she falls in with a group of Japanese kids who speak broken English; one of them, a photographer for a music magazine, tries to convince her to take a job in Asakusa with a theatrical revue of naked girls. But Kristin has now outgrown trading on her nakedness. In the week of the cherry blossoms when Kristin first arrives, Tokyo irrevocably roots itself in the present, before the rain of springtime capitulates to the ongoing drizzle of Tokyo timelessness; she prowls Ueno Park in the hail of the dying blossoms unaware that this is the rare Tokyo moment when yesterday, today and tomorrow are clearly delineated by the explosion of trees. Cauldrons of incense fill the air with scent.

Several months into what now outdated Western calendars quaintly call "the third millennium," Kristin has arrived not only in a blizzard of cherry blossoms but atomized time; on the Ginza a panorama of small dancing white dots stretches out before her. The entire city is garbed in surgical masks. Everyone wears these masks on the train, in the streets, along the docks, at the park, so as not to breathe in the epidemic of demolished time that fills the air like pollen. Everyone in the city wears surgical masks except Kristin, who flaunts some unconscious arrogant conviction that she's beyond the reach of time's virus.

In her ryokan near the bay, she doesn't have much in terms of possessions. There are only some books, the Occupant's coat and some clothes, including a blue dress that fits a little better now. On the walls she's tacked some of the news clippings she brought with her from Los Angeles. Every day she returns to her room to find that the maid has taken them down and stacked them neatly on the small ankle-high tea table in the corner of the room, and every day Kristin tacks them back up. Clearly the maid's aesthetic sense is offended by the clippings on the walls. Since she is a maid, it's not her place to protest, but since she is Japanese, it's not quite possible to acquiesce to the Western barbarity of news clippings tacked to the walls.

At twilight, from the window of her room, Kristin sees the pixeled black waves of the bay rolling in. At night, she sees a beacon out over the water that's too bright to be a window but too close to be a star. She can only assume it's a lighthouse of some kind, except that when she walks down to the wharves in the morning and looks out over the bay, there's no lighthouse to be seen anywhere, or, for that matter, anything that might make such a light. Every night she stares out the window trying to figure out what this light is. Every night she finally falls asleep a little after midnight, waking three hours later to the sound of foghorns from the ships sailing into the bay bringing the fresh tuna for the morning marketplace. In the morning she walks down to the docks and to the huge open market where she eats fresh sushi for breakfast and, barbarous Westerner that she is, offends the stall vendors by asking for too much wasabi, the strong green horseradish that she actually prefers to the fish.

One morning while standing out on the docks looking out over the water, her eyes still peeled for the source of the night's bright slashing light, eating her rolls of tuna and her eyes tearing up at the rush of wasabi in her head, Kristin suddenly remembers something. She suddenly remembers being a little girl back home in Davenhall and standing with her uncle on the banks of the river, staring across the water as she's staring now. On the other side of the river was a woman waiting for the ferry, too far away for Kristin's little eyes to make out distinctly; Kristin might even have taken her for a man, at first. The woman was staring back at her. From time to time, her uncle waved to the woman.

Remembering this now, Kristin feels fairly sure this was her mother on the other side of the river. But whether her uncle actually told her this or it was just some idea she got in her head on her own isn't clear. The ferry lumbered through the water toward the small dock on the other side, but when it reached the dock, the woman hesitated, and soon the boat embarked again without her, sailing back toward Kristin. Kristin remembers her uncle seeming as confused by this as the little girl was, and nothing is more terrifying to a child to realize the grown-up she is with is as confused by something as she is. On the other shore, as the ferry glided back across the river toward Kristin and her uncle, the woman's shoulders seemed to sag. Her head hung in something even a little girl could recognize as defeat, and then the woman turned her back and walked away.

As the last of the cherry blossoms dies in Tokyo, Kristin buys a blank journal from a small bookshop. She begins to write what she calls the Book of the Falling One-Winged Bird, named after the scorch mark that the lightning made on the Occupant's time-capsule that afternoon in Black Clock Park when she and Yoshi dug it up. She might have called it the Book of Millennial Memory, but it sounds too much like the Occupant, and it's also a title that would have no meaning anyway in the place she's in, since in Japan the Western notion of a millennium has no mean-ing. In her book she records everything she remembers, begin-ning with standing by the river as a little girl looking at her mother on the other side.

Her second week in Tokyo, Kristin is sitting in a fast-food restaurant full of Japanese teenagers, writing feverishly in her book, when two young women next to her strike up a conversa-tion. They are both Japanese. The one who speaks a little English seems a few years older than Kristin; the other is probably in her late twenties, maybe thirty, and asks Kristin many questions, using her friend as an interpreter. Kristin might be suspicious of all the questions except that the two women seem so guileless and pleasant, and the older woman is most fascinated with the memoir that Kristin is writing so intensely. It turns out that Mika was a geisha in Kyoto some years ago, before deciding—as she puts it to Kristin through their interpreter—to come "out of the shadows and into the light." Now she is madam of the Ryu, one of the rotating memory hotels set amid the bars and brothels and strip joints and massage parlors and pornography shops of Kabuki-cho.

This is how Kristin gets her job as a memory girl at the Hotel Ryu, on the "Avenue Shimada" that is informally named—since none of the streets in Tokyo have real names—after one of its most persistent and dangerous visitors. Gleamingly modern, but punctuated with old photographs and disenfranchised memen-tos, the Ryu waits at the top of an anonymous flight of metal stairs, a sepia light shining above the door. Within its outer shell, the hotel is a large three-story revolving cylinder whose doorway, at certain times of the day or night, slides into alignment with passages that open up into various entryways and exits to differ-ent parts of the city. Inside the hotel the memory girls assemble for the customers, who make their choices and disappear with the girls into private booths lit in the magenta or marigold or pale blue colors of twilight and morning, and cordoned off by curtains or sliding doors. The tiny booths are just large enough for a love seat and small table for two, on which sits a small

vase with a single white rose watched over by the serene porcelain mask of a woman's face above the doorway, placed there
to transfix the customer and arouse old, impotent recollections.

In the Hotel Ryu, Kristin's dirty-blond hair, undistinguished
in America, is very popular with the Japanese businessmen. But
more than the hair, it's her empathy that attracts them; because
she is not Japanese, her memories are considered more likely
to be authentic, rather than the prefab memories found at most
of the other Kabuki-cho establishments. Kristin recounts for her
customers her recollections of Davenhall and Los Angeles and
all the memories the Occupant spent inside her, sometimes embellishing them slightly with other recollections she's picked up
along the way, though she's careful not to steal any of the other
girls' material. If a dream is only a memory of the future, in
Tokyo she finds one has no need of memories of the future:
memories of the future are the only kind they have in Tokyo.
Memories of the past are Kristin's stock-in-trade. Unlike those at
the love hotels on the surrounding streets, the transactions inside
the memory hotels do not involve sex. As she talks, old Kai-san,
or Doctor Kai, her most loyal customer, just puts his hand on
her knee, listening in quiet reverie.

After a while Kristin moves out of her ryokan to live full-time
on the third floor of the Ryu with the other girls. In her own
tiny chamber she can put away her books and tack her newspaper clippings to the wall without the maid yelling at her, though
she misses the mysterious beacon of light that shines in the
night, and even the sound of the foghorns at three o'clock in
the morning from the boats sailing in with their fish. Like the
other girls, she learns the rotating hotel's schedule and where
the hotel's exits will release her at a given moment; the Ryu is
the hub of a wheel of memory on an amnesiac landscape, and
the long shimmering tubular tunnels are spokes that lead out
into Shinjuku and Ueno and Shibuya and Roppongi and Asakusa
and Ikebukuro and Harajuku and the other neighborhoods of the
city. Sometimes Kristin emerges at the core of old Tokyo near
the Imperial Palace and its moat, sometimes on the monstrous

boulevards beneath buildings that twist up into the sky as labyrinths of glass, with protruding translucent domes that are like cataract eyes, invisible by day and glittering at night. These boulevards and buildings approximate the way the city is gray in the sunlight—confounding and enervated, vanishing into the mist off the bay—and then takes on a different identity at nightfall: exhilarated and thrilling, the pachinko parlor of the Twenty-First Century, the funhouse of the soul.

At these moments Kristin, her body humming for a release her mind is too exhausted to pursue, steps into the Tokyo borne of light and noise, the Enola Gay having been only the first and gaudiest pachinko parlor of all. In Japan's nuclear birth and the subsequent announced death of its imperial god, the grit of the past has been liquefied and frozen into a million windows in which a million disconnected images and juxtapositions now flash, geishas and the Ginza, buddhist shrines and beautiful bondage queens, serene tea ceremonies and crazed cabdrivers careening through the maze of Tokyo, windows full of images of the Tokyo soul. After she's been in Tokyo a while, Kristin soon begins to notice everywhere the small gleaming time-capsules, in the larger temples like the Kobayashi Shrine not far from the hotel, and in smaller shrines in tiny homes—gleaming time-capsules smuggled in from the West with their dates of original interment. The entire city is littered with time-capsule shrines in homes and on the streets, in the ryokans and temples, each date constituting the beginning of a new age following the death of the old one on the first of January 1946 and the void of time in between, during which the Japanese Emperor was in free fall from divinity, and the Japanese empire in free fall from meaning. When the Emperor confessed to his people he wasn't God, it blew them out of the Twentieth Century altogether, into the Twenty-First, well ahead of everyone else: after all, what did the Japanese need the Twentieth Century for anymore? What had it gotten them but Nagasaki and No God? Now a million new epochs and a million new empires fill Tokyo, and a million new emperors have been born from the time-capsules, in the form of a piece of rock with unreadable graffiti or a wristwatch broken at a particular hour, or a postcard of a showgirl in a Las Vegas casino. In one such epoch the emperor of the new age is a tiny black coffin that holds a tooth and a piece of charcoal and a single long, scrolled strip torn from a picture of a naked woman having sex. In another he's a used condom.

About the time she begins her journal—sometime around the death of the blossoms—Kristin knows she's pregnant. For a while she's more tired than queasy, but more queasy than she would have expected, having always thought of herself as having a stomach strong enough for anything. I'll get fatter, she realizes gloomily, just when the blue dress she took from the Occupant's closet that last night in L.A. was starting to fit. But my breasts will get bigger, she consoles herself. She admonishes herself that she should have been more careful.

Otherwise, she's so sanguine about the prospect of having a child it confuses her a little. She can't imagine being less pre-pared for such a thing. But almost immediately, before it even evolves into a decision that has to be made, she has made it, she has decided to have the baby, and while at first she resists the impulse to name him, she decides to name him Kierkegaard. Kierkegaard Blumenthal. Or, if he should later so prefer, finding the full name cumbersome or, more important, deciding Kier-kegaard was full of shit, Kirk Blu. In the mornings she opens the window of her room at the Hotel Ryu and bares her belly to the city, disturbing people in the streets. Having grown up in the dead silence of her chinatown back home, she means to toughen up little Kierkegaard by exposing him early to the din of reality. The world isn't going to whisper for you, little boy, she whispers to him, her hands on her stomach awaiting a response.

In her bath at the Hotel Ryu, she soaks in the warm water, staring at her stomach, thinking more and more about her own mother waiting for her on the other side of the river, only barely noticing anymore the date that the Occupant wrote on her body, *29.4.85.* Having left the Occupant because she would not be the vortex of chaos, Kristin now refuses to acknowledge that everywhere she's gone and everywhere she goes, in a city where time is atomized, everything breaks down. She refuses to acknowledge how she's become a conductor of chaos since she left the Occupant, beginning with Yoshi's rather electrifying end on the knolls of Black Clock Park, and continuing with the key to the truck and the key to the San Francisco penthouse that she had taken from Isabelle and Cynda and left—on purpose? by accident?—on the small table next to Louise that last night they slept in the Occupant's house. Kristin has refused to acknowledge the way she sets into motion pending cataclysm, the way she makes all the monitors and compasses go haywire; on this matter she is, as she herself would put it, a point-misser.

If nothing else, she might at least wonder how it is she alone walks through Tokyo without a surgical mask, inhaling without consequence the time-contaminated air. As she walks through Ueno Park, she doesn't see how the cherry blossoms shake loose from the trees in panic; as she rides the subways she doesn't realize that it's not typical for every subway train in Tokyo to break down all the time, that in fact in Tokyo the subway almost never breaks down, except when she's on it. As she walks through the deranged electronic vegas of Akihabara, with its hundreds of open electronics shops and stores and stalls of televisions and stereos and computers seeming to topple over one another, she takes no note of the televisions crazily changing channels, the stereos suddenly blasting songs no one has ever sung, let alone heard, the computers crashing in homage to her. She doesn't even fully grasp the situation the night she rises wearily, nauseated, from her tatami mat to go downstairs and meet her best client. Straining to put on her blue dress, fastening the last button, she finally takes note of the *29.4.85* on her body and realizes with a start that today happens to be the twenty-ninth of April, the fifteenth anniversary of the fading date. She counts on her fingers the time difference and calculates that in L.A. at this very moment the twenty-ninth of April is just beginning to dawn, and then she goes downstairs to meet Doctor Kai, only to find him sitting in their booth, eyes peacefully closed, literally as still as death.

Doctor Kai had just gotten to a particularly important and difficult part of his memoirs. As it happened, the old man was actually from America, or at any rate had spent a great deal of his life there, which might have accounted for his special rapport with Kristin. By the time he returned to his Japanese homeland some ten years ago, after more than forty years of living in the States, his wife was dead, his disgraced and disowned daughter Saki had once again dropped from sight, and so all Doctor Kai had left was a memory so American in content and process, he explained to Kristin, that few Japanese girls understood.

Kristin understood. I can see the nuclear halo of Nagasaki across the bay—she recounted his words later in her journal— from my hometown of Kumamoto that August morning in 1945, around eleven o'clock, like the neon halo of Las Vegas: a great glowing star: I was twenty-six then. That was how Doctor Kai began. Over the next several weeks he returned every evening, distraught on the occasions Kristin wasn't available, patiently waiting for his time with her on the occasions she was occupied with someone else; he had just gotten up to somewhere around 1988 or '89, a particularly painful recollection of the last time he saw his daughter and exiled her from him forever with his silence, when Kristin said, We'll finish tomorrow night—and re-served him a slot in her schedule.

Racked with nihilism, choking on his words, the old man had said to her, "We are living in an age of chaos."

"Yes," answered Kristin, "I've heard."

Sitting beside the old dead doctor in the dark of their booth while waiting for someone to come for his body, having finished her story, Kristin notices something in the palm of his cupped hand, which rests on the seat at his side. Without taking it from his hand, she nonetheless cranes her neck around to try and make out what it is. She so convolutes her body in order to identify what the old doctor holds that she almost winds up sitting in his dead lap; that's when she sees it's a claim ticket, with a number. The next afternoon Mika presents Kristin with the ticket, explaining as best she can that it seems only fitting to all concerned—though Kristin has no idea who that might be—that the ticket should be bequeathed to her. Without Kristin's knowing what it claims, nonetheless it is an odd and disappointing inheritance. Kristin can't help wondering why it couldn't have been ten or twenty million yen instead. But on her first day off from work, even as she wakes more nauseated than she's yet been during her pregnancy, Kristin leaves the Hotel Ryu and takes the late-afternoon tram out across the bay to where Mika has told her she'll find the address on the ticket. The white tram on its white track juts south out over the black water apparently toward nothing at all, or nothing that Kristin can see, until the tram turns east, in the direction of a small man-made finger of island curling into the bay from the city.

Then there's no missing it. Even from out over the water several kilometers away Kristin can suddenly see the monumental aquariumlike structure that sits on the island, its previous invisibility a trick of the Tokyo light, where the gray of the bay and the gray of the sky and the gray of the wide-open brick plaza on which the building sits all run into each other. With the turn of the tram and the shift of the hazy light, the tremendous aquarium suddenly reveals itself as an interlocking piece of sea and sky in a completely elemental universe of water and air and stone, a huge patch of sky swimming before her in crystal-blue blocks of glass, covering the equivalent of several square city blocks and stacked some thirty stories into the air like massive cubes of ice frozen together, filling the horizon. Even from several kilometers away, before the tram pulls into the station, Kristin can make out the thousands of silver time-capsules floating throughout the building in a lattice of intersecting interior canals. Dwarfed by the building, the tiny figures of hundreds of people can be seen standing around the perimeter looking in. When the blinding glint of the sun off the peak of the aquarium reflects into her eyes, Kristin suddenly realizes that the light she used to see from her window when she lived at the ryokan was the moon off the top of this glass building that is otherwise rendered transparent by both night and day. A fuji mist surrounds the aquarium's highest spires.

Of course, Kristin thinks nothing of it when, just as the tram pulls into the station, it lurches and, for the first time ever, in an audible gasp of confused machinery and technology, breaks down. Baffled attendants and security guards help the passengers off the cars onto the platform. Kristin and the other passengers descend the steps from the open station and make their way across the gray brick plaza toward the time-capsule aquarium; in the open empty expanse between, nothing else can malfunction as Kristin passes. Near the building, signs presumably direct Kristin, but they're in Japanese. Several pedestrian corridors run beneath the aquarium from one side to the other, through which people stroll looking up at a distant and obscured sky beyond the water and glass. On the outer glass walls, condensation forms from the frigid temperature inside, and little kids run their fingers through the moisture.

Inside the front entrance and at the far corner of a huge interior lobby, with the last of the twenty-ninth of April 1985 faintly receding into her flesh, Kristin shows her ticket to a man behind a booth and he points her to the other end of the lobby down a glass hallway. The ceiling of the inner lobby rises hundreds of meters above her, its glass balconies full of people circling the edge; and all around her, as though floating in the sky, countless capsules gleam in the sun, shining through the glass like metal stars. From one of the structure's upper suspended ramparts, a little girl being pulled along by her impatient mother releases a red balloon that Kristin watches float higher and higher up into the glassy trellis overhead, a drop of blood disappearing down the drain of the sky. As she makes her way to the claims department, she notices what appears to be a number of security people running excitedly in the other direction, and far off she can hear something like an alarm, harsh and bleating, less a bell than a buzz saw. A few other people in the building look around at the sound. But no one seems especially concerned.

At the claims department Kristin finds she has to wait her turn with a crowd of other claimants. The rather unsettling blast of the distant alarm continues. After ten minutes, when Kristin gets to the window and presents her ticket, there's another flurry of men in uniform rushing through the hall, and finally people seem to be wondering what's going on. Three minutes later, the woman behind the window counter presents Kristin with the capsule.

It's still wet and cold, just fished out of its glacial coffin somewhere in the upper glassy catacomb. It's round and very shiny as though it's been polished, perfectly unmarred except for the small number etched in the rim that matches the number that was on the claim ticket. Kristin is studying the capsule when several policemen come in and start saying something very emphatically, and an announcement blasts out from an overhead speaker at a frightening volume. Kristin has no idea what's being said, of course, which seems inconvenient, since everyone around her, from the waiting claimants to the woman behind the counter to the policemen themselves, responds with nothing less than sheer panic.

From all corners of the lobby, across the glass ramparts above her, there's a terrified stampede for the main door.

Clutching her time-capsule, Kristin runs with everyone else. There's a crush in the doorway, among people almost too civilized for sheer survival; it puts Kristin at an advantage. Bigger than many of those around her, including the men, she bulls her way through. Outside, hundreds of people are now fleeing from the colossal aquarium across the open gray plaza, couples divided and frantically looking for each other, women scooping up children, younger people moving older people as fast as they can. At the tram station in the far distance, passengers who have finally gotten off the broken-down train and are just starting to make their way across the plaza stop in their tracks, wondering what's happening. Sirens wail in the distance and flashing police cars appear on the horizon, speeding along the thread of land that connects the city to the small island, along with a stream of screaming fire engines and ambulances, while security guards from the aquarium are blowing whistles and desperately motioning everyone away from the building. Kristin keeps looking back over her shoulder, irritated that she's apparently the only one in these circumstances who doesn't speak the stupid language. But none of the others around her seem any more certain of what's happening than she is, and when she finally stops at the edge of the gray plaza to turn and look back at the aquarium, as though waiting for the entire situation to explain itself, with a cop yelling at her and gesturing for her to move on, the situation explains itself.

There's a crack, like lightning but not lightning, and an explosion from a corner of the building, and a wall of water is launched at Kristin in a flame of glass.

Things never happen in slow motion like people say. Things always happen much faster than people can know or comprehend: what happens in slow motion is the memory of the thing later; it's surprisingly vivid, rendered in more detail than seemed possible to register at the time. Later Kristin will remember the event with more precision, the swirl of the new river roaring across the plaza as millions of liters of water burst from the building, carrying thousands of time-capsules like bullets. The power of the onslaught has only begun to wane when it reaches Kristin, hitting her so hard it instantly springs loose from her arms the capsule she's been holding as she goes under. To those around her who see her, in her light blue dress not entirely dissimilar to the color of the water, it looks as though only Kristin's face is left—a blond head bobbing among the waves. Under the water, perhaps from the sun above her, perhaps from some detonation in her mind, there's a white flash before her like a Moment, a submerged imploding star of faith and memory, and going through it, she's surprised to find herself back above the water's surface, gasping and flailing for the capsule she had held, grabbing it back into her possession as a torrent of other capsules surf past her and into her. One swipes a gash across her face. The water furiously sweeps her farther from the aquarium, its rapids unsure where to carry her, until she's finally deposited in a wave near the top of the tram-station steps.

SHE can't be unconscious for long. She wakes to what she first believes is an astounding sun in her eyes.

But it isn't the sun itself, it's the sun's reflected blaze off the water and glass that fill the plaza in a lake of light. Kristin rolls out of the sun into the shade of the overhang of the tram station; cut everywhere, bleeding, she assumes the pain in her side is from several cracked ribs. She dozes a little more until—after what's been a remarkably silent and stupefied catastrophe—she wakes to the air finally filling with cries. Raising herself, she expects to see a holocaust in front of her, and in fact water and glass are everywhere, and across the plaza people lie hurt and, for all she knows, dead. She expects to see people crying over relatives and friends, she expects to see people crying at carnage, but that isn't what people are crying about; they aren't crying about the ruptured building or the dashed bodies. They're crying because in the fall of twilight the flooded landscape is covered with thousands of beached and gutted time-capsules, their contents strewn from the shores of the aquarium out to the bay of the city. First in tens, then in hundreds, people wade through the water from one capsule to the next, many ripping from their faces the surgical masks that then float out into Tokyo Bay like dead white cherry blossoms.

In the light of the moon over Tokyo, this goes on through the night. Finally one of the nurses making the rounds of the disaster reaches Kristin; in broken English she confirms that Kristin has probably cracked two or three ribs, and explains there isn't much to be done about it except give her some pills for inflammation. Kristin's bleeding has stopped. Slowly and painfully she gathers up her capsule and waits another hour for a repaired tram to take her home. At the Hotel Ryu she doesn't see anyone, none of the memory girls or their clients, as though the Tokyo night has been wiped clean of memory, and she goes straight to her room up on the third floor where, for a while, she sleeps. She has a great deal of pain in her side from her ribs, and later in the night, when she wakes, it's with a start so violent she suspects she's fractured her rib cage more by turning in her sleep; but then the pain, no longer just in her ribs, is irresistible, and she stumbles in terror through the dark hotel to the toilet down the hall. She makes it to the toilet just in time to see the glistening white rain of Kierkegaard Blumenthal run from her body.

It still doesn't occur to Kristin, even after what's happened this afternoon, even with what happens now, that she's a vortex of chaos after all. Irrationally, all she can think is that she shouldn't have stood in the window of her room all those mornings, exposing her pregnant belly to the din of the city. All she can think is that if she had it to do all over again, she would have gladly taken her little boy back to the silence of the delta town that starved her of her dreams; all she can think is that it's because he was starved of his own little umbilical dreams that the glistening yolk of little Kirk Blu has broken, emptying from her. *Noooo*, Kristin moans, and drops to her knees sobbing. She begs him to come back. She drops to her knees retracting every stern admonition she's given him: I promise I'll make the world whisper to you, she cries, and scoops him up in a puddle, holding him in the cup of her hands and splashing herself with him, on her face and neck and breasts, until she can't distinguish the tears of her eyes from the discharge of her uterus, until both have seeped into her and she's bone-dry.

When Kristin wakes the next morning, it's the first day of the Year 33 in the Age of Apocalypse. She slowly sits up, exhausted, profoundly aware of nothing inside her. She has no idea what time it is, but it seems still early and she wants to go back to sleep, and wonders when Mika will knock on her door. She opens the window of her tiny chamber and lies back down staring at the rare generous blue of the Tokyo sky. For a while she rubs her stomach absently, as though hungry, though she's not hungry. She rolls over onto her side and for several seconds lies looking at the image of the scorched-black one-winged bird on the time-capsule that sits against the wall. She closes her eyes and opens them again, and the falling black bird is still on the steel cylinder, and she pushes herself back up painfully, her side killing her, and scoots across the tatami mat to look at the capsule more closely.

Because at this moment she isn't thinking so clearly, she doesn't immediately understand what happened. She has it in her head that maybe someone broke into the hotel during the night and switched capsules on her or something. But then she remembers the water smashing her and tearing the capsule she held from her grip, and she remembers going under and then surfacing, and grabbing the capsule that was in the water in front of her; Doctor Kai's capsule, she imagines, is now somewhere at sea, sailing to Hawaii or the Philippines or Australia. She wonders who will find it.

It isn't a matter of coincidence that the Occupant's capsule has returned to her, she does know that. In the midst of everything else that confuses her, she would really have to be a big point-misser to believe anything ever really has to do with coincidence. Though she knows the contents of the capsule will link her to the Occupant forever, as morning comes through the window of her room, she works at prying open the capsule with the spoon for the morning tea. She's so stunned by the single item she finds inside that she just puts it back in. Wrapping the capsule in a small blanket, she huddles in the corner of the room and closes her eyes; and cradling the capsule to her breast, untouched by a stranger and unkissed by chaos, she dreams.

ANGIE, the old man says. Twenty years after Kristin's flight to Tokyo and the Occupant's to Brittany, in the old condemned hotel penthouse by the Dragon Gate of San Francisco's Chinatown, Carl wakes to a secret as old as memory. Angie, he says in his sleep, waking himself with it; but this time the name doesn't disappear as before, this time when it flits across his mind and he says it out loud, it hovers there, in the air just beyond his lips. For a moment, the zero of his maps threatens to answer as before; but in the next moment, as her name still lingers, there is no more zero, any more than there's an answer that matters to his mysterious coordinates on the wall. What matters is that the x factor that rendered him zero wasn't the remembering, it was the forgetting; and now he remembers and so, with perhaps more relief than true peace, with perhaps more hope than true faith, he is slipping back into a more contented sleep than he's known in days, when the building begins to shake.

LET'S say I had it to do all over again: and I changed everything. Let's say I gave myself over a little more to faith and a little less to vision, let's say I could take back the first lie that broke a heart, let's say that in settling for something smaller I in fact gained something larger. Let's say that everything I did, I never did; let's say that everything I never did, I did. Let's say that having exploited chaos in terms of my own imagination, I learned to trust it in terms of my life; let's say love won every struggle over cowardice. Let's say I didn't *think* so damned much. Let's say I dared to suspend myself in the moment between breaths. Let's say I found a way to say one comforting word to her the night she cried, or even to just reach over and touch her. Let's say I had the courage of my sensuality, thus overcoming my depravity; let's say I had an emotional fortitude to match the tenacity of my ambitions. Let's say my dreams were not so attached to the tangible rewards that I was smart enough to know didn't matter.

Let's say I was incapable of despair, because despair is not a grief of the heart, but a grief of the soul.

As he lies in the shadows of the ancient village tower of Sur-les-Bateaux, the last thing the Occupant sees is the smile of the girl standing before him, the last thing he hears is her reply.

Let's say, he hears her tell him, that sometime, somehow, not in this life, not in this millennium, but in another, one of your own, that begins tonight and ends a thousand years ago, you will have another chance.

AT first she doesn't realize she's dreaming. Since she's never had a dream, she doesn't know how to identify one; rather she believes that the small flicker she sees on the far side of the darkness, on the other side of unconsciousness, is the dream itself, which she approaches across some limbo between consciousness and sleep. It's like the flicker of a gunshot in the distance, except as it grows closer and larger, it has a sound of its own. It's as though this small flash is on the far horizon of a vast veldt she's crossed, and as she grows closer to it she believes at first it's a time-capsule, glistening in the light of a star she can't see, until she finally identifies the sound coming from it as crying, and when she finally reaches it, she sees it's a baby sitting on the ground waiting for her. He stops crying and looks up at her, blinking.

And she wakes. Or rather she's awakened, in a flash of nausea, by a bubble breaking the surface of her dream and reclaiming its place in her womb.